And Give You Peace

Also by Jessica Treadway

Absent Without Leave and Other Stories

And Give You Peace

❖ ❖ ❖

A NOVEL BY

Jessica Treadway

Graywolf Press

SAINT PAUL, MINNESOTA

Publication of this volume is made possible in part by a grant provided by the Minnesota State Arts Board through an appropriation by the Minnesota State Legislature, and by a grant from the National Endowment for the Arts. Significant support has also been provided by the Bush Foundation; Dayton's Project Imagine with support from Target Foundation; the McKnight Foundation; a Grant made on behalf of the Stargazer Foundation; and other generous contributions from foundations, corporations, and individuals. To these organizations and individuals we offer our heartfelt thanks.

"Burnt Norton" from FOUR QUARTETS by T. S. Eliot, copyright 1936 by Harcourt, Inc. and renewed 1964 by T. S. Eliot, reprinted by permission of the publisher.

Published by Graywolf Press
2402 University Avenue, Suite 203
Saint Paul, Minnesota 55114
All rights reserved.

www.graywolfpress.org

Published in the United States of America

ISBN 1-55597-315-9

1   2   3   4   5   6   7   8   9
First Graywolf Printing, 2001

Library of Congress Catalog Card Number: 00-101778

Cover design: Julie Metz

For my sisters, Molly and Laura
And my beloved Jack

"It's a poor sort of memory that only works backwards," the Queen remarked.

Alice's Adventures in Wonderland
Lewis Carroll

1. We are the Dolans

Q. Why do we call a possible answer to a mystery a "clue"?

— F.B., Guilderland, N.Y.

A. A clue, originally spelled "clew," was a ball of string in medieval England. The word was used repeatedly in the retelling of the mythical exploits of the Greek hero Theseus, who killed the minotaur. Theseus was the only one to escape the monster's deadly labyrinth on the island of Crete. He found his way back from the underground maze by retracing the string he had begun unwinding when he entered, thus following the clew.

I once saw a policeman in the Public Garden helping a blind woman feed sugar to his horse. This image—the cop gently lifting the fingers folded around the sugar cube, the blind woman's sudden smile—is why I went to college in Boston and why I moved back after the deaths, although I didn't realize this until years later when I began looking for meaning in small, forgotten things.

The summer I was twelve, my family took a driving trip through New England. We went on a boat tour of Boston Harbor and visited the USS Constitution. On the lowest deck of the old ship, between the hammocks and cannons, a guide in a naval suit pointed at my youngest sister, Meggy, who was five. "Can you take this and scoot down to the other end of the deck?" he asked, handing her a folded black satchel. I felt the momentary piercing of not having been picked, but at least it was Meggy he'd chosen and not Justine, my middle sister, the one most often noticed by the world.

Meggy nodded, accepted the satchel, and made her way—lips pursed, pink sneakers squeaking—away from us and other members of the tour.

"When I say 'Go,' run to me as fast as you can, okay?" The guide was a college student whose enthusiasm for his summer job was still new, as it was early in the season. Meggy nodded again, brushing aside a stalk of her dark blond bangs. She wore purple shorts and a T-shirt that showed the Cookie Monster munching a cookie and giving the thumbs-up. The guide said, "Ready, set, go!" I held my breath as I watched my little sister, clutching the black bag with crossed arms to her chest, pitch across the floor. When she reached the guide, he gave her a clumsy pat on the head as we all applauded, and Meggy leaned back in flushed pride against our mother's knees. My father reached over to rub her hair, and I raised my own hand to push at a pimple on my chin. It was the summer I stopped being cute, and I kept waiting for the shock and the hurt of it not to feel so fresh.

"Okay, say this little girl was a boy, and it was the early 1800s," the guide instructed us. "That bag would have been filled with gunpowder. Can anybody guess why they would use children to run ammunition between the guns?"

"Low to the ground," a man in the back said, chuckling as if he'd made a joke, but the guide told him, "No, you're exactly right. Powder Monkeys, they were called. Young people were also more expendable," he added. Behind me, I could feel my father growing tense.

"As you can probably imagine, anybody who ran ammo became a key target for enemy fire," the guide went on.

Justine, who was nine, asked, "What does that mean? You mean they just killed all the kids?"

"Well, not all." The guide blushed as my father clapped his hand over Meggy's ears.

"What's the matter with you?" he said to the guide. He took Meggy over to a corner, and I could see that she didn't understand any of what was going on.

"Sorry," the guide told my mother. He was humble or perhaps young enough to seem genuinely chagrined.

"It's not your fault." My mother pulled out a compact, looked at herself in its mirror, and waved vaguely in the direction of my father and Meggy. "He's oversensitive." The small tour crowd dispersed, in deference to the guide's loss of composure.

"Let's blow this Popsicle stand," Justine said, and once again I marveled at my younger sister's sophistication. She was always making adult-sounding declarations that I had never heard. She'd bought half a dozen bangle bracelets at Quincy Market that morning, and impatience made them sing against each other, up and down her arm. We left Old Ironsides a few minutes later to catch the boat back to Boston. I remember vividly the ride across the water, because it was the only time I ever saw my father refuse to pick up Meggy when she asked him to.

"Too hot, honey," I remember him saying. Then he moved by himself to the other side of the boat. My mother offered to take Meggy onto her lap, but Meggy shook her head and plunked down between Justine and me. The breeze tangled the hair of all three of us girls together. My mother took a picture, and when it came back we made it into a family joke, how we appear to be three heads on a single body—six arms and legs and eyes, thirty fingers, each of us looking happy to be part of such a freak.

Later the same day we drove up to Salem in the afternoon and visited the House of the Seven Gables. I was trying to read Hawthorne's book about the house, but it was slow going, and I gave it up in favor of an illustrated history of the Salem witchcraft trials. I became fascinated with the stories of girls my own age who suddenly started throwing fits, their bodies convulsing as they accused neighbor-women of casting evil spells.

To me, the most interesting detail was that the whole thing began with two girls who dropped an egg white into a glass of water and tried to tell the future from the shapes it made as it moved. The egg-and-glass method was an early variation on the crystal ball. But instead of the romantic visions they expected to see, the girls divined the image of a coffin in the spreading egg white, and went berserk. (Of course when I got home I wanted to try the fortune-telling trick myself, but of course—because we were never allowed to touch raw eggs—my father wouldn't let me.)

After we left the House of the Seven Gables, we went to get ice-cream cones and sat eating them at a picnic table near the center of town. My father had not been feeling well earlier in the day, when we took the tour boat back from the Constitution, but when we'd been on land again for a few hours his appetite returned. I finished my cone first, lay down in the grass, and began to imitate the wide-eyed witch-girls writhing and screeching, tongues wagging as they plucked at their hair. My father was amused, and so was Meggy, who plunked her cone down on the table and came over to imitate me.

But my mother and Justine were embarrassed. "Mom, make her stop," Justine said, in the voice that had recently agitated my father into composing a riddle: "What's nine and perfectly fine, but inclined to whine?"

"She looks like a total retard," Justine added, and at that exact moment, a family with a retarded boy walked by us. I had paused in my rolling-around routine to gauge the level of my mother's disapproval, and I saw the boy just as my parents and sisters did. He was younger than me, closer to Justine's age, and he had the big head, jutting jaw, and uptilted eyes I later learned to identify as features of Down's syndrome.

He was walking between his mother and father, who turned to look in our direction, but not directly at us, when they heard Justine's remark. Both of their faces wore the same expression—not anger, which would have been easier to witness, but sadness and a chagrin of which they were both clearly ashamed, but which they had learned to forgive in each other and, so, in themselves. Worst of all, I could tell they forgave Justine.

"Oh, shit," Justine said. It was the first time I had ever heard one of us swear in front of our parents. Instead of scolding her, my mother echoed, "Shit." The boy and his parents were beyond us by then. He was wearing sneakers with neon orange laces and a *Star Trek* baseball cap. The father had a camera slung over his shoulder, and that night in bed all I could think about was whether they had any pictures of the boy that made him look normal, and if so, whether these were the ones they sent out at Christmastime.

My mother told Justine, "Honey, you have to be careful. You can hurt people's feelings." My mother's cone was dripping from the bottom as she said this, and she turned it sideways to stop the ice cream from flowing out either end. It had her full attention, but my father was still looking after the couple and their retarded son. I could tell he wanted to catch up with them and apologize, or say something to make them feel better. But he didn't know what this might be. A few hours later at dinner, when my mother could tell that it was still bothering him, she said, "Tom, remember when we lived on Mercer Street, the sampler that old

Russian lady had in her kitchen? *When you live next to the graveyard, you can't weep for everyone.*"

My father looked puzzled, as if he didn't have the slightest idea what she was talking about. Justine said, "Who lives next to a graveyard?"

"It's just a figure of speech, honey." My mother spoke into her restaurant napkin, so we could barely make out her words. Her lips left the stain of a kiss in the folded cloth.

At the time, of course, I had no way of knowing the psychic torture my father had suffered earlier in the day, when he refused to hold Meggy in his arms on the boat as it sped through Boston Harbor. During dinner, I thought I understood what was troubling him. As my sisters and I flashed "see-food" at each other and giggled into our milk, I believed it was the memory of the retarded boy and his parents I saw haunting my father's eyes.

He was the one who named me Anastasia, after the youngest of the four duchesses in the Romanov family executed during the Bolshevik Revolution in 1918. My father believed the legend that Anastasia had survived the firing squad, escaped Russia, forgotten her own identity, and lived to be an old lady in the United States.

My father's thoughts turned often to the assassination as he had heard it described once in a documentary. Members of the Tsar's family were awakened in the night, led to the cellar, and told that they were going to be shot. Nicholas, the father, asked the Commandant, *What? What?* The Commandant repeated what he had said and ordered the firing squad to get ready. Nicholas turned to his family and said nothing further. His wife and the children uttered a few incoherent phrases. "What do you think they were trying to say?" my father wondered aloud, as he told me the story of my name. My mother got mad at him for giving me all the gory details, but my father said I should be prepared for how much it was possible to suffer in this world. "Do you think they said 'I love you' or 'Good-bye' or 'Don't leave me'?" he asked me, and I could tell he didn't really expect an answer; he just couldn't help speculating aloud. "Or do you think it was just sounds of terror coming out?"

When the shooting started, three of the daughters did not die right away. Something made the bullets ricochet all over the room, and when they tried to bayonet one of the girls, they found that the Grand Duchesses—Anastasia and her sisters—were wearing corsets studded with diamonds. "That's what saved her," my father said. "She played dead but she really wasn't, and somebody helped her get away. But imagine living the rest of your life, if that happened to you. Imagine *wanting* to live, after that."

I used to look up Anastasia in those Name-Your-Baby books. It comes from the Greek for "one who shall rise again." When I was younger, it comforted me to believe that I might come back to life somehow after I died, like the rumor of the real Anastasia. But now I know I wouldn't want that—now, I can't imagine a prospect more frightening than eternity. There has to be some relief.

My middle name is Grace, for my maternal grandmother, and our last name, Dolan, came straight off the boat with our Irish grandfather. My youngest sister was named after our mother, Margaret, but there is no story behind Justine's name. My parents told her it was because she was an original, but I don't believe Justine ever took this as a compliment.

The number of letters in each of our names—Anastasia Grace Dolan, Justine Carolyn, and Margaret Olivia—adds up to nineteen. It was important to our father that they all have the same sum. We didn't ask him why, because by the time we were old enough to wonder, we already had a sense that it was one of the things he would never be able to explain.

Being the oldest of three daughters is one of the first ways I think about myself, and it's one of the first questions to come up in friendships, at least between women. Do you have any brothers or sisters? Where do you fall in the line? The answer helps put the two new friends in some kind of balance, gives them a landmark to show where they're starting from.

If I meet another oldest, I know she understands things about me already, as I understand them about her. If I meet a middle child, I assume she is like Justine, who always made sure to be noticed, not to get lost in the crowd.

And if I meet the youngest in a series of siblings, especially sisters, I must endure the short shock to my head and stomach that is all too familiar to me now. I know it's coming and I know it will recede, but I expect it will never leave me entirely, and I wouldn't want it to. Painful as it is, it's something to count on. Justine feels it, too. I think we both imagine it is Meggy in that moment, reaching through this other family's youngest to touch us where we live.

It depends on the person who's asking, what my own answer will be. If I sense sympathy—not necessarily pity, although there are times when I want that, too—if it seems that he or she will understand what I am surviving without, I might tell the truth. In the old days, when early death was more common, people were accustomed to giving a qualified count. A mother would say she had "eleven children, six living." Remembering this, I might tell someone, "I had two sisters, but one died," so that I don't have to feel I am betraying Meggy, the way I do when I give the other answer, which is that I have one sister, Justine, who is three years younger than me.

Another choice is to try to be like the little girl in the poem by Wordsworth. When a stranger asks how many children are in her family, she tells him seven, including a brother and sister who lie in graves in the churchyard. "Then ye are only five," the stranger tries to convince her, but the child insists, "Nay, we are seven!" So sometimes I try to get away with responding that I have two sisters, but then there are the follow-up questions that leave me stammering: Where do your sisters live? What do they do?

And even when I tell the truth, that one of my sisters is dead, it does not always end there. More people than not, when they hear this, will say they're sorry and look distressed, and we agree in that moment, without saying anything, to talk about something else.

But there is the occasional new acquaintance who will, after the murmur and the wince, ask, "How did it happen?" There are two kinds of people who pursue the question like this, and I have come to understand how important it is to distinguish between them. One is the person who has learned that life is worth living only if you admit it all. That there is nothing that can't be imagined, nothing you can't say out loud. These are the people I can end up loving, who can be my friends, because what did happen I *never* imagined, and it feels good to have company there.

The other people who ask are the ones who hoard disasters, who collect sad stories like chits they can cash in against the misfortunes of their own lives. The more of these people you meet, the better you become at identifying them before you give too much of yourself away. They're the ones who use the opportunity of a commotion in one room to check their teeth in the mirror of another. Anything could be causing the commotion—a dropped punch bowl, a heart attack—but the first thing they think, before going in to find out, is that they can check their teeth now without anyone noticing.

To these people, I say, "It was a long time ago," as if that is an answer, as if that's what they want to know. If they persist, I say, "She died young," and usually those words, along with the look on my face, are enough to make them back off. The few times someone has pressed me beyond that, I said, "She was shot to death." There must be something final in my tone when I say this, because no one has ever gone on to ask, *By whom?*

It's different when you talk about a parent. It's not so shocking to say your father's dead. Hardly anyone ever wants to know the details; the fact alone is enough, that branch of your tree has fallen, you're held up now by other things. It doesn't leave you swinging in the air like the loss of a sister. I don't think anything does.

This is the way they died: our father went into Meggy's bedroom on a humid Wednesday morning at the end of June, four months before Meggy's sixteenth birthday, and shot her through the head with a gun none of us had ever seen before. Then Dad walked around inside the house for a while. Through the kitchen window screen the next-door neighbor, Mrs. Waxman, saw his shadow, running a glass of water and drinking it. She saw and heard the TV in the family room being turned on—the sounds of a musical, children singing— and almost immediately it went off again, the picture collapsing like a star in the center of the screen. Our father went outside to trim the rosebushes. But after he trimmed them, he cut the blooms off, too.

Then he went back inside the house, to his own bedroom, and shot himself by putting the gun in his mouth.

By that time Mrs. Waxman had gone downstairs to start her laundry, so nobody heard anything—no shot, no body falling. Justine found our father when she came home to change clothes for a party that afternoon, and the police found Meggy when they arrived a few minutes later. Our dog, Bill Buckner, had been locked out of the house, and by the time police arrived he was going nuts. At first they thought he might have witnessed what happened, through the windows, but then they figured out that he was just hungry. After they fed him he settled down in the place where the roses had fallen.

All of this was documented in the police report, after they interviewed Mrs. Waxman. "In his mouth?" I remember my mother asking. "He put something as dirty as a *gun* in his *mouth*?" She seemed almost more surprised by this detail than by the suicide itself. But then the police told us that he'd done it on top of the Sunday newspaper, spreading sections over the place he assumed his body would hit. "Well, that makes more sense," my mother said, as if this made her feel better.

If I am grateful for anything about that day and what happened in it, it's that Justine did not see Meggy, did not look into the corner bedroom, before she ran out of the house and over to the Waxmans', where she whispered "ambulance" and then threw up until she fainted.

She played dead but she really wasn't.

But yes. She really was.

They used the ambulance for Justine; our father and Meggy were not carried out until the police had gone through the house. They took fingerprints from the water glass my father had left in the sink.

Even Meggy's diary, from which the most recent pages were missing, became part of the case.

They put things in plastic bags, the way police do on TV: rug fragments, threads, the piece of Meggy's rubbing blanket—she called it her "rubbie"—that lay tucked under her good cheek. Meggy would have been embarrassed to know she had been found with her rubbie. And she was wearing a nightshirt spotted with old stains from her period. When I learned these details, I couldn't help realizing that this is where the expression comes from: *I wouldn't be caught dead*.

But when she went to bed with her secrets the night before, she had no reason to believe she would not be alone with them, under the covers, until she got up in the morning.

At first, my mother insisted that there had been a mistake. The deaths could not have been the result of murder and suicide, she told the police. It had to be foul play.

But the police showed her a letter our father had written for our mother and Justine and me. That night, our mother told us she'd burned the note without reading it. Hearing this, Justine laughed because she thought our mother was making a bad joke.

"No, I mean it," our mother said.

"Yeah, right. You burned Dad's suicide note." My sister actually snorted; it was a vulgar, piglike noise she would have mocked in another girl.

"I thought it was best." My mother squeezed her own fingers inside each other until both hands turned white. "I didn't want the last thing we remembered about him to be a bunch of rambling that didn't make any sense."

"How do you know that's what it was, if you didn't read it?" I asked. For an astonishing moment I thought I might strangle her.

My mother coughed. "I'm just assuming," she said, but something was still caught in her throat and she coughed again. Justine and I waited. "Based on his state of mind." Then she told us she thought it would be simpler, if anyone asked, to just say there had been no note.

But the media had already gotten hold of it—not the note itself, but the fact that one existed. The woman on the TV news called it "blood-spattered," but at this our mother made a sound of disgust and muttered something about sensationalism. She said that the note had actually been very clean, considering. There was only a trace of red in the top corner. It might have been a smear of Justine's nail polish, excess blotted from the edge of a finger against whatever scrap of paper happened to be around.

But it was not nail polish. We know, because they did tests. The note was folded neatly when they found it on Dad's dresser, next to loose change and his keys and the plastic photograph cube that contained pictures in only three of the six squares.

I keep the photograph cube on my own dresser now; neither my mother nor Justine wanted it. The first picture is the one my mother took on the boat that day in Boston Harbor. Then there's a snapshot of our whole family taken by Mr. Waxman at a barbecue in our backyard two summers before the deaths. Justine and Meggy and I sit with our legs crossed, at our parents' feet. On one end, my dark hair tilts toward my sisters' fairer heads. Nobody quite knows why I was born with this complexion, with brown eyes and skin that might have been blessed by the Mediterranean. My sisters and my mother have blue eyes, my father hazel, and according to the laws I learned in tenth-grade genetics, I shouldn't belong to this group.

My father's sister, Aunt Rosemary, insists that she remembers an uncle with my same coloring, but he never came up in any other conversation, and I'm pretty sure she invented him to make me feel better. When she got to the tenth grade herself, Justine took to calling me a mutation until my father made her stop.

And I remember once, when we were little, someone commenting on how different I looked from Justine and Meggy, and my mother saying that they hadn't quite gotten the recipe right the first time around. I must have seemed upset because my father told her, "I can't believe you just said that, Margaret."

"Oh, she knows I don't mean anything," my mother said. "Right, Ana? Daddy's too sensitive."

In our family photograph, my father's eyes appear dark and slitted above his smile. Here he looks sinister, although he was not. Between Meggy and me, Justine hugs her legs, her chin resting on a bare kneecap, her watchband slid all the way down to the base of her bony wrist. Meggy's braces flash in the sun.

My father is the only one touching some part of everyone else in the family. He has to stretch himself to do it—to lay one palm on Meggy's shoulder and the other on mine, while his shin supports Justine's back. Next to him, her hand on his arm, my mother looks as if she is about to say something. I have heard photographs referred to as frozen time, but whenever I look at this one, I think of it as a moment in motion. My mother—her white neck looking fragile in the noon light, her short hair waving away from her head—still waits to utter whatever it was.

The third picture is cut from the cover of a theater program. When she was nine years old, Meggy played the title role in the Ashmont Repertory's production of *Annie*. She didn't even have to audition for the part. The repertory's director, Mr. Spelich, was also the elementary-school music teacher, and he took my mother aside one day and asked how she'd feel about Meggy being in the play. "It's a lot of work, and some late nights, but I think you'll be glad you let her do it, in the long run," he advised. "She has perfect pitch, and she's a remarkable actress. I don't know if you realize."

"We had some idea," my mother told him, although in truth I don't think any of us had ever really noticed that Meggy could sing. Because she was the youngest, her voice was often crowded out. She liked to stand in front of her mirror and perform, using a hairbrush as a microphone, but Justine's stereo was always on at the same time, and her music was all any of us could hear.

In our town's *Annie*, Meggy was a star. With her long hair tucked up under the curly orange wig and her features accentuated by shadow and rouge, her expression of hopeful innocence reached all the way to the auditorium's last row. When she finished her solo as the abandoned daughter imagining the parents who will return for her someday, there was a moment of stunned silence in the audience before it exploded in applause. On opening night I sat between my parents (Justine was watching from a dark rear corner with the first in a series of junior-high boyfriends; I'm not sure she saw or heard much of anything that happened on the stage), and while everyone around us clapped and whistled for Meggy, my father sat motionless in his seat, unable to hide or remove the tears shining on his face. Across my chest, my mother passed him a tissue, but he wouldn't take it. His eyes were fixed on the stage, as if he had been hypnotized by his own daughter. Although I was fifteen then and thought myself too old to care about such things, I felt a chill of jealousy at the effect Meggy had on him—she had made him feel *awe*—which I knew I never could.

After the cast took its bows, we went back to find Meggy. Along the way we accepted congratulations from our neighbors and friends, and from people we'd never been introduced to but who, because of the size of our town, knew us anyway. I'd expected that Meggy would be flushed with pride and excitement, but instead she was sobbing in the arms of Haley Goldberg, our dental hygienist, who'd played Miss Hannigan. When Meggy saw my parents, she broke away from Haley and went to my father, who folded her into his arms. "I kept thinking about what if I didn't have you," she mumbled, barely getting the words out between shuddery breaths. She took care to address both of our parents, but we could all tell it was Dad she grieved most in her fantasy. I looked at my mother and saw her lips go tight as she understood this, too. Our father picked Meggy up and carried her out the back door, past clusters of admiring coos. When we got home, he was the one who tucked her into bed. In the morning he was ready to call Mr. Spelich and withdraw Meggy from the play, but my mother convinced him not to. And Meggy herself seemed fine after a good sleep, as if she didn't even remember her sorrow of the night before. My mother and I went to all of the other performances, but my father, saying he couldn't stand it, stayed home.

The show had been videotaped, though, and often he would watch it, late at night when everyone else was in bed. When I came home after graduating from college that summer, just before the deaths, I kept finding the worn-out *Ashmont Rep* tape in the VCR. By then, Meggy was spending a lot of time with her friends, trying on makeup and trading clothes, and she only clucked whenever our father called her "Annie," in an effort to win her back.

"Get over it, Dad," she'd say, in the sarcastic, world-weary tone she and her friend Gail inspired in each other. "I'm not your little orphan-girl anymore." Then she and Gail would giggle and go off to call some boy, leaving my father with the ghost of his foolish hopes still fading from his face.

The videotape was one of the things the police took from the house when they searched it for evidence. They watched the first half hour before deciding it wasn't relevant. Later, when I lay in bed next to the investigating officer, he told me that the cops had not even recognized Meggy in the starring role. I was glad my father wasn't alive to hear him say it.

The final photograph in the cube on my father's dresser shows my sisters and me laughing as we fall out of a human pyramid. Justine and I are kneeling next to each other on all fours in a pile of leaves while Meggy loses her balance on top of us, one knee wobbling on each of our denim backs. Her hair, long and loose that day, falls in front of her forehead and across one eye above her laughter, making her look like a giddy pirate. The camera caught us on our way down into the leaves, all three of our mouths opened in the same pleasurable surprise.

We learned how to make the human pyramid from Justine, who was a cheerleader. When she was in her uniform I was a little afraid of her, even though I was older. Something about the confidence she put on along with the flared skirt made me shrink before her. I knew, of course, that the orange *A* sprawled across the chest of her sweater stood for Ashmont, but there was a part of me that also suspected it was a code for some secret language I would never be allowed to understand. Justine knew this and didn't use it against me the way she might have with a non-sister, a girl she could afford to offend or threaten, whose worship she would welcome and perhaps even invite. Between us, my rank in the family—my firstness, which all oldest children cherish, no matter how much we complain—gave me a power each of us knew would belong to me as long as we both should live.

Meggy, when she was little, begged Justine to teach her the cheers. Sometimes as I practiced with the two of them, I imagined I belonged to that species of girl you could identify purely by posture from far away. We pushed the sofa to one side of the living room and jumped and clapped and shouted until we were out of breath or until our parents made us stop.

But they—our parents—were also infected by the cheers, especially the old standard that our school's teams raised in the locker room or on the bus to away games, and which Justine took to singing around the house:

> We are the Eagles, mighty mighty Eagles!
> Everywhere we go-oh, people want to know-oh
> Who we are. So we tell them:
> We are the Eagles, mighty mighty Eagles!
> Everywhere we go-oh, people want to know . . .

And you kept repeating the words until you got sick of them, or you grew hoarse, or somebody told you to shut up.

One Sunday, when we were driving down to our grandparents' house for dinner and somebody in a Cadillac cut us off at a light, my father hit the steering wheel with the palms of both hands and yelled "Goddammit!" at the windshield. It was his favorite and, as far as I can remember, his only epithet. He was usually able to expel all his rage in the space of these three syllables, after which he was calm.

On the day the Cadillac cut us off, he aimed the aftershock smile at our mother, who sat next to him in the front seat. "Doesn't he know who we are?" he said, referring to the Cadillac's driver. Mom just looked at him for a moment, and then she caught on and smiled, too. Together they began to sing, and from the backseat the three of us joined in—

> We are the Dolans, mighty mighty Dolans!
> Everywhere we go, people want to know
> Who we are. So we tell them:
> We are the Dolans, mighty mighty Dolans!

Of course, if anybody I knew had been within hearing distance, I would have slumped way down in the seat and rolled up the window.

Even remembering it now makes me blush at how corny it was. But privately, among the five of us, it became a family refrain, especially when our parents were arguing. Say Dad was making a fuss about raw chicken in the refrigerator not being wrapped tight enough, or about somebody leaving a drop of egg white on the sponge. Next to the poison from lead paint on windowsills, diseases from eggs and chickens were among the potential invasions he dreaded most.

When his anxiety was highest, we couldn't have chicken in the house; when we did, he was the only one who could touch it before it was cooked. He buried the plastic wrapping in newspaper, which he then put into its own garbage bag and rolled into a tight twist. He brought the whole package outside to stash in his car trunk, so he could dispose of it far from the house.

And once, when he'd bought a week's worth of groceries but the cashier sneezed while packing them, my father wheeled the bags out of the store and directly to the Dumpster, where he tossed the entire purchase, canned sauces and all. If we had pancakes for breakfast, only he could crack the eggs into the batter, and the eggshells went the same way as the blood juice of the meat. (Years later, I would miss my father whenever I saw Phil Hartman playing the Anal-Retentive Chef on *Saturday Night Live*, while around me everybody laughed.)

Sometimes our mother just watched, without saying anything, when our father went through these elaborate sanitary routines. But other times she grew impatient and couldn't help showing it. She'd watch our father scouring the spot where an egg had leaked, and she'd say, "For God's sake, Tom, it's an *egg*, not a body fluid."

My father seemed to understand that his behavior was difficult to put up with, but he couldn't help it. He would ask her not to be so sarcastic, and she would say she couldn't help *that*. If the mood wasn't already ruined beyond repair, Meggy could start up the *mighty mighty Dolan* cheer and make everyone smile. It had to be the right moment, but when it worked it was one of those magic formulas every family has, a silly set of words reminding us of what's really important, that we belong to each other and this is how we know.

Justine was in junior high when she made her first cheerleading squad. Meggy was eight then, and I had just turned fifteen. Dancing alone in front of my mirror, I could move my body in a way I didn't mind watching, but when it came to gym or intramurals, I was the spastic sister. This was not a name I invented for my own masochistic torment; I heard somebody giggle it once as I passed the playing field with Justine. I was one of those girls who hates every minute of gym class except when the teacher blows the whistle to signal the end. On the soccer or hockey field I just tried to stay out of the way when the ball came to me, and let my teammates knock me down, if they needed to, in taking over the play.

The worst was cross fire, which we played on rainy days, the boys' and girls' classes combined. It was one thing to play the version we all learned in elementary school, where, if you got hit with the ball from the other side of the center line, you were out of the game. Many times, I would put myself in the direct line of these shots, so I could go sit on the side until there was only one person left and it was time to start over. Once, I was darting out when a ball bounced off my shoulder and hit Heather Shufelt in the ear. Even after I apologized and said that it wasn't my fault, Heather started a rumor that I wore boys' underwear.

When we reached high school, they taught us a different form of cross fire. Now, if you were hit, you had to go to the strip of floor at the back of the other team's territory, collect the balls that got past them, and try to hit them from behind. If you nailed someone, you earned your way back in. It meant that the game never ended, and you had to defend on all sides; you could never be safe. I suppose the teachers thought it was good for us to learn this lesson, a preparation for life. I never knew anyone who genuinely liked this version, except maybe Phil Cunningham, who was six feet tall, hid gin in his locker, and could never be hurt.

I knew I was a disappointment to my mother, who, as a teenager, had been a member of the All-State girls' basketball and field-hockey teams. And my mother didn't consider cheerleading a real sport. So it fell to Meggy to carry on the athletic tradition. She played basketball and soccer and ran the hurdles at track meets, her legs blurry flashes over the level slats.

After she died, the Kiwanis Club founded the Margaret O. Dolan Memorial Scholarship, which grants five hundred dollars each spring to a graduating senior girl who excelled in athletics throughout her high-school career. The school invites my mother, Justine, and me to the ceremony every year, but none of us has ever attended. We always receive a copy of the award program and, sometime over the summer, a thank-you note from the most recent winner. The notes usually start off by saying, "I didn't know Margaret, but . . ." and end with some variation of, "I will do my best to honor the memory of your daughter's and sister's name." After three years of reading remarkably similar letters, I finally figured out that the school must keep them on file somewhere, so that each new recipient will have a model to consult when her mother forces her to sit down and write to us.

Meggy's favorite sport was baseball, probably because everyone in my mother's family had been a devoted Mets fan since Casey Stengel days. Every April our grandfather, who had connections because of his position in the Presbyterian church, took us down to Shea Stadium for the home opener, and once our grandmother caught a home run off Mookie Wilson's bat.

Meggy wanted to play baseball, but when the Little League in our town wouldn't let her, my mother organized a separate league for the girls. By the time Meggy was in high school, the league had eight teams in each of three age groups, and my mother, as founder, was honored at the end-of-season banquet every summer.

We all used to go to Meggy's games together in her early playing years, when she was an outfielder. The spring my parents separated, only a few months before Meggy died, she was promoted to pitcher, but by then it was usually only our father who went to watch her play. I was at college in Boston, Justine was busy with her friends, and our mother had moved out. She wasn't all that far away—an hour and a half or so west, to the town (actually, it liked to call itself a "hamlet") of Delphi. But of course it was a different school district, so after our mother left in March, Meggy and Justine stayed behind in Ashmont to finish out the year.

Mom was going to turn down the job at the Delphi newspaper when they offered it to her, because she couldn't take Justine and Meggy right away. But Justine told her, *Go ahead, it's only for three months, we'll see you on weekends, we'll be fine.* I remember realizing that our mother's absence, and our father's distress over it, would actually benefit Justine during that final semester of her senior year, when it came to staying out late and going unchaperoned. She moved into the guest room at Sue Shooby's. Justine and Sue and their friends liked to hang out at the Cat House, the attic of Sue's garage, where the Shoobys stored their old couches and where all the cats in the neighborhood sunned and slept during the day. At night it became a party den for the kids in Justine's crowd, the room rocking with shrieks and music, the air sour with filched beer.

So Justine was never around to talk to whenever I called that spring, but it didn't seem to bother my father. This should have been a clue to me that he was preoccupied by something deeper than the divorce, but I only recognized the clues afterward, when it was too late to do anything but feel guilty.

I graduated from college in May, watching through drizzle as the marching band formed a crooked *1988* on the football field. My parents and sisters came to Boston to attend the commencement as a family, and we went out to dinner afterward. My father kept looking at my mother, but whenever she caught him, he looked away. Meggy tried to make everyone laugh with her imitation of Pee-wee Herman, but we were all distracted by the energy it took to keep our grief within bounds, and in the middle of her shtick she had to stop suddenly and swallow. When the tears appeared on her cheeks nobody said anything. My mother handed her a clean napkin while my father raised his hand for the check.

After the ceremony my mother wanted me to go back to Delphi with her, but I wasn't ready to leave home. Instead I returned to Ashmont with my father and sisters, to the house on Pearl Street that other people—a family named Crowell—would soon call home. Our father had rented an apartment in Grandview Arms, staggered stucco units with a communal

Jacuzzi and badminton court. I could no more picture my father living there than in an igloo, but he seemed surprisingly resigned to it as the Fourth of July approached. That was moving-out weekend; his suitcases would go across town to the Grandview's square, white, empty rooms, and my sisters and I would help the Crisafulli brothers load our belongings onto the truck they would drive out to the condo in Delphi, which my mother had already bought with money her parents gave her.

The condo was small, but Justine was scheduled to start college at Syracuse, our mother's alma mater, that September, so the extra bedroom at the new place would really be Meggy's alone until she graduated from Ashmont High.

But Meggy and our father died at the end of June. By then, she had already decided she didn't want to play softball anymore. She told Dad it was because she wanted to spend her last evenings in Ashmont at the town pool, but he didn't believe her and he kept pestering her about it until finally she said, "Okay, okay, if you really want to know, I can't stand going to games knowing you're afraid you'll see Mom there. It makes me sick that you can't even look at each other; it makes me want to puke." Then she flung her Parrelli Hardware team cap at him in a little fit of drama and went outside to sit on the swings.

Later, she told Justine and me that she'd overheard our parents talking on the phone. Our father was crying, pleading with her not to go through with the divorce, saying it would be too much for Meggy to handle. "But *he's* the one," Meggy told us. We'd turned up the radio in her bedroom so we could talk. Meggy and I were eating Chips Ahoy cookies straight out of the blue bag. Justine, who always wanted to be thinner than she already was, sipped at her seltzer. "The three of us are handling it just fine."

Meggy was almost sixteen then. Although we never said anything about it, we all sensed that *the three of us* was changing in ways we could not guess. I remember going to the last game she pitched. I watched from the top bleacher, the aluminum under my bare legs hot from a long day's sun, which came in slanting at that hour and made the field hard to see. My sister's face was only a shadow under the bill of her cap, and her hair hung in wheat braids between her shoulder blades. Gail Harvey, Meggy's best friend, had hair of the same length and color, and when they were younger the girls asked for matching clothes at Christmas and pretended to be twins. Occasionally, from a distance, even my mother and Justine and I mistook one for the other. The only person they never fooled was our father, who could pick out his favorite daughter instantly across three playing fields.

Before each pitch, I remember, Meggy would tap the bill of her cap for luck. Her windup was slow but the ball flew fast from her fingers, and she struck out many of her opponents.

In the younger teams, you got a strike counted against you only if you swung at the ball and missed. But in the major league, where Meggy played in the end, the umpire would call it if you just stood there while a pitch went through the strike zone and over the plate. By then, you were supposed to have some judgment. You were supposed to be able to tell if what was coming at you was something you should want.

2. The universe is unfolding

Q. Is there a "method" for eating animal crackers?
— *E.S., Cheviot*

A. According to a spokesman for the National Biscuit Company (Nabisco), which in 1902 introduced Animal Crackers in those little boxes with the string handles (the boxes themselves were supposed to be used as Christmas tree ornaments), there is no official etiquette for eating the baked goodies. However, based on hundreds of letters to the company, it is known that most children prefer to nibble first on the back legs, then the forelegs, then the head, and lastly the body.

Criminally speaking, nothing much ever happened in Ashmont, which lies just south of Albany between the Hudson River and the Helderberg mountain range. Sometimes kids spray-painted graffiti on the brick walls of the junior high, or tipped a parked car on its side, but unless your father went off the deep end, you didn't have to worry about being shot to death in your own bed.

We moved to Ashmont the summer I was nine. For weeks I didn't meet anybody on our new street except Russell Stinson, the Vietnam vet who lived next door to us and sat on his front porch, in his wheelchair, smoking and calling out to cars. The realtor had warned us about him. "He's a little loud sometimes, but completely harmless," she said. "It's more of a nuisance than anything else."

All the girls in the neighborhood who were my age already seemed to belong to their own crowds, and I was afraid to ask them if I could be let in. Instead I sat on the porch, listening to Russell and reading books from the fourth-grade list my father had requested from my new school. (My favorite was *The Long Secret*, which I could have finished in a few days but managed to stretch out for an entire delicious week.) I kept hoping someone might approach me as I read—I held the books with the most intriguing covers up to my face so they could be seen from the sidewalk—and invite me to play. This didn't happen, but I consoled myself with the idea that at least I would be ahead in my reading when school began.

Even as a first-grader, Justine found her clique right away. She spent entire days at the town park with other six-year-olds whose mothers made a habit of hanging out by the pool, drinking Diet Cokes, while their kids played Marco Polo in the shallow end. Justine had already been to three birthday parties and to Saratoga to see *The Nutcracker* by the first day of school.

My mother didn't seem to notice that I did everything alone, or with her and Meggy, but my father stopped one morning on his way to work and sat down next to me on the top porch step, where I was watching ants crawl across my toes. "It's hard, isn't it," he said. If he had told me to cheer up or tried to make me feel better, I would have continued sulking. But when he said what he did, I felt my face fold and then I turned into the jacket of his suit, wanting to make myself small enough to fit inside his pocket. He held me until I finished crying. It was only a short burst, but it left a circle of wetness on his suit coat. I was afraid it would make him nervous—like dirt or germs—but instead of going inside to change clothes he kissed me on the forehead, gave me a complimentary Zenith Realty pen from his briefcase, and went on to work, still carrying the stain of my sadness on his shoulder.

In Ashmont, in the summer, you could be reading on your front porch when you found yourself dozing to the blended buzz of lawn mowers, the ice-cream truck, basketballs slapping driveways, and children splashing and screaming in backyard pools. On snowy days you could count on one of your neighbors to give your car a push, especially if other neighbors were watching from their windows. If you painted watercolors or took pleasant photographs, you could show them on the walls leading into the library. The air you pumped into your bike tires was free. The police station stood across from the Shamrock, and on their lunch hour, officers went over there to drink beers with the men they would decline to arrest later the same night, when they stopped cars for creeping or veering and found their friends at the wheels. Everybody felt taken care of, and there was the sense, even for those of us who didn't understand why we went to church, that God knew who we were.

The day my father and Meggy died was hot and sticky. The weather had been like that for a week. At Justine's high-school graduation the Friday before, two grandmothers had fainted, and the news was filled with warnings about a hazardous quality to the air.

I had a baby-sitting job that day. I'd started working for the Melnick family when they only had two children, Donald and Sarah; then, while I was in college, Josh was born. Nostalgia, more than the money, was what made me agree to take care of all three kids for a whole day. I knew that after my sisters and I moved out to our mother's condo in Delphi, I wouldn't be running into the Melnicks at the park or the post office anymore. We had all finished packing, and there wasn't much to do except sit around and absorb our father's gloom as we waited for our family's failure to become official.

Mr. and Mrs. Melnick were catching a 7 A.M. train to New York, so I got up at 5:30. My father was sitting at the table in the kitchen when I came into the room and switched the light on. I was so surprised to see him there that I sucked in a gasp.

He turned when he heard me and seemed to smile. The early-morning fluorescence caught the dampness of his hair, just washed, where it was smoothed at the sides of his head. He had scrubbed his face so hard I could see the pores stinging in red flesh.

"Hi, honey," he said, but it sounded more like a question than a greeting.

"What are you doing up?" I asked, taking the chair across from him.

He shrugged. "Couldn't sleep. I had a dream about Mom."

Although I dreaded the answer, I knew he expected me to ask. "What was it?"

"She was having some kind of operation. They were knocking her out. The doctor came over to me and said, 'We'll be opening your wife up in a minute, sir. But I wanted to let you know, as a courtesy, that during the surgery, you'll be the one doing the bleeding. We gave her the option, and she chose you.'" When he said this last line, my father sounded as if he couldn't get enough breath, and there was something new in his eyes that I hadn't seen before. Or maybe something that had always been there was suddenly missing; I couldn't be sure which.

I told him, "It's just a dream, Dad. She wouldn't do that."

"I know," he said, but he didn't sound convinced. "I'm not going to work today," he added, playing with the spoon in the sugar bowl. I couldn't tell whether he wanted me to approve or to try to talk him into changing his mind.

"Well. Maybe you need a day off." I didn't point out that he'd missed more days of work at Wolf Subaru than he'd shown up for, since I'd been back home. "If you haven't been sleeping, you should get some rest. You and Meggy could go to a movie or something."

"Where is Justine, again?" He was trying to concentrate, I realized— to recall what he already knew.

"Lake George. Remember? A bunch of them went up last night."

"And when is she coming back?"

"I don't know, Dad. She's not exactly living here anymore." I waited for him to remember that Justine was hardly ever home except to change clothes—as she would be later that night when she found his body—but when he didn't respond I said to him, "Listen. I'll leave the Melnicks' number by the phone, in case you need anything. Okay?"

He laughed slightly, sounding not at all amused. "What could I possibly need?"

When I went to leave, he stood up and insisted on giving me a hug, a long one, and though he held me close, there was no strength in it. "Be good," he told me. It was only later that I realized what he'd said, instead of his standard "Be careful."

"Well, you too," I said, a little confused, trying to smile.

"I never wanted to be like this."

"What?" I turned from the door, not sure I'd heard correctly because he had murmured whatever it was.

"Nothing." He smiled back and gave me a wave. "Never mind, honey. Anastasia." He lingered over my name, giving it the elaborate, Slavic-sounding pronunciation he once used to amuse me when I was a child. "'Bye."

I started out the door and turned back one last time. "Listen, let Meggy sleep in, okay? She was up late watching TV."

"Okay." My father was staring at the tablecloth. A gnat hovered above the sugar bowl, and when he didn't even move to swat it away, I felt a quick drizzle of dread.

It was not a premonition, exactly. A few days after it happened, I tried to remember if my body held any foreboding as I walked away from our house, down the same street I had walked every school day to the bus stop since the fourth grade. But it was pity I felt, more than fear. He'll go to bed, I thought, and Meggy will be nice to him, bring him tea and toast as if the problem were in his stomach. She'll stick around the house today, tell Gail to go ahead without her to the pool. There was no real reason to think Meggy would do this and give up a day with her friends, but I wanted to believe the scene I had conjured. I resolved to call home at lunchtime and check up on things.

When I got to the Melnicks' house, the kids were already having their cereal, and from the moment their parents left, the day was a frenzy of play. We spent the morning making forts in the backyard; for lunch we made pizza, and I gave each of them a piece of dough and let them put on whatever they wanted for toppings—they chose chocolate chips, marshmallows, and broccoli, which Josh, the baby, called trees. He went down for a nap after he threw up, and I thought about calling my father and Meggy then, but the older kids had started a game of croquet and demanded that I play. When Josh woke up I took them to the park to go swimming, and we camped out on our towels by the kiddie pool. I was in the water with the baby when I heard someone call my name, and I looked up to see Matt Lonergan squatting beside me, slurping the last of a Dr Pepper.

"Where's Meg?" he asked, wiping the brown drops from his chin. "I tried calling her this morning, but there was no answer."

"Really?" I grabbed Josh's hand to keep him from splashing. "What did you want?" I hadn't meant to be rude, but his question surprised me. Matt was a year older than Meggy and they'd been in the same pre-school class, but by the time he was old enough for T-ball, he left her behind. Over the years, when our neighborhood had its annual block-party barbecue, Matt usually made an appearance only to grab a hot dog before climbing back up to his tree house, which was the scene of a noisy and endless intergalactic war. Until I left for college, I only saw him mowing lawns or riding his bike. In the summer when the screens

were in, we could hear him fighting with his father, Ed, a town select-
man who came home drunk most nights and yelled at his wife, Kay,
who was my mother's best friend.

Now Matt was seventeen, about to be a senior, and he towered so
high above me at the pool's edge that he blocked the sun. He hesitated
when I asked him why he was trying to reach Meggy. "Well," he said,
"no real reason. We were talking about going to see *Alien*, maybe. No big
deal." I could tell he was trying to sound nonchalant.

"Well, our dad stayed home sick today," I told him. "Meggy might be
doing something with him."

The night before, we'd watched *Cheers* with our father, and then he
went, uncharacteristically early, to bed. He shut the door, which was
also unlike him. In front of the TV he hadn't laughed at the things Meggy
and I found funny, but we didn't mention this to each other. Instead she
stayed in the living room long after I'd settled down in bed with a book.
When I woke up in the middle of the night, I could still hear the TV.
I went out to the living room to see if she'd fallen asleep on the couch.

"Are you awake?" I asked. A talk show blared in the background, but
except for the glow from the TV, the room was dark. As I moved to turn
on a lamp she made a sound of protest, but the room was already lit, and
I saw she was sucking her thumb. "What's the matter?" I asked.

"Nothing." She frowned and slid her thumb out. Then, in a whisper:
"Ana?"

"What?" Huddled into a corner of the couch, she looked more like
my little sister—the girl in purple shorts and Cookie Monster T-shirt—
than the angular, moody young woman she'd become during the past
year. I hadn't returned home as much to visit during that year, my last at
college, and it shocked me each time I saw her after being away. She was
already taller than either Justine or me, and she always wore black clothes,
as if her most fervent wish was to blend into the background. My father
often brought home blouses with bright colors from expensive stores,
but she never put them on. "I can't stand all that black," he said to me
one night, when it was just the two of us for dinner. "She looks like
Morticia on *The Addams Family*. Or Zorro, for God's sake."

"She's fifteen, Dad. We can't tell her what to wear."

"I know," he said, but I could tell he didn't believe me. "Remember those little dresses she used to have? Remember the one with the strawberry pocket?"

"We all wore that dress. Aunt Rosemary gave it to me."

"Oh, right," he said, but I knew he didn't have any memories of the same dress on Justine or me.

The night before she died, Meggy appeared to be deciding whether she should confide something. Finally she shook her head and said, "Never mind."

"But what's the matter?"

"Nothing, I said." She smiled, but I could see her mouth quiver. "Go back to bed."

"You sure?" I knew there had to be more, but I was still halfway asleep, and I felt the word *bed* luring me back.

Meggy nodded without meeting my eyes. "Okay, then," I said. "Good night."

"'Night," she murmured, drawing a cushion close. The TV remained on and in my room I fell asleep to the sounds of people shouting at each other and contemptuous applause.

Now, at the pool, I considered telling Matt that it seemed Meggy *had* had something on her mind. But since I didn't know what it was, I decided not to say anything. "I'm sure she'll be home soon," I said. "When you get back from swimming, try again."

"Okay." Matt hesitated, and I thought he was about to say something else; he looked nervous, but I told myself he was only squinting at the sun. He gave me a slight, almost guilty smile and headed off toward the pack of teenagers gathered by the deep end of the pool. When they were younger, they all used to sit here in segregated circles. The girls would paint their toenails as they passed around *Seventeen*, while the boys played tapes of the B-52s on a boom box. Now the sexes blended in a miasma of laughter, the bodies under their bathing suits ropy with suntanned desire.

When I returned the Melnick kids to their house around five o'clock,

I called home and the machine picked up. I wasn't worried, because there was any number of things Dad and Meggy might be out doing. Still, I felt a pulse of alarm when I remembered leaving my father in the morning, the vacant look in his eyes as he hugged me good-bye. But Meggy would have helped him out of it, by now. She would have taken him to a movie that would have them both laughing. Something silly, starring Bette Midler or Chevy Chase. When I got home he'd tell me about it: "I know I was a little off when I saw you this morning, but Meggo cheered me right up."

I was browning ground beef for supper tacos when the doorbell rang. "Can you get that, Sarah?" I called into the TV room. When the bell rang again, I swore and turned the stove down. Donald, the eight-year-old, was blocking my way, holding up a sloshing Sprite bottle.

"Did I show you my collection of fluids yet?" he asked solemnly. "It's in here."

"Just a minute, Don," I said. At the screen door I saw two men in police uniforms, and felt a prickle shoot through me as I tried to remember what I had done wrong.

One of the cops asked me, "Are you Anastasia Dolan?" Josh was hiding behind my legs, but he peeked around the side as I opened the door.

"Yeah," I said, hearing the wariness in my voice. Suddenly it occurred to me that something must have happened to Mr. and Mrs. Melnick—a train derailment, a sniper in Times Square. "Josh, go in there with Don and Sarah, okay?" Reluctantly he padded away, still looking over his shoulder at the big men in uniforms.

"We have some upsetting news," the officer said. He looked familiar, but I wasn't sure where I had seen him before. "Bad news," he added, as if clarifying what he'd said at first. In the kitchen, the meat was still sizzling, and I said, "Let me just turn off the stove," and the other officer told me, "I'll get it," and he clumped heavily back toward the kitchen. While he was gone I said to the first one, "You hungry?" and he started to smile but then caught himself, and this time he put a hand out to touch my arm.

"It's your father and your sister," he said. I thought he meant it as in,

There's your father and your sister, as if they had somehow entered the Melnicks' house, behind me, and I hadn't seen them yet. I wasn't even sure which sister he was referring to, although instinct told me he meant Meggy.

"I'm sorry, Ms. Dolan. But we got a call about an hour ago, we went to investigate, and—they've suffered fatal injuries." He cleared his throat when I just frowned at him, and added, "They've died."

I remember I felt the impulse to laugh; by the time the words reached me, they were pure gibberish. "I have to feed the kids," I said to the officers, backing my way down the hall and into the kitchen, reaching out to keep my balance against the wall. The officers looked at each other, then followed me.

In the kitchen, I picked up the wooden spoon I'd been stirring the beef with and added seasoning to the mix. The first officer, the one I knew from somewhere, said, "We need you to come with us. Ms. Dolan?" He came over to the stove and lifted a hand as if he thought I might need support, but when I didn't sway or fold, he held back his touch.

"I can't. The kids." I gestured at the three of them, lined up in the doorway of the family room. I concentrated on making out the scar above Sarah's eyebrow, the bristles of Donald's crew cut, the baby's pillowy knees. "Call me Ana," I told the officers, hearing what I said but still making no sense of it. "They're hungry. Their parents are in the city watching a play."

"I'll stay with them," the second man told me. "You go ahead with Officer Garhart—with Frank here."

"Oh," I said, "Garhart. Monica's brother. You used to chase us around the house in your Herman Munster mask."

"Guilty," he said, and smiled, but then I saw him remember his purpose here, and his face grew solemn again.

"What'd she do?" Sarah asked the officers, and I could tell she was afraid to look at me. Then that concern slid into second place. "Frank's a silly name," she said. "What are you, a hot dog?" She cracked up at her own joke.

"I was named after a singer my mom liked," Frank told her quietly, but he was looking at me.

I said, "Sinatra?"

"No. Zappa."

"That's funny *too*," Sarah said with delight.

The other policeman, who had offered to stay behind as baby-sitter, took off his belt and handed it over, with the gun still in its holster, to Monica Garhart's brother. "Nobody did anything wrong, you guys," he told the kids. "There was an accident." Then he took off his badge and held it out to Josh, who looked at his sister for permission before accepting it. I watched all of this, the movement of moments in front of me, without seeing or, it seemed, breathing—but I must have breathed; lungs work, don't they? even after the mind shuts down. I let Frank lead me by the elbow out the door, not feeling his touch. The children called 'Bye behind me and I called back, without turning, Be good, but it was my father's voice and not my own saying the words.

On hard legs I went to get into the backseat of the police car, because that's how they always did it on TV. But Frank opened the front door instead and helped me into the passenger seat. Lois Phelps and her elderly father were sitting on her porch across the street, and I saw them both lean forward to get a better look. Three houses down, a children's kickball game on the Shoobys' front lawn paused in midplay as the kids gathered to watch from around the Frisbee that served as home plate. It was only after I was inside the car that I saw the metal lattice-wall behind me, separating the backseat from the front. "Sorry," Frank said, seeing me notice. "The cage car was all we had free."

"I've never seen the inside of a police car before. In real life, I mean." I was suffocating, slowly. Something I couldn't see pushed down on me and made the landscape shrink.

"Well, then, I guess you've never broken any laws. Or been caught at it, anyway." Static flickered over the radio, and Frank reached to turn it down. "I guess if I punched you up in our computer, I wouldn't find a match."

I was having trouble comprehending. When he said, "punched you up," all I could think of was him punching me in the stomach, and this puzzled me, but in the next instant the puzzlement vanished, along with the memory of what he'd just said. "Where are we going?"

"I need to take you to the station."

"Could I go home first? I want to get a sweater." It was the end of June, still hot and light outside, but I was shivering. When he didn't say anything right away, I turned to look at him and saw a wince cross his face. "What?" I said. Something about his silence made the juice in my stomach go sour. "Where were they?"

"Where were they?" he repeated. Later I would understand that he just wanted to delay my knowing, but at the moment I almost believed he was mocking me—the way children, to be annoying, will echo whatever you say.

"When they had the accident." I had it all laid out in my mind: the busy parking lot at the Cinemaxx, somebody speeding through a stop sign and broadsiding my father's car. Meggy putting her hands up against the windshield; my father, knowing what was about to happen, throwing his arm across her to keep her from hitting the glass.

"Actually, Ana, they were home." We had reached the police station, which had been converted to its current use ten years earlier from our old elementary school. Frank parked at the curb, where we used to line up for our buses at the buzzer signaling the end of each school day. I could almost hear the shouts from that time, as if they had been etched indelibly in the atmosphere—*You retard! McCarry's a fairy!* as he switched off the ignition and turned to me in the seat.

"What do you mean, they were home?" I said. "How could they have an accident at *home*?" I felt a rush of hope: if they had been home, that meant they were safe, which meant that all of this had to be a mistake.

"Let's go inside first, okay?" Frank got out and came around to my side to open the door, like an old-fashioned date. While I was waiting for him, I looked down at the siren controls on the panel between the seats. *Yelp*, read one of the dial settings. Underneath that was *Wail*.

I followed him inside the building, to the foyer. It was here that Gordon Zukowski, in fifth grade, put on Mrs. Teague's wet rain bonnet and started singing I *Honestly Love You* like Olivia Newton-John, making Abigail Knott laugh so hard she peed straight through her underpants onto the floor. In high school Gordon was arrested for soliciting sex in the Shamrock, but that was a long time away from happening (so was Abigail Knott's self-induced abortion the night before SATs) when we all went to school here together and left our muddy rubber-tracks in the hall.

Now that it was a police station, you rounded a corner by the old Teachers' Lounge before you came to the reception area. Frank got there first, and before I came in view of the desk, the man sitting there asked him, "Hey, did Tom Dolan really do his daughter?" Then he saw me and his face blanched as he realized who I must be.

"Jesus, Len." Frank turned on his heel fast, as if afraid he might have to run after and catch me. "Ana, listen. Come here." He led me, again by the elbow, over to a bench by the water fountain, which had been lifted in the wall from the design of grammar-school days. I still didn't understand what was happening, and I didn't believe my father and Meggy were dead, because of what Frank had said about their being at home. And the only times I had ever heard the expression "do," in terms of a man doing a woman, it meant he had had sex with her. So it couldn't be my father and Meggy the officer was talking about.

"I hate this," Frank said, and I could see sweat dotting his upper lip. "I've never had to tell anybody something like this before. But your father and your sister—Margaret?"

"Meggy." Even though it was our mother's name, Meggy hated *Margaret*. She thought it made her sound like an old lady.

Frank winced again. "Okay. Listen, Ana. They're dead, and it looks like a murder-suicide. It's pretty clear. It looks like your father shot—Meggy— and then shot himself."

"That's impossible," I told him. I actually felt relieved. If he had told me they'd spun into oncoming traffic on the bypass, there would have been no reason not to believe him. The idea of my father with a gun, let alone of him shooting Meggy, was absurd.

Yet even as I thought about how to say this to Frank, I remembered the look on my father's face that morning as he sat at the breakfast table.

I thought about how odd it felt to know that he had stopped being aware of me even though I was still in the room. And I knew, even though my mind hadn't caught up with the feeling, that what Frank told me was true.

"Where's Justine," I said. I didn't even have the energy to make it sound like a question.

"She's at the hospital. No, don't worry—he didn't—God, let me start over." Frank bit his lip. "She was the one who—she came home, and that's how we knew something happened."

"She saw them?"

"I think it was just your father. Then she got sick. You know, shock. She started throwing up and couldn't stop." He took a deep breath as if he might be feeling nauseated himself. "I believe she also made some gesture toward hurting herself—probably just an impulse, but she cut herself with a stone from the walkway in front of your house. A sharp edge, I guess. They brought her in for observation to make sure she was okay."

"I want to go there." My voice sounded dead.

"You know, your mother's on her way out here from—where is it, Delphi? Don't you want to wait for her? Besides, I think they might have given your sister something to make her sleep."

"I don't care. Take me." I had forgotten I had a mother until Frank said the word. Maybe not forgotten, exactly. But it was my sister I wanted to see.

"Okay." Frank sighed and supported me as I stood up from the bench. The hours after that, in my memory, all converge at a single point, the sensation of being led down the hospital hall to the room where Justine lay curled on a bed in the children's wing. On the way I passed the lounge, where kids on crutches or attached to machines watched cartoons on a VCR. From a distant room came a cry: "You promised! You promised!" and the sad sound of parents trying to soothe.

When I reached Justine, she was facing the wall, away from me, and even when I touched her shoulder she didn't turn. I yanked her roughly, and when her body fell toward me I saw that she was asleep. Or not asleep: they had taken the chemical equivalent of a hammer and knocked her out—every trace of emotion and intelligence had been erased from her features so that her face was remote and blank. She still had on the clothes she'd come home in, a denim shirt over a tank top, and cutoff shorts so tight and tattered that my father would never have let her wear them out of the house if he'd seen her, if he'd been in his right mind.

A white gauze bandage was wrapped around Justine's left arm, below the elbow. The next day she would tell the doctor it had been an accident, cutting herself with the stone, and he would release her. "Wake up, Justine," I told her, pinching her cheeks before Frank could stop me. "Wake up. Come on. Wake up." The idea that I didn't have access to her, at that moment, seemed the worst of all things to bear.

But then the doctor came in, and he pulled me gently away from Justine. "Let me give you something," he suggested, putting a needle in, and I spent the rest of that night sleeping beside my sister. It wasn't until morning that we saw our mother; she had been sedated, too, and we woke up before her.

Our mother had a bruise on her forehead. She told us that when the Delphi police came to tell her what had happened, she'd collapsed, and they hadn't caught her before she hit her face on the door.

But Frank told me, later, that this was a lie. (That wasn't the word he used, but it's what it came down to.) He'd talked to the Delphi officer, who said that when my mother understood what he had come to tell her—that Meggy was dead—she took hold of the edge of the doorway and banged her head hard against the wall. That was when she collapsed, the officer told Frank. I decided not to ask my mother about it, or even to tell Justine. In fact, I managed to forget this detail myself, until just now.

The rest of that day and the next is unclear to me, except for a conversation I had with my friend Ruthie after the funeral. Our mother and Justine were watching TV with the Waxmans, and Ruthie and I spoke in low tones at the kitchen table. She was wearing a long T-shirt that said *Take Me Drunk, I'm Home*, and she had her feet up on the rung of the chair I sat in.

"But Ana," she kept saying, "why did this happen?" At the time I thought she was being inexplicably cruel by forcing the issue, but now, looking back, it seems more likely that she was just trying to make me focus. I think it scared her, my being so soupy. That's the word she used. "Look at me," she'd say, but I couldn't; I didn't want to recognize her or anything else.

Much more vivid in my memory is the following night, Saturday, when Frank came to see us at the Hudson Motor Inn. My mother and Justine and I had been staying there since the deaths. Kay Lonergan had offered to put us all up, but it was hard enough going to the Waxmans' house for the reception. We wanted to be as far away from Pearl Street as we could, until things were wrapped up and we were free to go back to my mother's condo in Delphi. There was an inquest scheduled for Monday, and when that was over, Frank told us, they wouldn't need us to stay in town, as long as we were—to use his word—"reachable."

The motel, which was located at a juncture of highways just outside town, was cheap and what Justine called cheesy: two double beds and an imitation-wood bureau with a TV bolted to one end. Our room was at the end of the first-floor row, next to the parking lot and the pool, and Justine had to turn the volume up loud to drown out the noise of kids calling, "Marco!" "Polo!" on the other side of the drapes.

The first night we spent there, my mother asked if either of us wanted to sleep with her.

"What?" Justine said, looking away from the bureau mirror, where she was experimenting with parting her hair on different sides of her head.

"I mean, does anybody want to share my bed?" Mom made a what-do-you-think-I-mean gesture, putting both hands out to the side. "Somebody has to double up."

"We'll take this one," Justine said, patting the spread on the other bed. My mother said "Fine," and I could tell she was hurt, but I was glad Justine had declared the arrangement. It was what I wanted, too.

We'd spent the afternoon picking out headstones and what we wanted engraved on them. We ordered takeout from the motel restaurant, but only Justine ate; the rest of it went into the basket beneath the TV. Frank

Garhart knocked at about eight o'clock. Standing in the doorway of the motel room, he told us what to expect. With his blond hair in a buzz cut—he'd probably been to the barber's on his lunch hour; there were nicks on his neck—he looked like a freshly shorn von Trapp brother. And there was some of that—*von-Trappness*—in the way he spoke, a slightly formal lilt to his voice that I hadn't detected before, as if afraid he might be corrected at any moment for the wrong grammar or faulty choice of words. "The coroner will ask some questions, mainly the ground we've already covered," he said. "It's pretty routine." He held his officer's hat in his hands, turning it over and over in the room's sour light. My mother, supporting herself by pillows against the headboard of the near bed, looked up from her crossword puzzle and blinked. On the other bed Justine lay prone, watching a movie on HBO.

"Get me out of here," I said to Frank in a low voice, though I doubted my mother and sister were conscious enough to care. I followed him out to the parking lot, looking for a police cruiser. "Where's your car?" He gestured at a beat-up Impala with a bicycle rack on the back. "Wait— you're not on duty?" I asked, and he blushed and shook his head.

"Just got off. I told them I'd stop over and see you folks on my way home." He blushed again on the word "folks," and he rubbed the back of his head, as if he thought it might be possible to mess up the neat nap of his hair. "Is there someplace in particular you want to go?" He looked as if he wasn't sure he should be offering, but when I reached for the passenger-side door he beat me to the handle and held it open.

I said, "Can we just drive?" From the corner of my eye, I saw that he was watching me as I tucked myself into the seat. We kept the windows down as we circled the town, and then he began taking the short roads toward its center. We traded childhood stories about the places we passed—the time I fell asleep reading *Helter Skelter* in one of the library's bean-bag chairs and woke up with a shriek, thinking it was Charles Manson and not the librarian tapping my shoulder; the time he got his tongue stuck in the end of a garden hose at the Lawn Ranger. Both of us had stolen from Woolworth's (I took a tube of Chap Stick; he managed to smuggle out an entire twelve-pack of Upper Deck baseball cards), which was a Crate&Barrel now.

"I bet you don't have a record, either, though," I said to Frank, after he confessed his technique of wearing his father's old army fatigue jacket on his shoplifting missions, the better to stash the loot. "You must have been good."

"Actually, they did catch me one time." A shadow crossed his eyes and I could see that the memory pained him. "The last time. They called my father in; I guess they knew he was a cop. He asked the security guard to leave us alone in the room. The guy said, 'Okay, but just for a minute. No rough stuff, right?' He must have thought my dad wanted to beat me up." Frank paused and gripped the steering wheel. We were stopped at a light.

"Did he?"

"Oh, God no. My father wasn't the beating-up type. He just sat across from me in this little room and said, 'Son, I'm disappointed.'" Frank lowered his eyes briefly and snorted a laugh without the mirth. "I wish he had hit me."

Something in his voice made me ask, "Is your dad still living?"

He shook his head. "He was killed in a car crash chasing a scumbag, excuse the expression, seven years ago."

"Oh, yeah. God, I remember. Monica was out of school for a long time." I thought of the first day I'd seen Monica Garhart back in the hallways, after that. She was stooped and stunned, bumping into people, and I remember thinking, This is what you look like when one of your parents dies.

"That must have been hard," I said after a moment. "The scumbag lived, right?"

"Yeah." Frank's features hardened as he pressed the accelerator. "They got him off on a technicality. Nothing ever happened to him."

I looked out the window at the teenagers gathered in front of the Toll Gate Ice Cream Shoppe, where just before closing you could get two cones for the price of one. A girl in a ponytail screamed in pleasure as her boyfriend drew a streak of his soft-serve swirl down her neck, then leaned closer to lick it off. I felt Frank's eyes focusing on the side of my

face. "But at least that was an accident," he said. "My father. I can't imagine what it must be like—"

"That's okay," I interrupted, sticking my head out the window to get
more air. It made my eyes sting and I closed them, blind in the night's
mild breeze. We drove like that for what seemed a long time, though
when I finally pulled my head back in and opened my eyes to look at the
clock, I saw it had been only a few minutes. My hands trembled on top
of my knees.

He pulled into a dark gas station and stopped the car. "Should I take
you back?" He reached across the gap between us, his one hand fitting
over both of mine, and—though I expected the opposite—I felt the
shaking stop.

I thought of the room at the motor inn where my mother and
Justine would be silent as they waited to fall asleep. "Please, not yet," I
told him.

"Then where?"

"Do you live around here?"

"Not far. By the post office."

"Can we go there?" I imagined a rented room strewn with bachelor
clutter. A place where it would be easy to lose something, if you needed to.

"You want to see where I live?" Frank took his hand away and put it
back on the wheel.

"Well. Unless you had plans."

"No. I just—well, yeah. Okay. We could have a beer or something,
I guess."

Neither of us spoke again until he pulled up in front of a one-story
brick house on Salisbury Avenue, cut the engine, and turned off the lights.
"You live here?" I said. It was a real neighborhood, with trees and swing
sets, backyard decks and roll-around grills.

"Why not?" He got out of the car and came around to my door, but I
already had it open.

"I don't know. It's just so grown-up."

"Well. I'm a grown-up," he said. "Don't tell." Although it was silly
and didn't really mean anything, I laughed. When I let it ring longer

than I meant to, he lifted a finger to his lips and whispered, "Ssh—screens."

I nodded, feeling distant from myself and a little out of control, as if a wire had lost track of its circuit inside my brain. He'd left a light on for himself, and the door opened easily under his key. "Have a seat," he said, switching on a lamp in the living room. There was a couch along the wall and two chairs behind the coffee table, and I chose one of the chairs. "Just let me hit the men's room a minute," he said, then blushed at what he'd called it. "I'll be right back."

While he was gone I looked at the photographs on his mantel—there was one of him and Monica as children, laughing on a raft—and then I caught sight of an Ashmont High yearbook propping open a window on the other side of the room. I pulled the book out and let the window down, and I was looking at Frank's senior picture when he returned clutching pilsner glasses, two opened bottles of Budweiser, and a bowl of chips. "Oh, God," he said, when he saw what I was doing, but he smiled. In the photograph he looked smart and serious, like a young man with a plan. But there was also a drawn, gray expression around his mouth that made me see he had suffered.

"I can't believe you're actually named after Frank Zappa," I told him, setting the book on the table between us.

He smirked a little. "Actually, that's one of those family lies. It was really Frankie Valli. You know—'Big Girls Don't Cry'? But by the time Zappa came on the scene, my mom was eating and sleeping rock and roll." He poured the beers and watched the heads settle. "One of my earliest memories is of being locked accidentally in the bathroom, banging on the door, and her not being able to hear me over Sergeant Pepper. I remember crying so hard my nose bled into one of her yellow towels." He took a sip of beer so small that he might have been tasting wine before telling the waiter to go ahead and pour. "Anyway, she started telling people she'd named me after Zappa. It made her seem younger than she was."

"How old was she when she had you?"

"I think nineteen. She was a little wild back then." He paused, considering whether to continue, or maybe just trying to imagine his mother that long ago. "She was pregnant when she met my father."

"What do you mean? You mean—" I stopped myself, not sure I should finish.

Frank nodded. "My father wasn't really my father. Oh, of course he was, just not biologically. He never knew I knew, though. I overheard my mother and my aunt talking about it when I was twelve, and my mother begged me not to tell my father I'd found out. She said it would kill him." He lifted his beer and gave the hollow laugh again, into his glass. "In fact, she didn't just beg me—she bought me a drum set, to keep me quiet. She didn't have to do that." His lips lingered at the rim and he stared beyond me, though I was sure he wasn't aware of it. "The last thing I ever wanted to do was tell my father what I knew. Not just for his sake. Because if I didn't tell him, and we didn't ever say it out loud, then it might not really be true. You know what I mean?" He shook himself free of his reverie to meet my eyes, and I nodded. "God, sorry," he said. "I'm rambling." He held out the bowl of chips and though I wasn't hungry, I took some.

"No. It's interesting," I said. "I'm trying to think what it would be like to think all along that someone was your father, and then one day, *bam*, he's not."

"Well, it wasn't really like that. He *was* my father—the way I felt about him didn't change." Frank crunched deeply, leaving a piece of chip at the side of his mouth. "In fact, if you want the truth, I made myself think that my mother was lying about the whole thing, for some reason. We never talked about it again." His tongue felt around for the errant crumb. "Of course, that makes no sense, and I know she wasn't lying. But it was what I wanted to believe."

"It's weird what people will tell themselves," I said. He looked at me and I could tell he expected more, but I picked up my glass and drained the beer in a series of swallows. I hadn't had anything to drink in a long time—not since graduation weekend—and right away I could feel it seep into my senses.

"Hey, hold on." Frank raised his eyebrows and leaned forward to take my empty glass, as if I might be planning something dangerous with it. "Take it easy, there."

I shrugged off the warning and picked up the yearbook again. "Was that picture taken before your father died, or after?"

"After." He put his own beer down carefully, using *Sports Illustrated* for a coaster. "Why?"

"I don't know. I would have guessed it, though. It's like you look older, or something, than most people. Like you've been through more." I squinted to make out his senior quote. Where others on the page had chosen *Free at last* or *Party on!* as their final words of wisdom before graduating, Frank's selection was from *Desiderata*: "No doubt the universe is unfolding as it should."

"Do you really believe that?" I asked.

He shifted in his seat. "Yeah. I know it sounds corny, but I guess I have to. If I didn't think there was a reason for some of the stuff that goes on, I'd blow my brains out. Oh, God." Immediately he leaned forward to slap his glass down, and beer spilled over. "God, Ana. I'm sorry."

"It's okay," I told him, though his words had caused beer to come back up in my throat. For a moment I was afraid I'd spew it out, but I managed to force it back down. "Let's see," I said, trying to make him feel better, "you were three years ahead of us, right? That means Monica and I should be back here somewhere." I flipped through the yearbook until I came to the photographs of underclassmen, arranged alphabetically by homeroom. First I found Monica, laughing between Tammy Hummel and Erica Grenier. "She was always so popular," I said to Frank, "your sister."

"I bet *you* were popular," he said, but we both knew he was just trying to be nice.

I asked for another beer, but instead Frank poured the rest of his bottle into my glass. "Take it easy," he said again, and when I put the glass down and took hold of his fingers, like an infant grasping, he started to pull back, then let me squeeze the fingers, tight, until the tips turned red. When I saw what I was doing, and that it hurt him, I loosened my grip, drew his fingers up to my lips, and kissed them with a suction sound.

"Ana." Frank's voice was gentle. "I should take you home now. I mean, back to the motel."

"No." Although my thoughts darted through my mind before I could catch them, I could tell that I sounded petulant as a child. This time I found his mouth and kissed him—it was more of a pressing together of closed lips, really—to keep my own mouth from shaking.

He pulled back and took hold of my shoulders. "Ana—"

"What's the matter?"

"We can't do this."

"Why not?" Almost without realizing what I was doing, I joined him in his chair and was half-sitting on his lap. As I reached for the belt of his uniform pants I felt again that strange surge of electricity crinkling the folds of my skull. "Hey," I said, touching his hip where a holster would be, "what happened to your gun?"

He had been holding his breath, and now he let it out as he answered. "I put it in my car trunk before I went to the motel. I didn't want to—remind you guys of anything."

"Like what?" I said, then laughed. Frank sat completely still, like a child afraid to make any movement in front of a growling dog.

"That's so sweet. That is so sweet," I added, drawing the words out until they sounded as if they made no sense, and this must have startled Frank, because he flinched. Seeing this, I felt tears collect in a hot rush behind my eyes.

"Oh," Frank said. "I'm bad with crying. Please don't cry, okay?"

"I can't help it," I told him. The sobs came in shivers; it was the first time I'd cried since he told me, four days earlier, that my father and sister had died. I almost fell off the chair and he drew me closer, balancing my weight across his knees. Finally, when I couldn't control the convulsions, the spastic movements of my body against his, he lifted me to a stand and pressed me close to him, the way you thaw something frozen by hugging it to your warmth.

This time I kissed the top of his blue shirt, just under the collar. I kept kissing and crying until the fabric was sodden and I felt calm again. But just as soon as I recognized the calmness, as soon as it lit in one place, it flew off and away again, leaving my head to buzz.

"Come on," I said to Frank, pulling him back toward what I knew must be the bedroom. There were no lights on except for the fluorescent yellows and greens flickering from the tubes of a fish tank on a shelf in the far corner. It was like walking into the Boston Aquarium, the way you feel a part of the giant circular swim. "Come on, Frank. Zappa." The syllables tickling my tongue made me giggle. I unbuttoned his shirt, pulled it off, and let it drop to the floor. He tried to say something, but I wouldn't let him; then we were next to the bed and I flopped us down on it while lifting my lips to his as if they were my sole source of oxygen.

"Wait a minute." He gulped, then sputtered. "I have to swallow." He pulled away so he could look at me and took in a deep breath. "This isn't good." He closed his eyes, but before he could open them again, I had my hand in his pants and he was moving under my touch.

"Oh, shit," he groaned, and I knew he wouldn't stop me. My few sexual experiences, in college, had been drunken rounds of naked grappling that left me gasping in pain without making a sound. Technically, I was a virgin—my muscles always clenched to prevent penetration, which nobody but Justine knew. But this felt like the right—the only—thing to do. I brought Frank to orgasm with my hand; as he was about to ejaculate, he rolled to the other side of the bed and came into the sheets. He lay there, his back to me, for a few moments, catching his breath. "Oh, shit, Ana," he said, when he turned again to look at me. His lips were swollen where we had both bitten them. "We shouldn't be doing this."

"Too late," I whispered. I drew his sweaty face to mine and slipped my tongue in his mouth to keep him from speaking. "Now me." I could tell he wanted to protest but I also knew he wouldn't dare. I didn't care that he thought it was a mistake. I didn't care about anything except changing the way I felt.

I slipped off my own shirt and flung it to the foot of the bed. At first Frank averted his eyes, but then he rose up next to me, reached over to unhook my bra, drew it off, and began rubbing my breasts with the backs of his fingers. Not knowing what else to do, I turned toward him, took his other hand, and pressed it flat against my stomach. I had only ever had orgasms by touching myself, but now I wanted it from outside, and I felt the pressure building, the anticipatory tingling in my crotch as Frank's hand slid down from my stomach and between my thighs. With his other fingers, he pinched my left nipple. "Ow," I said, trying to bat that hand away, but he pinched harder and I thought, *He must not have heard me.*

By then he was stroking me and I caught my breath. My nipple was being squeezed between fingernails and the pain made a noise in my throat, but at the same time he moved his fingers inside me and in a few seconds I came, hard, though I still felt the pain through the pleasure, in the tenderest flesh of my breast.

He took his hand out and pressed it against my crotch to feel the pulse beating as my breath came back. He kissed the nipple he'd pinched so tight it would show the red dents for days to come. "Did you hear me?" I whispered, gesturing at the raw breast. "Say that part hurt?"

"I thought you liked it." He tried to put his tongue on the injured skin, but I covered it with my own hand as a shudder seized my body without warning. He lifted his head and took his hand out from between my legs, and I saw that he looked stricken. "I thought it would help."

"Oh," I said. "Okay. Well, thanks." I pulled the covers up over myself, feeling mortified and ashamed. "Sorry."

"You're not the one who should be sorry." He put a hand up to brush my hair out of my face. "I didn't really hurt you, did I?"

"No. I mean, a little. But you're right. Maybe it did help." I turned toward him and pulled my legs up to hold myself closer. "Besides, I'm the one who assaulted you." We made slight laughing noises to cover our mutual chagrin. "Would that be sexual battery?"

"No. That's when the other person doesn't want it," he said.

We lay in silence for a few minutes. In the corner, the fluorescent tank hummed as fish soared through vertical bubbles. Although I tried to hang onto the sensation of his fingers inside me—the feeling of being filled—it had begun to recede as soon as he took his hand away, and now I was only myself again, and my father and sister were dead.

We began to talk, quietly, inhaling each other's breath as our heads lay on a single pillow. We remembered nursery school in the Methodist church basement and pony rides at the Altamont Fair. After we'd laughed about the time he panicked during his sixth-grade performance as Dick Deadeye in H.M.S. *Pinafore* and had to ad-lib both his lines and the song lyrics, we were silent again. I felt in danger of falling asleep. But then something dislodged itself from memory, dropping straight to my stomach and jolting me back awake. Although I'd never talked to anybody outside the family about it before, I told Frank about the day my father set his car on fire.

"He kept having these dreams that the car broke down and then exploded or something," I said, speaking quietly across the pillow and into Frank's ear. "Whenever he had one of them, he'd be afraid to drive the car for a week." I waited for him to make a comment, but he just told me, with his eyes, to continue.

"My mother kept having to bring him to work and then pick him back up. She told him to have the car checked out, if he was so worried, and he did—but, of course, nobody could find anything wrong. He wouldn't believe them, though. He was sure they were missing whatever it was.

"So this one day—I was in fifth grade, I think—I'm riding the bus home from school and we turn onto the bypass, you know, by Radio-Shack, and I hear the other kids shouting and look out the window and see all these police cars and fire trucks up ahead. There was this car on the side of the road, totally burning, and I didn't recognize it at first, until I saw the license plate and realized it was my father's."

"God," Frank said. "You mean he was right, and there was something wrong with the engine?"

"No. He torched it himself." In spite of what I was saying, I felt a small smile play at my lips.

"What are you talking about?" He shifted to get a better look at my face, and I knew he thought I was putting him on.

"He couldn't stand thinking about it—*imagining* it—anymore. It was like he had to do it himself, because his dream was so real, and he was so sure it would come true." I hadn't realized that I understood any of this until I heard it come out of my mouth. "But if he waited for it, he'd have no control, and it could have happened at any time. This way he could just get it over with."

"Wow." Frank gave a low whistle. After a pause he added, "Well, I guess I can imagine that. A kind of superstition, with a twist."

I smiled. "Sounds like a new drink. 'I'll have a superstition with a twist.'" But even before I got the words out, I had to throw my arm across my eyes as sudden images of my father's face that morning, and of Meggy's swallowed confidence the night before she died, seized all the space before me. "Oh, God," I said, bouncing my fist on my forehead, "last week at this time, they were still alive."

"Ana. I'm sorry." Frank caught my hand and stopped it, then began stroking my hair behind my ears. I concentrated on the rhythm of his breathing until I could match it to my own. "Did you know he had a gun?" he asked.

"No. I don't think he did. I mean, he must have gotten it just for this." But I didn't want to start thinking, in such violent detail, about what my father had done. "What about the videotape of *Annie*?" I asked, remembering the items of evidence the police collected from our house. "Why did you take that?"

"You sure you want to talk about this?"

"I'm the one who brought it up."

Frank began to shrug, then seemed to realize it was too casual a gesture, given the subject. I felt his arm go around the top of my head and I closed my eyes, to savor for a few seconds the illusion that I was safe. "Well, it was still on," he explained, gently. "The VCR. Whenever there's a tape that looks like it might have been viewed recently by—by someone involved in a crime, we confiscate it automatically, in case it has any relevance or contains any clues." He fell silent, perhaps hoping I'd forget what I wanted to know.

"*Confiscate.* What a word." I raised myself on one elbow to look down at his face. "Well?"

"Well what?"

"What did you think?"

"Of what?"

"The *tape*. What were we talking about?"

This time he shrugged without apologizing. "We only watched a half hour or so. It was just an amateur performance of something, right? A musical?" He furrowed his brow. "Why? Were you in it or something?"

"Not me." I moved away slightly. "Meggy. She was *Annie*. Couldn't you tell?" Although it wasn't my intention, my voice sent out irritated rays.

Frank shook his head. "No, I missed that."

"How could you? I mean, she was the star."

Now he rose on an elbow, too, and collapsed mine so he could pull me closer. "The guys at the scene—*we*—didn't necessarily know what she looked like," he whispered, holding me tight against him. When he saw that I didn't understand, he added, "What she looked like when she was alive."

"Oh, my God." I dove under the covers and thought I would be sick, but he brought me up to the air again.

"You okay?" he asked, still whispering, and I nodded, even though my heart had caved in and I thought I might die. Frank placed his hand over my chest, but it took several minutes for my breathing to slow again. "You're okay," he told me, patting. Then he mumbled, "You don't look like your sister, you know," and though I'm sure he only meant to distract me, it made me feel worse. I put my head on his bare chest and prayed to fall asleep, soon hearing above my head the sound of his soft snoring into my hair. I dozed in and out, half-waking a few times to shimmers of light bouncing toward me from the fish tank, but it took me several moments to realize where I was when I felt Frank start as he woke above me and craned to see the clock.

"Ana, get up. It's 3:30." He moved a hand down my shoulder. "Come on. I have to get you back."

"Okay," I murmured, but I made no move to leave his bed. He pulled his arm gingerly from under my head, got up, and took some clothes out of a drawer. Swiftly, he put on sweatpants and a T-shirt with *Police Benevolent Association Softball League* stitched in the shape of a ball over his chest.

"Meggy played softball," I said. Through the haze of near-sleep I saw my sister getting ready to pitch, the bill of her Parrelli Hardware cap creased down the middle of her forehead, her braids hanging beneath her shoulders. Closing my eyes, I could hear the voices from the playing field: *Good eye, heads up, batter batter batter.*

"Whoa," Frank said, "don't fall asleep on me." He put a hand out. "We'd better hurry, in case they miss you."

I swung myself off the bed so fast it made me dizzy, and he caught me as I swayed. He kept hold of me as I put my shirt back on, then let me lean against him as we walked through the house and outside. I wasn't drunk, though I wished I were. Something else—grief, or fear, or the wish that I hadn't awakened—made me stumble. "Aren't you afraid of what people will think?" I asked, realizing what they would see if they looked out their windows: the neighborhood police officer assisting a wobbly young woman from his front door, a few hours before dawn.

"Nobody's up now," he told me, and he seemed to be right. We saw not a single light on in any of the houses all the way down the block. The air felt already damp, containing the drizzle forecasted for the next day. At the motel Frank walked me to the door of our room, and I had to wake Justine up to let me in.

"Where have you *been?*" she said, grumbling back into bed.

"Just answering questions," I told her. Frank leaned toward me and I put my hand up to warn him away, but he ignored me and touched his lips to my forehead while Justine's back was turned. Before I closed the door, he made a sliding motion to remind me to bolt it behind him.

3. Some of us are out of breath

Q. How old is the institution of permanent marriage?
— *H.T.O., Selkirk*

A. There was considerable freedom in early history to initiate and terminate marriage without formality. Christianity, however, decreed that sex relationships that were considered to be marriages must be monogamous and should be characterized by faithfulness, especially on the part of women. At one time the marriage union was indissoluble. The doctrine of indissolubility of marriage was given special importance when marriage became a sacrament, notably in the 4th century through St. Augustine.

My mother went back to work at the *Delphi Oracle* two weeks after the deaths. Her editor told her she should take off as much time as she wanted, but my mother said she needed to get back into a routine. She wouldn't know what to do with herself if she had all that time on her hands.

I had been planning a vacation on Cape Cod that July with my friend Ruthie and some other people from college, but I canceled it, as Justine canceled her job as a coach and counselor at a cheerleading camp near Rochester. We shut ourselves in the condo's living room with the shades drawn tight. We made a fortress of the couch and its cushions, and at night we slept together in the sofa bed, because neither of us wanted to use the bed in the room that would have been Meggy's.

Neither Justine nor I had menstruated since the deaths, though our mother remained regular. Justine and I sat around waiting to bleed again. If one of us ever had to leave the apartment alone, to go to the dentist or the post office or an appointment with Nora Odoni, the other was always standing at the window, watching, when she got home. Nora was the therapist we all saw after the deaths, sometimes together but more often separately. Mom was the first one to meet Nora, in the hospital, where they took her after she lost control at the funeral. She started screaming and crying and calling out Meggy's name, and she threw her handkerchief at our father's coffin but it fell before it touched wood, so she started taking her clothes off and throwing them before Kay and Ed Lonergan grabbed her and took her outside.

Nora Odoni was Greek, and I spent most of each therapeutic hour listening to the way she pronounced words with an accent that made even "murder" sound elegant. I kept my appointments for a while longer than my mother and Justine, who quit after a couple of weeks.

When we met as a family, Nora said our grief was like rice boiling inside a pot with a stuck lid: if somebody didn't do something to relieve the pressure, the whole thing would explode. I asked her if she didn't think oatmeal would make a better emotional metaphor. Justine hated the doctor because she couldn't bring Meggy back. She never said this directly, but a sister can tell.

While our mother was at work, I read novels and Justine watched TV: Phil Donahue, soap operas, the Olympic track and field trials from Barcelona, and—at night, to keep us all from having to talk to one another—sitcoms and Movies of the Week, except when they were pre-empted by the presidential conventions. The only things we always had to switch off as soon as they came on were police dramas, or anything else that might show a gun, anyone shooting or being shot. Using a note-book of graph paper and a system intelligible only to herself, Justine kept elaborate track of selected dramas (the hundred-yard dash, what Erica was up to on *All My Children*, delegates for Dukakis and Bush), forti-fying herself with snack chips and candy bars.

She had begun eating out of control on the day of the funeral. Since the night she discovered our father's body, she had not been able to keep any food down, and her face above her violet collar looked as white as the light of the candles on the bier.

At the gathering afterward at the Waxmans' house, Justine would not leave our mother's side. I moved in a slow circle around the living room, saying *thank you* and *no thanks* and *I don't know* and *I know*. It was only the second of July but already there were a few fireworks, and every time I heard a pop in the sky I flinched, imagining the sound of the gun my fa-ther had used. I couldn't taste my food or feel any part of my body, except the headache of sunlight beating between my eyes. My friend Ruthie had come from Boston for the funeral, and she always managed to get her arm around me just when it seemed I might fall without realizing.

I watched people go with hesitation to the Waxmans' window, the one that looked out on our yard, and peer through it as if they might see something that could help them believe what had happened. The ones who spent the most time drawing the curtain aside and looking for clues were Meggy's friends, both boys and girls, who came to the funeral as a single shuffling body and left soggy wads of Kleenex in the pew. In the family room, one of the kids had turned on the tennis at Wimbledon, but Mrs. Waxman hurried in and slapped off the TV.

My mother and Justine sat together on the couch, and people kept bringing them plates of food. Both refused, shaking their heads and trying to smile. Toward the end of the afternoon Lois Phelps approached, twisting her hands in front of her. "I'm so sorry to have to do this," she said. "This is so awkward." She seemed to be appealing to my mother for help, but none of us knew what she was talking about. "My niece's son is being christened in Ithaca tomorrow," Lois went on, her voice getting louder as if she thought it might drown her chagrin. "Isn't it funny— well, maybe that isn't the right word, but doesn't it always happen this way? Doesn't it seem like maybe God plans it so a birth comes right after a death, to maybe show us something?" She flushed with desperation as the words spilled out.

"To show us what?" My mother wasn't even blinking.

"Well," Lois said, "I guess maybe I don't know. I'm sorry, I'll just get out of your way, then. The thing is, I need my quiche dish back."

The silence that came after her request, among those of us sitting around the coffee table, felt like slow motion. We all looked at where the broccoli-and-mushroom quiche sat among the other offerings; there was only one piece gone from the fluted plate. Justine, who brought raw cauliflower and carrots to school for lunch, snacked on heads of lettuce and, candy-wise, had not let so much as an M&M pass her lips since the day her gym teacher called her Tubster when she was ten, picked up a fork and ate the rest of the entire quiche as Lois Phelps stood there watching with an expression of discomfort that melted into disgust. Our mother also watched, though I don't think she understood what she was seeing. "Oh, dear," Lois said at one point, as Justine scraped up a huge forkful of crust, but no one seemed to hear her. When Justine had finished, she went into the kitchen to wash the dish, and she brought it back out to Lois wrapped in a plastic shopping bag from the Gap. Then she sat back down and ate what was left on the table.

Later, in the night, Justine was sick; but the next day she fell to eating again with the same desperate energy, her teeth grinding through each bite. When my mother finally came to and asked her what she was doing, Justine said "Nothing," and my mother didn't pursue it. After that, Justine started eating in secret.

The first day our mother was scheduled to go back to work after the deaths, my sister slipped out of the sofa bed early. I knew she was trying not to wake me up by the way she walked on the balls of her feet, and even when she stubbed her toe on the bed frame, she stifled a curse. She took my mother's car without asking permission. Half an hour later she came back carrying a bag of groceries, a globe of broccoli sticking pointedly out of the top.

"Where'd you go?" I asked her. I hadn't gotten out of the sofa bed yet because I saw through the blinds that the day was going to be beautiful, and I wanted to put off the sunlight as long as I could. "Well, where does it look like I went?" Justine began unpacking the food—tomatoes, sprouts, cantaloupe—and Bill Buckner trotted over to see if there was anything for him.

I wanted to say, *I know you snuck away to eat something. You can't fool me. I know you were sitting in the car behind the Price Chopper, stuffing Devil Dogs into your face.* But I didn't say any of these things. Instead I went to sit up in the sofa bed, and as I tried to step out of it, the mattress folded, clapping me inside.

"Goddammit!" I was more shocked than anything else, though in that first moment when my face was pressed against foam rubber I had to move my head to breathe. Then I heard my mother come out of the bathroom and start laughing, and I knew from the sound that she was bent over with how funny she found it. Didn't this happen to *That Girl* once? Didn't an old commercial for the show go, *What other girl could get her head/Caught inside a folding bed?* Around me the mattress started shaking as I let my own laughter go. "Hey," I said, hearing my words from far away, as if underwater. "Help."

My mother said, "What's that, honey?" as she moved toward where I was trapped. Her words contained mischief and a little bit of mirth. "Could you speak up?"

"Mom, come on." Justine's tone indicated that she saw nothing amusing about it at all. "Let's get her out." I felt the edges of the mattress being pulled away from each other, and my mother and Justine opened the bed wide enough for me to roll out onto the floor.

My mother said, "Look, it's a girl!"

"This bed isn't safe," Justine declared. She crossed her arms over her chest and added, "No beds in this family are."

I felt as if somebody had punched me quick, the surprise going deeper than the blow. I knew Justine was referring to the fact that Meggy died in her bed, but if anyone had overheard her, it would have sounded like something else. In the days after the funeral we got wind of the rumors being passed around town, and one of them was that my father had been molesting Meggy, and that he killed himself and her either out of guilt or because she had threatened to tell on him. Of course, nobody ever said anything to us directly, so we couldn't very well go around announcing, out of the blue, that our father was not a child abuser.

When Justine made the crack about beds, my mother took in a slow breath and put a palm across her stomach.

"I can't believe you said that," I told Justine.

"I can't either," my sister said. She sounded the way she did when she came back from the dentist and her mouth was still numb. "I'm sorry, Mom. I didn't know that was going to come out."

"I know." My mother nodded. "Never mind." She tried to smile, but her lips were twitching. She started for the kitchen, and I saw in her face the decision to forget what had just been said.

One day at the beginning of August, a few weeks after our mother had gone back to work, I snapped off the TV abruptly and said, "There's no way she didn't read that note."

"What note?" Justine asked automatically, though of course she already knew.

I didn't bother answering. Justine pulled herself up from the couch. She wasn't used to carrying the new weight she'd gained in only six weeks; I'd never seen anyone put on pounds so fast, and it made me think that her cells had been screaming *More! More!* for years since she'd started depriving them, and now were hoarding all they had missed. The rapid change made her movements awkward, though behind them still lay the cheerleader's grace.

She followed me into our mother's bedroom, where I began going through the drawers. "You shouldn't," she told me, not because she thought it was wrong in a moral sense, but because she knew how our mother would react if she found out we'd gone through her things. I ignored her and began rummaging through underwear, sweaters, jewelry, and even—on the top shelf of the closet, in a cardboard filing chest—the divorce papers, which had never been signed.

"Nothing," I said, shoving the file back up. "Goddammit."

Justine's hesitation gave way to curiosity and she said, "What about with her souvenirs?" Like a character in a movie, I snapped my fingers and said, "Of course." But when we went to the desk in the living room, took out the old Thom McAn box and lifted the lid, we saw immediately that nothing had been added to the contents we expected to find.

"I guess, in a way, that's good," Justine said, her mouth twisting a little as she replaced the box in its drawer. "It would be kind of fucked if she kept her husband's suicide note in the same place as her swizzle stick from the Governor's Ball." I knew she was disappointed and also relieved, because I felt the same way. I picked up my book again and Justine turned on the TV, and when our mother came home that night she didn't notice anything out of place.

We did have Meggy's diary—that, my mother didn't burn. Meggy started keeping it only that New Year's, having received the journal from Aunt Rosemary for Christmas. It was a beautiful date book, with a faux-marble cover and thinly ruled, gilt-edged pages. You could fit a lot on those pages, although Meggy usually only filled the first line for each day. When the police gave it back to us after determining there was nothing they needed inside, each of us took our time before reading it; the idea that we were invading her privacy was still too fresh.

But finally, we needed to read it. At first I thought it was funny, the way Meggy had kept track of the weather each day (at the top of each page was a chart with check boxes for *Clear, Cloudy, Rain,* or *Snow*), along with her homework assignments and the first days of her period. As if, in the future, she would have cared about accounting for any of these things.

But as I began flipping through the book, looking for anything personal, I grew more and more frustrated with each page. These were the months leading up to the murder and suicide—the months leading up to, and following, the day our mother moved out. Yet Meggy made only the slightest mention of this event, and nothing else that could help us to understand what was going on with her—*inside her*—in the last year of her life. She kept notes like a reporter: *March 7: Mom gone. May 21: Ana graduated. May 23: Ana home.* After this last entry, she'd drawn a smiley face, and when I saw it, my heart gave such a heave that I understood why people speak of hearts *breaking.* I could only look at that page once. Every other time I read the diary, after the first time, I skipped over that day.

The last entry we had was the one dated June 27, two days before she died. Meggy had written, "Fight with Gail, its not really her fault." The next two pages had been ripped out of the book.

"Maybe she just got mad and tore out blank pages," Justine suggested, but I knew we both believed that the missing entry contained some kind of clue.

A few days after Justine and I searched without success for our father's suicide note, our mother came home waving an envelope that turned out to be filled with dollar bills. I was reading *Beloved* and Justine was watching Oprah, who had just returned from a commercial break to say, "We're talking about how coming out of a coma changes your life." Mom shouted, "Hey, I won!" as she stepped through the door. "Hey, you guys, I won the pool at work." She hoisted the money like a trophy above her head.

"What pool?" Justine said. She was lying on the floor with an arm across her forehead, and I knew she felt sick from having just consumed an entire sleeve of chocolate pinwheels on the other side of the bathroom door.

"We all put money down on when and where the Toothpaste Burglar would finally be caught." My mother opened the refrigerator door, considered what was inside, then closed it again without choosing anything. "I had him down for the twenty-fifth, two in the afternoon, over in Westwood, and guess what? They got him that exact day at one-thirty, in one of those new houses on Westwood Ridge." She slapped the envelope on the counter to punctuate her achievement.

The Toothpaste Burglar had been on the loose in central New York since the spring. He stole the things burglars usually do—stereos, TVs, jewelry—but when he left the houses, he always wrote a message in his victim's own toothpaste on the bathroom mirror. Sometimes the messages themselves were disappointing and unoriginal—Fuck you or Ha! or Eat shit (of course, the newspaper didn't print the actual obscenities; our mother gave us those details).

But the more recent break-ins seemed to have taken a spiritual turn. The last few messages had been the same: God weeps with us, scrawled in Crest or Gleem across the glass. He was becoming careless, letting his handwriting become more identifiable than at the beginning of his reign. Psychologists interviewed for the newspaper suggested that he wanted to be caught. Police Sink Teeth in Burglary Probe, the headlines of the Oracle winked.

"He's just this little man, it turns out, who wasn't even selling the things he stole." Our mother was still looking for something to eat, and she finally settled on a dish of cold creamed corn left over from who knew when. "They found it all piled up in a corner of this little room. When the police got there, he answered the door naked and held his hands out for the cuffs."

Justine and I looked at each other, and I knew that it was not the specific information about the Toothpaste Burglar we were responding to, but the smile on our mother's face. It was an odd sight, at once foreign and familiar, and it made us wince. The few times I'd felt a laugh rise in me that summer—when we watched reruns of I Love Lucy, for instance— I always wanted to say "Sorry" or "I couldn't help it" to Justine.

On the day my mother won the Toothpaste Burglar pool, Justine and I searched for evidence of that same shame in her. But we didn't find it, and though we said nothing to each other about it then, I knew we both realized we'd lost something that could never be retrieved.

Now, I believe that we would have been better off to follow the therapist's advice, and do what our mother did: find something to take us out into the world each day and pass the hours in the presence of other people who might have known and understood our situation, but who weren't submerged in grief themselves. At the time, I didn't understand how my mother managed. "You'll probably think this sounds silly," she said, the day I finally worked up the courage to ask her, "but I just pretend Meggy's away at camp." She was watching herself in the mirror, tying a scarf around her neck. "And Daddy I was used to living without." Since the deaths, she had started calling him "Daddy" again, to Justine and me. For months before that, while the legal papers were in the works, he had been "your father." Now we noticed that when she met someone new, she told them she was a widow. When she saw the looks we gave her, she reminded us, "Well, the divorce never was final."

When my friends tried to reach me that summer, I let the machine answer and made myself forget to return the calls. I continued reading novels—Sophie's Choice, The Color Purple, Of Mice and Men. I didn't know that I chose them for a reason, but when I look back, I realize I was seeking a common theme. See what we can survive, if we have to. Look how much human beings can bear.

Over the summer, Justine went up two sizes. I went through twenty-three novels, but don't ask me what they all were.

The only one I couldn't finish was Jude the Obscure. When I got to the part where the oldest brother hangs himself and his siblings by nooses from coat hooks and leaves the note, "Done because we are too menny," I put the book away. Not because it was so sad, but because I didn't believe it. Children don't commit suicide, I remember thinking. Children get killed.

My mother had been working the general assignment beat at the *Delphi Oracle*, covering everything from county politics to the Central Tier's annual tree-sitting contest, for four months when my father and Meggy died. She had been a journalist since just after college when she was hired by the *Knickerbocker News*, which came out every afternoon except Sunday. This was in Albany, where many things—streets, restaurants— are named after the Dutch.

It was on the newspaper's bowling team that my parents met. This is the most unromantic way I've ever heard, at least among the stories of my friends, whose fathers first approached their mothers across dark rooms at dances, or caught their eyes over the head of other straphangers on the bus.

My friend Ruthie swears her parents met like this: her mother was on a college choir trip to San Francisco and had arranged to meet a male cousin, twice removed, in front of a certain coffee shop at a particular hour. When the time came and a man walked up, she said the cousin's name like a question, and the man smiled and said yes. They went inside and sat down and ordered, and by the time their pastries arrived she caught on that he wasn't the cousin she had arranged to meet, and the man confessed but said he couldn't help it, her voice was so charming and her face so sweet, he had run the risk to see where it would take him, and he was glad he had.

So by then she was flattered and couldn't hate him, and she forgot about the cousin who might be waiting out in the darkness, searching for a face that would look familiar to him though he had never seen it before. By the time they left the coffee shop, it was late and cooler. The man and the woman who eventually became Ruthie's parents went walking, arm in arm. They were both visitors to California, and on their honeymoon they returned. Ruthie herself had never been there. I'm saving it, she said.

But my parents met on the bowling team of the *Knick News*. My father, who sold advertising space, was the captain of the team. Bowling was a sport he was accustomed to, as he had grown up in Albany near the Lucky Strike Lanes. My mother was a novice at bowling when she joined the newspaper, but she picked it up quickly and within weeks she had the highest average of all the women in the league. At the end of the season, Tom Dolan and Margaret Ott won the Golden Bowl award for the Cutest Couple, and the *Knick* ran a picture of them, their cheeks touching behind the trophy. The headline over the photo said, *Bowled Over*, and the ring on my mother's finger caught the camera's flash as the diamond appeared to explode.

At first my mother's parents disapproved of my father because he'd started working straight out of high school and had no college plans. But one Sunday, when my parents took them out for dinner after my grandparents came up to Albany for a church meeting, the conversation turned to Hemingway, and my father said he was the most overrated writer of all time. By accident, he'd voiced an opinion with which my grandfather thoroughly agreed. Beyond that, they both believed that most people knew this truth about Hemingway, but were afraid to say so. So my father got points for the courage of his convictions *and* for the fact that he read so much on his own.

My parents' first official date was to see the movie *I Want to Live!* It wasn't until we got a VCR that I watched the movie myself. My father rented it one night soon after our mother had left, when I was home on spring break and both of my sisters were sleeping over at friends' houses. When he popped the movie in I felt vaguely guilty, as if I were stealing something from my mother.

But then I became engrossed by Susan Hayward's portrayal of Barbara Graham, the condemned woman who remains blithe and irreverent even in the face of her own execution. For the first time I recognized, in Hayward's saucy performance, the source of a gesture my father always made whenever we asked him for something—the pantomime blow on a pair of pretend dice for good luck, followed by their roll against an invisible wall. Like Hayward's character, he would pretend to read how they came up and then tell us, "No dice" or "It's a deal!"

And there was the dialogue between Barbara and her lover, which echoed a refrain from my childhood. "Life's a funny thing," the man muses. Barbara quips back: "Compared to what?" My parents exchanged these lines often, and though the context always seemed to change— sometimes they'd have just finished a fight, other times it was after kissing—my sisters and I took comfort in the familiar tune of the words.

In less specific ways, the movie reminded me of my mother. She was no criminal, but in her personality she resembled Barbara Graham. I could imagine my mother ordering a hot-fudge sundae as her last meal and insisting that she be allowed to wear her shoes into the gas chamber, because she looked better in them than she did barefoot.

But I could also imagine her clutching a stuffed tiger in her jail cell to remind her of her babies back home.

My mother was the only female reporter in the newspaper's city room. Until she was promoted to general assignment, she started where women writers had always worked before her, in Fashion and Features. For a while, she wrote a column of television reviews, under the pen name of Chan L. Turner. (Just to set the record straight, the column and the pseudonym existed at the newspaper long before she did.) There was a local talent program called *Teenage Barn* and my mother panned it, based on the performance of a nine-year-old blind girl who, on the night my mother watched the show, sang a song about dead love. My mother didn't think it was appropriate for such a young girl to be singing dirges, and she said so in print. The *Knick* received a dozen angry letters, most implying that anyone who could criticize a handicapped child must have stone for a heart, and one woman from Schuylerville recommended that Chan L. Turner be sent on the next slow boat back to China.

My mother still has those letters, in the old Thom McAn shoe box with her newspaper clippings, old press badges, and the bowling photo—her souvenirs. When she showed them to Justine and me one night (Meggy was still a baby, already asleep), my mother began laughing as she remembered the slow-boat-to-China part. But with the letters spread out in front of her, her face turned flat and I was afraid she was going to cry. They had hurt her feelings; they called her cruel.

My mother was Chan L. Turner straight out of college, when she was twenty-two. Later, while she was dating and then newly married to my father, she covered hard news: deadly fires, a crash at the Albany airport, cases before the New York State Court of Appeals.

She became pregnant with me at the time of the newspaper strike in the city. She picketed the downtown office with other reporters, asking for higher wages and better hours. I always liked knowing that I was involved in a protest even before I was born. It made me feel sensitive and special, as if I could detect injustice from the blind side of the womb.

But instead of raising her salary they laid my mother off, and she didn't have much to say about it because she was six months gone with me. This was back when you could smoke and drink if you were pregnant, but you had to leave your job. I was born on the first day of spring, a slushy Monday, and they brought me home to the apartment on Morton Avenue, where they had set up a bassinet in the bedroom, under curtains the color of phlegm. I slept in that space under the window for the first months of my life. You will say I can't possibly recall anything that early, and you will probably be right. But my heart insists it remembers the white of that window, the circle of sun on the sheet in the mornings, and the blunt light of moon through the shade. I remember the feeling of wanting to move, or to be moved, out of the painful brightness and into the balm of gray. After I moved into my own bedroom, my parents would find me bunched at the crib's foot in the morning, my head under my duck-bordered blanket, turned from the slatted rays.

Although I could not have known the words then, I had a clear sense of light and shadow, and of frustration, then relief. It is my earliest memory, and I see myself from both above the crib and inside it, the way people who almost die on the surgeon's table are said to see themselves.

When I was a freshman in college, taking Introduction to Psychology, I wanted to write a paper on early memories. I asked my friends about what they remembered, and I took notes in the cafeteria and in the common rooms of the dorm. Then my professor told me I had to write about something more relevant, based on library research. I chose conditioning—the dogs, the bells, the spit, and the morsels. I'm not sure what I learned from it that I didn't know already, but I remember it made me hungry.

On my own time, not for credit, I continued to ask people about their memories and to write down what I heard. By the end of the semester, I had a folder filled with napkins and scraps of paper, each representing one person's first impression of this life. It may not have been very scientific, but I did find some consistencies.

For example, many of the memories involved vivid physical sensations or perceptions of color. My freshman roommate said she'd never forget falling out of her baby carriage when her mother ran over a rock, and landing cheek-first in a snowbank to see the world skewed sideways as the ice bit into her skin. My friend Ruthie said her first memory was of red: of wearing her favorite red corduroy overalls in the car with her mother driving to buy a carton of Winstons in the red-and-white soft pack. "God, I loved those overalls," Ruthie said, and I looked away when I realized that her eyes held sudden tears.

My favorite of the memories I elicited was from someone I didn't even know very well, the boyfriend of a girl who lived down the hall from me at school. We were sitting together in the lounge—he was waiting for her to get out of the shower, and I was ripping haircuts I liked from her copy of *Mademoiselle*—and when I was finished making a little pile beside me of the magazine heads, I asked him about the first thing he remembered. He thought for a moment, and then he said, "Okay, got it. I was being toilet trained, and my father put me on the little plastic pot, and when I was done he clapped for me—I can't believe I'm telling you this—and he went to lift me up, but he lost his balance and fell back against the bathroom door. He had just painted the door that morning, and it was still wet. He was wearing a green sweater, and fuzz from the sweater stuck to the wet part of the door. They never did anything to get the fuzz off until we moved, like two years ago."

He didn't ask me why I wanted to know, but he seemed surprised at what he'd told me. "I saw that door every day of my life until I was sixteen, but I didn't know I remembered how that fuzz got there," he said.

Ask anybody: people believe they won't recall the dimmest, most distant silhouettes, but they will. I have thought about how better off we all might be if the summits of the world could start this way, with an exchange between presidents about the songs their mothers sang them or about sweet naps in the grass.

My mother stayed home with the three of us until Meggy was in nursery school. To bring in extra income, she worked as a freelance editor of environmental reports for the state. Although they never let us kids know directly, it was clear that my father didn't make enough money, especially once we moved to Ashmont. For the first eight years of my life, he sold insurance. Then, after we moved from Albany out to Ashmont, he got his realtor's license. My parents led us to believe it was his decision to leave the insurance agency, but I knew better because I'd overheard them talking in the kitchen one night when they thought I was asleep.

"I just think it's the wrong field for you, hon," my mother had said. "It eats you up. You're too nice to the customers, you worry about what they can afford." Her voice was gentle, as if she were explaining something to one of us. "No wonder they can't keep you on."

"I can't help it," my father said, and I could hear him drumming his fingertips on the table. They had pieces of paper spread out in front of them, dozens of numbers scribbled in their own hands or printed out on the stark faces of bills.

"I know you can't. It's one of the things I love about you. But let's face it, you just don't have the killer instinct."

I could hear the papers moving over the sound of my father's sigh. On the stairs, my foot was falling asleep beneath me. I would have to move soon; my father was already beginning his nightly ritual of checking the locks on the doors and windows, looking under beds and in closets to make sure nobody had sneaked in. "Houses are different from insurance," he told my mother while sliding the back-door bolt into place. "Real estate I think I could do." When we moved to Ashmont he got hired by Zenith, which had sold us our house, but within six months he was looking for work again. He ended up selling cars, which was what he was doing—or *not* doing—when he died.

The day after I eavesdropped on my parents' conversation from the top of the stairs, my mother took my sisters and me to our grandparents' house, an hour and a half down the Thruway to the Catskills in the clattery Nova. It was a school day, and that morning I was trying to decide which color tights to wear under my corduroy jumper when my mother came into my bedroom and said, "I'm having an idea."

She got up and stood in the doorway, so she could speak to my sisters and me at the same time. "Do you guys want to go to the game farm?" she asked, loudly, so as to be heard over the scratchy sounds of *Alice in Wonderland* on the child-size phonograph in the playroom. It was a narrated album, and Meggy loved to hear "The Walrus and the Carpenter" over and over again. Sometimes when she was supposed to be taking a nap, we heard her in her room repeating her favorite stanza to herself: *But wait a bit, the Oysters cried, Before we have our chat; For some of us are out of breath, And all of us are fat!* The last line cracked her up every time, invariably coming out in a giggled shriek.

When my mother suggested going to the game farm, Justine plucked the needle off the record too fast, and it made a screech. "But what about school?" She was only in first grade, but she was old enough to know what was breaking the rules.

"Well, it's up to you." Our mother bent down to lift Meggy, who had her arms up in the air. "I think it might be a nice day to take a drive and see the animals. It wouldn't be crowded, the way it always is on the weekends, and we could stop at Grandma and Grandpa's on the way back." She looked at me again. "What do you think, Ana?"

I hesitated. Although I knew you weren't supposed to admit it, I liked school. We were halfway through *Beezus and Ramona* in the Monarch Reading Group (we were all named for butterflies), and the weather was still summery; we would be allowed to go out to the playground for recess. The only thing I didn't like about school was when the hot lunch was spaghetti and Robert Turcio pretended he was eating worms.

"You love the game farm, Ana," my mother reminded me, though of course she didn't have to.

"But how come you would let us do that?" I was holding my gold tights, rubbing the fabric between my fingers as I tried to figure out why my mother was suggesting we play hooky.

She set Meggy down on the floor and took my little sister's hands in her own. Meggy stepped on top of Mom's feet and hung there, waiting to dance, her face turned up in anticipation and delight. She wore her favorite dress, the one with strawberries on it, and just looking at her made me feel a rush of love pool inside my chest. "Life is short," my mother said, stepping in a circle with my sister on her toes. When she saw that her words puzzled me, she said, "I mean, we have to make the most of things. Wouldn't it be a surprise if we went to the game farm today, instead of what we're all supposed to do? Grandma and Grandpa would be surprised, too, if we stopped by to see them." She took a tissue out of her pocket to wipe Meggy's nose.

"And the best part is, we'd be surprising ourselves."

When I was a little older and my mother told me about the job she had as a journalist before I was born, I understood more of what she meant, more of how "surprise" translated for her into "excitement," the world offering up possibilities you would never have imagined before the unexpected thing happened, before you heard the news. Whenever she talked about her job at the Knick—how the newsroom could be elec-trified by a phone tip about a fire in Pine Hills or a missing resident from the veterans' home—I pictured her sitting at her old Underwood as she banged out the story, looking as she did on the press credentials she saved in her souvenir box, her wavy hair pressed close to her head and the eye-glasses with wings turning up at the corners, as if the frames might take off and fly.

My mother was an intern at a newspaper office on the day of John F. Kennedy's assassination. Almost twenty-five years later, she could still remember the bulletin that had come in over the UPI wire. "*Kennedy wounded—perhaps seriously, perhaps fatally—by assassin's bullet*," she recited, show-ing off to the people around our table at Thanksgiving dinner, the year before our father and Meggy died. Mom would leave in the spring, but that fall we were still a family, and on Thanksgiving, which fell as it always does near the assassination's anniversary, we had the usual gathering at our house—my mother's parents; Aunt Rosemary; Ed and Kay Lonergan and their son Matt. Justine and Meggy had taken Matt into the family room to watch *Top Gun*, but I lingered at the table to hear everyone else tell their stories about where they were, and what they were doing, when Kennedy was shot.

My grandparents had just returned home from a church conference on that day in 1963, they remembered, and my grandfather initiated a prayer chain, which was a phone list of people who called each other when someone in the congregation, or the world at large, needed group supplication. (My grandparents took their names off the chain after my father and Meggy died, but I was always afraid to ask them why.) Rosemary, my father's sister, said she was cutting a typing class to smoke cigarettes in the alley behind the Blaine Secretarial School. My father worked for a tree-cutting service that fall, and one of the other men called the news up to him from the ground. "I thought he said Kennedy was shocked," my father told us, "and I thought, what's the big deal?"

Then it was Kay Lonergan's turn. "I was in my dorm room, reading *Atlas Shrugged*," she began, and Ed cut in, "No, you weren't.

"You were having lunch at the Rathskellar with me," he said. "I can't believe you don't remember this—don't you remember Dave Huff coming in and telling us Kennedy got shot, and I laughed because I thought he was kidding?" Ed had drunk most of the three bottles of wine we'd opened for dinner, along with a couple of Scotches before we sat down, and his voice and color had been rising throughout the meal.

"I know that's what you think happened, Ed, but you are sadly mistaken." Kay's own voice grew thick with conviction and a little bit of scorn. "I was reading *Atlas Shrugged* on my bed, and Marcie Keppler came in and started crying. You can call her up and ask her!" she cried, growing more frustrated as her husband shook his head.

"Well, you could call up Dave Huff, if he hadn't been killed in Vietnam," Ed said. "You were right there at the table. They turned on the TV over the bar and we all sat there and got loaded, waiting for the word."

"It must have been some other girlfriend, Ed," Kay told him. She looked at the rest of us with raised eyebrows, as if about to deliver a punch line. "Though we *were* engaged by then."

"It was you, dammit." He reached for the empty wine bottle and poured the last drops into his glass. The exchange between them had the feel of a tired comedy routine. Nobody said anything for a while then, and I wondered if dinner had been ruined; but when I raised my eyes to steal a look at my father, he winked at me. Later, in the kitchen, Kay told my mother, "I wasn't with him that day, you know," and my mother assured her, "I know you weren't. Men always get things wrong."

On the way to the game farm the day we played hooky, Meggy sat beside our mother in the front seat while Justine and I played Spit on the hump in the back. To pass the time we sang, as we always did on road trips. When our father was driving, we stuck to cheerful ones, like "I've Got Sixpence" or "Someone's in the Kitchen with Dinah."

But when she was in the car, my mother let herself sing some of her favorites, which were almost like church hymns, solemn and slow. "'Someone's crying, my Lord, Kumbaya,'" she would start up after a period of silence, the road rushing by under our wheels. "'Oh, Lord, Kumbaya.'" I remember that even when I was very young I understood why my father found it hard to bear those words, that tune. You couldn't hear them without feeling more than you might be ready for. Years later when Kay Lonergan suggested that "Kumbaya" be included in the funeral music, it took my mother only a moment to decide against it.

We did not go to the game farm often, and it was partly because of this that it was one of our favorite places. You walked around on ground spread with sand and sawdust, smelling animal and, on the best days, the rich weight of a coming rain. You went up to the pens to pet the goats and the llamas, and tried to get the peacock to fan its tail. In between, you ate popcorn and hot dogs from the snack counters, drank lemonade from a wax-paper cup. Looked at other kids and the grown-ups they were with, and wondered what it would be like to be any of them; went to the bathroom in trailers set on concrete, the walls shaking when you flushed.

Besides the animals, the game farm had playground toys—slides, swing sets, a jungle gym, and horses fastened to the ground on rusted metal coils. When we arrived, Meggy wanted to ride one of the horses, so my mother held her balanced on top of the plastic saddle. But this was too babyish for Justine and me, and we took turns on the spiral slide, letting out little screams as we wound our way down, even though it was not nearly as scary as we remembered or hoped it to be. When Meggy saw us she wanted to go down, too, so my mother said I could hold my sister in my lap, and Meggy leaned back against my chest and laughed as we slid. At the bottom I caught her, clutched her tight, and stood up before she could fly forward out of my arms.

After lunch, Justine wanted my mother to take her back to the monkey pens. She liked to imitate their sounds and watch them blink and grin. But the same noise and sight that fascinated Justine made Meggy afraid, so my mother told me to stay with the baby for a few minutes while she went with Justine. Meggy started to cry when she saw my mother leaving, but I took up her hands and put them together in the clapping song she knew from watching Justine and me—Miss Lucy had a baby, she named him Tiny Tim, she put him in the bathtub to see if he could swim—and she let herself be distracted in watching her own pudgy arms make the motions of the game. After a while, she grew restless and wiggled to be let off my lap.

I watched her chase some pigeons, then turn around in a circle as they became braver and even closed in a little, making her clap and squeal. I got up to throw away my Fudgsicle stick and get a drink from the stone-based fountain, and when I came back to the picnic table where I had been sitting, Meggy was gone.

I didn't feel scared, at first—she could not have moved very far in such a short time; I just wasn't seeing her, wherever she was. On the other side of the water fountain, I heard cars spitting up gravel as they pulled out or parked. "Meggy," I called, in the direction of the pigeons, "where are you?" The birds made their gulpy noises and flew aside when I walked near them. I did not see my sister anywhere, not by the snack bar or the toilets or the path that led up to the animals and their pens, where now I saw my mother and Justine holding hands as they walked toward me.

I knew I should move, but I couldn't; I just waited and watched as they approached, and I saw my mother's smile collapse as she realized that I was alone, and she dropped Justine's hand and ran the rest of the way to where I stood.

"Where's Meggy?" she yelled, and behind her, trying to catch up, Justine began crying.

"I don't know. I just went over there to get a drink, and when I came back, she was gone."

"Gone where?" My mother grabbed my shoulders.

"Mommy, I don't know." Then I cried, too, and a woman passing us with a stroller lifted her sunglasses and looked over.

"Have you seen a baby?" my mother asked the woman. "A little girl?"

The woman, confused, looked down into the stroller she was pushing, but my mother said, "No, I mean my baby," and the woman said, "You mean she's lost?" and when my mother made an impatient sound, the woman said, "No, I'm sorry," and pushed her sunglasses back down on her face.

"She's here, Mommy, she's somewhere," Justine said. Her face and voice were desperate. "Just please don't worry, just please don't look like that."

When my mother concentrated—on a book, a piecrust, or a crisis like this one—her eyebrows dove in toward each other and made her look mad. The expression on her face at these times was especially upsetting to Justine, even though my mother had explained to her that it wasn't anger, it was just how she looked when she was trying to figure something out.

But right now I saw—along with Justine, who took a step backward to join me—that my mother *was* mad, and I felt a chill in my stomach when I realized she was mad at *me*.

"You were supposed to take care of her!" she yelled, and the woman with the sunglasses, who had walked on ahead, paused to look back at us. "You're the oldest," my mother went on, and even though I sensed that she was out of control and would hate herself later for the things she was saying now, I felt a tremble begin so deep inside that I knew it would not dare show itself anywhere close to the surface. "All you had to do was hold onto her for five minutes. Goddammit, Ana, where did she go?"

But all I could say was, "I don't know," in a whisper, and my mother almost pushed Justine and me down on the picnic-table bench, telling us to wait, don't *move*, and she went off in the direction of the swings and slide.

It was then, after watching the hem of our mother's culottes flap against her thighs as she moved away from us, that Justine and I together saw Meggy in the shade thrown by the awning of the hot-dog stand, the other direction from where Mom was headed. Our sister squatted in the circle of shadow to look at something on the ground.

"Meggy," we said, together, and forgetting what our mother had told us, we both jumped up from the bench.

"Stay here," I said to Justine. "No, go get Mommy. Bring her back." She started running the short distance to the playground, her chubby legs still tan in September.

As I approached, Meggy looked up, and I saw that it was a stiff pigeon she crouched over. "Yuck," I said. "Don't touch that." Of course, this made her put out her hand toward the pigeon; all she'd heard was the word *touch*.

"No," I said, reaching to pick her up. "It's dead. It's yucky."

"Ana mean," she said, squirming, and as I carried her back to the picnic table, she threw kisses over my shoulder at the dead bird.

When my mother had Meggy back on her lap, she apologized to me. "Sometimes people yell when they're worried, honey," she told me. "It was just that she could have been anywhere. She could have been kidnapped or hit by one of the cars."

"I know."

"You just can't imagine how a mother feels."

"It was my fault," I said. "I was supposed to take care of her." I wanted my mother to smile and tell me it was all right, I had only made a mistake, but she didn't; she just kept putting her mouth next to Meggy's hair.

"Don't ever go away like that again," she said to Meggy, and I waited for her to add, "That goes for all of you," and when she didn't, I thought, *Well, Justine and I are old enough to know that without being told.* Still, walking back to the car, I felt as if the wind had been knocked out of me. I was aware of my breath—how much I needed it—and how it is really only our breath and blood and heartbeat, and not love, that keeps us alive.

The feeling of something bad having almost happened stayed with us all the way to our grandparents' house, and we did not sing. Meggy was the only one who behaved as she normally did, chattering and offering us animal crackers from the box my mother had bought her. She didn't seem to notice that the rest of us weren't responding in the way she was accustomed to. Mom kept her eyes on the road more intently than usual, and Justine and I knew enough to keep quiet even when we saw things to be excited about, like cows or a Ferris wheel.

They were both outside when we arrived. Our grandfather was sitting on the porch reading *Rabbit, Run.* (I remember because it seemed to me the title of a children's book, not one of the novels he always had open during our visits.) Our grandmother walked toward him from the backyard, where she had been sweeping pieces of loose tar left by the men who had refinished the driveway. She wore white knee socks and sneakers under her gardening dress, a green cotton shift faded by sun and detergent and time. When she saw our car turning in, she raised a hand above her eyes, trying to make out whose it was. A minute later, when she lifted her face to kiss us, I saw that her fingers against her forehead had left dark marks on the fair white skin.

"What are you doing here?" she asked my mother. "Don't the girls have school?" I was old enough to sense that although she was glad to see us, she was also preparing to disapprove. Next to me, I could feel Mom react to this tone in her own mother's voice.

"There was teacher training today," she told my grandmother, and it sounded so true from her lips that I almost said, *There was?* But right before I would have spoken, I caught sight of my mother's eyes, and I saw that she needed me.

"It's a day off," I said. "Like a holiday. We wanted to give you a surprise."

My mother sent me a grateful look, which made me feel as high as the sun. She sat down on the porch with her parents while Justine and I took Meggy inside to find the toys my grandmother kept in the sewing-room closet. We wanted the marble farm. This was a coffee can containing marbles of every size and color and condition, each labeled with a dot of cloth adhesive tape that carried a number. The names corresponding to the numbers—Chestnut, Black Beauty, Thunder, Blaze—had been kept in a notebook that was destroyed ten years earlier in the fire my mother's brother set in the attic when he was home during a college break and fell asleep sneaking a cigarette.

But the marbles themselves, the horses in their Chock full o' Nuts stable, survived. My grandmother asked my mother if she wanted them for us to play with, but my mother said no, she wanted to keep them in this house, they would be a treat when we visited. Although I was angry at her then because I wanted the marbles—they weren't just any marbles, but ones my mother had played with, held, and loved when she was a child—I also recognized that it was the fact that I could not have them, whenever I wanted, that made them precious.

We took the marble farm back outside and put down the pasture, a big plank of cardboard with glued-on Easter-basket grass. Meggy wasn't old enough yet to appreciate the various events of the horse show, but Justine and I were teaching them to her, as our mother had taught them to us. First was the high jump: you picked out ten marbles to compete and, one at a time, made them bounce on the cardboard over the high-jump bar, which was a Popsicle stick you kept raising. The victorious marble was placed in the winner's circle (one of my grandmother's old bracelets) and covered with a dandelion crown.

Next was the steeplechase, the elaborate course of which we never tired of setting up. It consisted of the cardboard tubes from wax-paper and toilet-paper rolls, taped together in a labyrinth, beginning where it was propped on the high end of a shoe box, ending in a soft cotton pile. You sent the marbles through the chute and listened to them wind their way through the tunnels, while you counted one-one-hundred, two-one-hundred, three. The marble reaching the end in the shortest amount of time won.

Justine and I took turns starting the horses off in the gate, but by then Meggy wanted to try, so we let her. She loved dropping the marbles into the open end of the cardboard, and each time she would put her eye up to the hole to follow where it had gone.

As we set up the farm, our mother was saying, "But I don't think that's really the point, Pop." If I tilted my head a little, pretending to move my eyes out of the sun, I could see her sitting on the top step, looking up with the weight of a favor on her face.

"Well, whatever the point is, Margaret, you're asking for money. And that gives whoever you're asking a certain right." My grandfather had turned the Rabbit book facedown on his lap. He often spoke quietly, so that you had to lean in when you listened; but when you heard what it was he was saying, you sometimes sat back again from its force.

"It's just till he gets his license," my mother said. "We'll pay it back when he sells his first house." I knew they were talking about my father and his most recent change of career. (When he was between jobs, my father liked to borrow another line of Susan Hayward's from the movie *I Want to Live!* When somebody asked her, "What's your occupation? What do you do?" she answered without missing a beat, "The best I can.")

"How much do you need?" my grandmother asked. My mother mumbled something, which I didn't hear, and a few seconds later my grandmother got up to go inside. When she came out, she took a check from her cotton pocket and gave it to my mother, who kissed her and tucked it carefully into her purse.

"You know how much I appreciate this," my mother said. "Listen, I'm not going to tell him where this came from, so could you please not bring it up?"

"Where's he going to think you got it?" My grandfather seemed agitated. I couldn't tell whether it was because of my grandmother's

having acted without consulting him, or just the tacit but tangible doubts
he'd accumulated over the years of my father's spotty job record and his
need to act on compulsions that had no ground.

"I'll think of something," my mother said. As if saving her from having to elaborate, Meggy made a noise that caused us all to look at her in
alarm. She was bending forward from her hips, her mouth open and her
face turning dark.

Justine said, "She just swallowed a marble."

My grandmother murmured, "Oh, dear God," and my mother was
with Meggy in an instant, turning her over so that the hem of Meggy's
dress fell above her head. The sound my mother made while she was hitting Meggy on the back was similar to the sound I had heard at the game
farm when Meggy was lost, but this one was worse—higher-pitched,
more panicked—and Justine and I sat there watching as Meggy sputtered and gasped and finally gave up the marble. Then she began to
scream.

"That's the second scary thing that's happened to her today," Justine
said. Moving closer to put her berry-stained hand on the baby's head,
my grandmother asked, "You mean Meggy or your mother?"

Once Meggy was in kindergarten, my mother gave up freelancing and
looked for part-time journalism work. When she couldn't find a regular
reporting job, she established the "Ask Us" column at the *Ashmont Star*.
The column appeared in each weekly issue on the same page as the Stork
Market, which listed all the new births in town.

As the Ask Us editor, my mother researched answers to questions that
bothered or intrigued the people who wrote or called in. Then she com-
posed a little narrative history about each one. Some questions were easy
("When were golf balls invented?") if you knew, as she did, the right
sources to consult. My mother always tried to alternate these with the
more specialized queries, such as, "Is there a club for people who collect
license plates?" (The answer, in case you're interested, is yes.)

The idea for Ask Us came from a phrase we traded often in our
family: *Tell me something I don't know.* Kids used to say it when they wanted

to ridicule you by showing that whatever you had to say was too old or too obvious for words, like that the gym teacher was a lesbo or that it was going to snow.

But one day a long time ago, when Meggy heard me say to Justine, *Tell me something I don't know,* our little sister missed the sarcasm in my voice and came over to listen for Justine's answer. Meggy must have been four or five then, and in her sharp, sweet face, I could see that she was waiting; that she thought I was genuinely asking Justine to teach me something new. So, feeling ashamed of myself, and loving Meggy's trustfulness more than I thought I could bear, I altered my tone and the look on my face and I said to Justine, "No, I mean it. Tell me something I really *don't* know."

Justine was suspicious, as of course she should have been. But then she saw that I was serious, and her expression changed to one of concentration as she tried to come up with an interesting fact. It had to be a good one, she knew—something that would impress both Meggy and me. She twirled her long hair around a finger (even then, she was practicing the gestures that would lay her foundation as a flirt) and bit at a fingernail. Finally, she took a breath and said, "A worm has a bunch of hearts all through his body, and if you cut him in half, you get two new whole worms out of one. And if you cut those worms, you get two more out of each one, and it keeps on going."

Well, I did know this; I had learned it, as she had, from the *Let's Look at Animals* book our father bought for us as a consolation prize, the day we had to cancel a trip to Cooperstown because there was a garbage spill on the Thruway and he didn't want us exposed.

But I wasn't about to let on to Justine that the worm fact wasn't new to me. "That's neat," I said.

"But how can it?" Meggy pulled herself up on the couch between us and leaned her head against my shoulder. "Have so many hearts?" So Justine went and got the book from their bedroom. The next day, when there was a lull during dinner, Meggy said to all of us, "Tell me something I don't know," and it became a game, instead of the insult it started out to be.

Ask Us was one of the most popular parts of the newspaper, because you found that people were asking things you also wondered about. "How did they get the horse's mouth to move on the old Mr. *Ed* show?" K.V. from Ravena would write, and my mother investigated until she learned that it was a simple case of applying a peanut butter-like substance to the horse's lips, prompting the animal to attempt to lick it off.

My mother wrote the Ask Us column for ten years. During that time, she answered more than a thousand questions. She always made fun of her job; for instance, on the day every spring that the Pulitzer prizes were scheduled to be announced, she pretended she was waiting for their call.

When she finally stopped writing Ask Us, it had less to do with the job itself than with my father and what was happening at home. I remember the day in February, four months before the deaths, that my mother decided to move out. It was a Friday, and I was visiting from college for the long Presidents' Day weekend. My mother came home from work and stood in front of the TV, where Meggy and our father and I were watching *People's Court*. Meggy was laying out a game of Solitaire on the rug, Bill Buckner's nose resting on her knee. Mom stood in front of the screen and said, "Listen to this," as she shook a piece of paper to get our attention. *My brother and I are curious about popcorn. How and why does it pop? What kind of corn is it? Who first discovered what it could do?* Then she crunched up the paper into a ball.

"Well?" our father said, after a moment. "Who did discover popcorn?"

"The Indians," she told him, her voice dripping exasperation, "but that's not the point." My father asked her what the point was, and she said, "The point is that I spend most of my time tracking down useless information for people who have nothing better to do than sit around and wonder about *popcorn*, for God's sake."

"But popcorn's important," Meggy said, without looking up from her game. She and her friend Gail had made their Black Pact at New Year's — a contest to see who could go the longest wearing only black clothes — and the jeans she put on every day were flecked with Bill Buckner's white hair. She tried to pretend she was smiling but it was more of a smirk, and I could see that she was going to say something she would regret, considering our mother's mood, even before the words were out. "It's excellent roughage. We learned that in health."

"Oh, very funny." My mother whipped the ball of paper over Bill Buckner's head and into the fireplace, where blue flames consumed it. "I guess this is all just hilarious to you guys. Nobody remembers that I covered Malcolm X and once interviewed Richard Nixon. I had Secret Service credentials. Now I'm just a big joke."

"Margaret?" From his reclining position on the sofa, our father raised himself up on an elbow. I felt my mother turning toward him hopefully; I could tell that she thought he might say something to comfort or contradict her. But he looked beyond her to the fireplace, where fragments of the singed paper had floated out onto the hearth. "Could you sweep those ashes up?"

My mother looked at him as if she couldn't believe what he'd just said. Meggy, who was between games, stopped shuffling and froze, because it was clear that something big was about to happen. We watched as my mother went to the kitchen for the hand broom and returned to brush the bits of charred paper into the dustpan. Then she went over to the sofa and turned the soot onto my father's head.

He remained motionless for a few seconds, though his eyes widened and panic swallowed the pupils. Then he began having trouble breathing. By the time he got up from the sofa, he was taking big gasps and still not getting enough air. My mother did not go after him; it was Meggy who, having thrown down her cards, ran to get him a glass of water. "It's okay, Dad. Dad, it's not really dirt, it's just paper. You can take a shower. We'll get you clean." She said the last four words more loudly and distinctly than the others, as if she thought they might get through.

"I'm okay," he said, though it was clear he wasn't. He gagged and choked. Meggy followed him upstairs, and we heard the shutting of the bathroom door. I turned up the TV to hear Judge Wapner's verdict. Without a word, my mother left the house, and through the window I saw her go across the street to the neighbors', where I knew she would sit down to a glass of wine with Kay Lonergan. At the kitchen table, they would take turns complaining about their husbands—one who scrubbed himself raw and still couldn't get clean enough, the other an elected town official with a tab at the Shamrock rivaling some people's VISA bills.

Meggy came back downstairs and told me, as if trying to convince both of us, "He'll be okay." The shower in my parents' bathroom ran through the entire six o'clock news. It was still running when Justine came home from a basketball game at 7:15.

"We lost," she said, flopping into my father's place and reaching for the box of Ritz crackers, which was all Meggy and I had managed to dig up for dinner. When none of us responded, she added, "Does anybody care?"

"Not really," Meggy said. "Could we talk about something besides cheerleading for a change?" Above us the shower faucets went off; Meggy and I looked at each other with relief, and Justine bounced, her ponytail bobbing, up to her room. When my mother came back from the Lonergans' she made up the cot in the basement and spent the night there. Within a week she was sending out resumes, and two weeks later an old friend from her early newspaper days offered her the job at the *Delphi Oracle*.

I had a list of questions I imagined, in my fantasies after the deaths, submitting to my mother in care of Ask Us. "Why did you leave? Why did Dad kill Meggy? Why did he kill himself?" And then the big one: "What did the note say?"—*Your daughter, Anastasia, At Large.*

But by then it was too late. She had already quit the job.

4. God's eyes

Q. I recently heard of a measurement know as the "jnd." To what does this refer?

— *G.H., West Saugerties*

A. The initials stand for the "just noticeable difference" between sensations. Researchers ask an experimental subject to judge between two stimuli—two sounds of nearly identical intensity, two lights of similar brightness or color, two weights that are nearly the same. By repeated tests, an effort is made to establish the exact difference between the stimuli that is needed to produce a single *jnd* of sensation.

The people who'd signed a purchase-and-sale agreement on our house in Ashmont wanted to back out of the deal after my father and Meggy died. The closing wasn't scheduled until the end of July, and in the meantime, word of what had happened made it down to the Crowells in Atlanta. When they heard, the wife contacted our real estate office to say that she'd changed her mind. The realtor, Gwen Schiff, called us in a panic to deliver the news. Justine and I were the only ones home; our mother was in Oneida covering a water-main break. I spoke to Gwen on the phone while gesturing for Justine to turn down the television, where she was watching a rerun of *Bewitched*.

"So what can we do?" I asked. Gwen was the top salesperson at Zenith Realty, where my father had worked for six months, nearly fifteen years ago, before they let him go because he hadn't sold a single property. I was surprised he had called them when it came time to sell the house, but he said there were no hard feelings, and besides, Zenith was the best.

"Well," Gwen said, and in the background I could hear her punching numbers. "I got the impression they might still be interested, if we came down on the price."

"Then do it," I told her.

"I mean substantially."

"I don't care. Just get rid of it."

"Are you sure you don't want to put it back on the market?" Gwen stopped her fingers from flying. I heard the flick of a cigarette being lit. "Although I'll be honest with you, it'll be hard to sell to anyone, at least anytime soon, because of—the history. If the Crowells are willing to renegotiate, we should probably grab it."

"Fine. *Do.*" I didn't even discuss it with Justine, because I knew what my sister would say. The house had remained in our father's name when my mother moved out, and he'd left everything to any children who survived him.

"All right. I just wanted to check with you." Gwen took a long drag, then lowered her voice. I imagined her cupping a hand over the phone. "Listen, we had the place cleaned. We brought in a company to do the whole thing—rugs, curtains, everything. You'd never be able to tell— well, you know."

"Good," I said, closing my eyes and trying not to think about what it must have looked like when the workers went in.

"I know you told the movers to take everything," she added, "but the last time I was over there, I saw some stuff in the basement."

"What stuff?"

"Just a few boxes. I didn't look inside. Do you want me to have them removed?"

I looked across the room at Justine sprawled motionless on the couch, watching the TV as intently as if God himself were addressing her from the screen.

"No," I said to Gwen.

"Well, then, you'll have to get rid of them yourselves. If the Crowells take us up on a lower price and they have to come up here for the closing, they'll want to move in as soon as they can."

"Don't worry," I said. Every time I talked to her, I felt like punching Gwen Schiff through the phone. She had come to the funeral, sat in a pew near the front, and cried, but I knew from overhearing my parents, all those years ago, that she'd been the one to suggest firing my father when he didn't produce. "I'll take care of it." I hung up without saying good-bye and then sat at the kitchen counter, tapping a pencil on the pad where I'd taken down figures without even seeing them.

When Justine's show was over, she sat up and looked at me. "Who was that?"

"We have to go back there."

"Where?"

"The house."

"When? Why?"

"That was Gwen. She says there's some boxes down in the basement the movers forgot to take." I decided there was no point in mentioning anything about the change in the sale price. "We have to go get them."

"Boxes of what?"

"I don't know. Maybe junk. But I don't want to take a chance; it might be something we'd end up wanting."

"What about Mom?"

"What about her?"

"Don't you think she'd want to go with us?"

"Yeah, right." In my sarcasm, I tried not to snort. Our mother had made it clear, when she moved out, that she was leaving Pearl Street for good. After the deaths and the funeral reception at the Waxmans' house, her resolve grew even stronger. "It won't take us long. If we go now, we can miss rush hour."

Justine said, "I don't exactly want to go back there."

"You think I do?"

"Why does it have to be today?"

"It doesn't. But why not get it over with? What else are we doing?"

"I don't know." She lay sideways again on the sofa. Sitting required more effort than she could spare.

I said, "There might be some things we forgot to save."

She stared at the TV for a long moment, then shrugged in an imitation of someone who didn't care one way or the other. "Why not?" she said, and the question seemed so absurd—there were so many possible answers—that I almost laughed.

We started the road trip singing along with Carly Simon, but the closer we moved to familiar territory, the quieter we became in the car. As we turned off the Thruway exit toward Ashmont, I felt us both hold our breath.

Do I have to tell you what it is like to go back home? You know by instinct the exact distance between every street sign, and just about every house has a name or a memory attached. This is where you took piano lessons from Mrs. Delmonte, who had an Italian accent and always made you crack up when she instructed you to use your "turd" finger instead of your third. If you go by the corner where the man in the lawn chair is always sitting with the schnauzer in his lap—making the dog wave its paws at the cars going by—but they are not there today, then their absence is as remarkable to you as the sight of the man and the dog would be to a stranger first passing through.

You know how long the lights take to change, the route of all the parades, what stood in that lot—the Cut'n'Curl, where you once lost a contact lens in a hair magazine—before the new bank was built. That the library used to be a funeral parlor, that Jimmy Garcia got killed playing chicken behind the old dump. You know this place—home—too intimately for your own good. Nothing should ever be this familiar, or have such a sure hold upon your heart.

"This is so weird," Justine whispered as I took the back way, a shortcut, to Pearl Street. It was the first time we had been on our old block since the day of the funerals. As we drove toward our house, I thought I could feel a thousand eyes staring out at us. Too late, it occurred to me that we should have waited for dark.

We went around to the back of the house, where the grass, which was too high, tickled our ankles. Our father had always been conscientious about the grass, as he was about the garden; he mowed the lawn on Saturday afternoons, and liked it most when the day was hot and he finished sweaty and satisfied, ready for the reward of a shower and an iced tea. I remember how he threw his head back as he drank, closing his eyes as if nothing he'd ever tasted had been so good.

Gwen had left the basement door unlocked. Ashmont was the kind of town where you could do this—safe, its citizens trustworthy, if only because they had reputations to protect. Justine and I sat in the car, in front of the house, for a good ten minutes. I had not parked in the driveway because we were trying to be as inconspicuous as possible. But if anyone wanted to see us, it was too late to avoid notice now. We shut the car doors quietly, like kids sneaking in past curfew, and moved quickly around the house to the bulkhead that led to the basement.

I went down the steps first, though Justine stayed close enough behind me that I could feel her breath on my back. "This gives me the creeps," she said, and I heard her shivering, even though the air was warm. "How come, out of all the time we lived here, all we can think about is that day?" It wasn't precisely true, but I knew what she meant. The deaths gave everything else we remembered a sinister sheen. Like the swing set in the middle of the backyard, and the picnic table in the corner: they reminded us of birthday parties, cake and ice cream that melted before we could eat it, the paper toot-horns we'd use to tickle one another's ears.

Yet we could not think of that laughter, the shouts and the singing, the dresses and hats and favor bags of Hershey's kisses, as anything but ghosts.

Same with the basement, once we stepped inside. All three of us had spent hours of our childhood down here with our mother, playing jacks and Spit on the other end of the rickety table as she folded the clothes. We came to associate the scent of warm laundry with the sensation of comfort, the rhythmic whish of the washer with the routine of carrying a dirty jumble downstairs and emerging later with a soap-smelling pile. I was very young when I realized that a basket of dirty clothes was heavier than a basket of clean. But back then I didn't understand why; in my childish conception, it had to do with good and bad, and God giving the reward of lightness to the pure, laundered load. To me it was a magical transformation that had nothing to do with the laws of nature, the density of soil and sweat, or the wringing motion of the spin. All I knew was that my mother seemed happier when the laundry was finished, and we could go upstairs again to the light of the kitchen and the feeling that all was fresh.

But now the washer and dryer had been moved out, and only one of the lights still worked, a single bulb trailing a length of sturdy green string my mother had borrowed a long time ago from my God's-eye kit. God's eyes—those designs you made by wrapping string around nails hammered into wood; stars and geometric figures and crossover patterns in bright colors of thick thread, which you pulled taut across a skeleton of nails. I had to stop making them when my father got it into his head that Meggy could pull one of the nails out of a board and swallow it. Not only did I have to stop making new God's eyes, he told me; I had to get rid of the ones I already had.

We used the many colors of string in that kit for years, to tie up newspapers, to wrap birthday presents when we ran out of real ribbon, even to extricate one of Justine's baby teeth when it was just hanging in its socket. Our mother attached one end of a length of red string to the tooth and another to the bathroom doorknob, but then she couldn't bring herself to slam the door to yank the tooth out, so I volunteered. It worked, but the force hurt Justine and made her mouth bleed, and though she didn't yell at me, I felt guilty. In the morning, we both found quarters under our pillows.

And we used the string to make the chain on this basement light switch longer, so that even Meggy could turn it on if she came down first. Now Justine and I looked at each other through the dimness, and when I didn't make a move (as the oldest, I always had the right of first refusal in such decisions), she reached up and yanked the bulb into brightness. We both blinked and started, suddenly able—before we were really ready for it—to see what was in front of us.

"Jesus," Justine said. "What did we do this for?"

Instead of answering, I went over to the hot-water tank, next to which the realtor had stacked the three boxes we were supposed to take. In the first box, we found piles of our old baby clothes—everything from stained T-shirts and sleepers to the antique christening dress that had been handed down through the Ott family for four generations. Here was the dress with the strawberry pockets, the plaid poncho, the jumper of calico wool. "Oh, God," Justine said, when we saw what the box contained, and though she quickly added, "If we came all the way here just for some stupid baby things, I'm going to be pissed," I knew that her exclamation came from shocked pleasure at recovering what we had loved once and had not now expected to find. If we went back to

Delphi with only these little remnants, her tone said, it will be worth the trip.

We put them aside to open the other two boxes. One was nearly empty, except for several newspapers, which at first we took to be cushioning for something else. But when we looked more closely, we saw that they were the front sections of the *Knickerbocker News* from significant dates in contemporary history: the day Nixon resigned, the day of the Kent State riots, the day Kennedy was shot. There was also a framed "dummy" front page that had been made up by the other reporters to send my mother off when she left the newspaper. *Ott Opts for Motherhood*, the top headline said, and, underneath it: *Knick Loses Ace Reporter to So-Called Normal Life*.

"I guess she was saving these once," Justine said, blowing dust from a yellowing photo of Patricia Hearst in her Symbionese Liberation Army uniform. "Should we take them back for her?"

"Let's not," I told her. "She went through all this stuff when she moved out. She must have left them here on purpose." I didn't add what I was thinking: *If she did want them, too bad. She had her chance.*

We put that box aside and pulled out the third and heaviest one, which had been layered with strips of thick packaging tape. The other two boxes had been labeled in our mother's slight, sloppy hand; this one carried my father's heavy deliberate letters, spelling IMPORTANT— SAVE.

We couldn't figure out how to get it open until Justine stood on her toes and found a wrench on top of the water tank. She ripped a slit down the center of the seal. "And now, Vanna, let's take a look at our prize," Justine said, holding the wrench up in front of her like a microphone. It took both of us to drag the box away from the tank and rip back the cardboard flaps.

What we saw made us smile first, then laugh to each other with our eyes, although there seems nothing funny in retrospect about a cartonful of keys, all loose and piled on top of one another like so many random coins. No two keys were on chains or connected by tape or twine; none was labeled or tagged; and there was no indication anywhere of what locks the keys fitted, how old they were, whether they had been discarded in this box or were being saved for the day when our father might need to open something and would try every key he had ever encountered, until one of them finally worked.

"Jesus," Justine said. She tried to whistle but it came out spit. "Did you ever see these before?"

"Of course not. What do you think?" I heard indignation in my voice without even knowing where it came from, but in the next moment I realized it was because I felt accused, and because I was instinctively defending my father, who was the guilty one. When had he begun collecting these keys, and why did he hide them, and what comfort did he derive from knowing they were here? He had always been a hoarder, but as far as we knew it was never in secret—he'd stick the most unlikely things (the cardboard of a paper-towel roll, an empty soap-bubble jar) on top of his current pile in the pantry, and our mother would take care of getting rid of them later, when he was out of sight. He couldn't bring himself to discard even a burnt match, at the exact moment it passed from utility into worthlessness.

As I recall, we chose as a family to see these behaviors, like his preoccupation with germs, as a quirky endearment, rather than a problem to worry about. Maybe we were just fooling ourselves; I guess, given the evidence, there's no question about that. As Justine would have said, *Duh.*

But it was just something we lived with, like the shedding of Bill Buckner's hair. I remember once Justine clipping her toenails and bringing them to my father in the palm of her hand. "Can I get rid of these, or does anybody want to save them?" she asked, and even he could laugh at himself. We never thought of him as sick or crazy. Even when he burned his car to the ground, my mother said it was time he got a new one, anyway. It was just *Dad.*

"There must be every key he ever owned in this box," Justine said, reaching forward to pick through them. The box contained double-sided keys, cap keys, keys to car models we never owned, even a few miniature, toy-type keys like the kind you might find taped to a child's diary at Woolworth's. "Should we take them, or what?"

"I don't see why. We'd never find out what any of them belonged to. Let's just leave everything, except the baby clothes." I went to pick up the first box, but Justine was still staring down at the keys.

"I know this'll sound weird," she said, not looking at me, "but I think I'd kind of like to have these. It just seems kind of sad to chuck them. Do you think we could?"

"Of course, if you want to. They're ours now."

"No, I mean could we *move* them," Justine clarified, kicking the dense cardboard. We each squatted down to take an end, then heaved and managed to shift the box only a foot or so before we had to set it down again. Justine had never been strong when it came to lifting. And though she had extra weight in her legs now, it didn't seem to help.

"Okay, forget it," Justine said.

"You're just going to give up?"

"Well, it's not working."

"Wait a minute. I'll bring the car around." I climbed into the daylight, got in the car, and backed it down the driveway, along the side of the house. At the lip of the lawn I hesitated only a moment before I drove over it and parked with the hatchback next to the bulkhead doors.

"I can't believe you did that," Justine said. From the look on her face you might have thought I'd landed a spaceship in the middle of a tub. We pushed and dragged the box of keys across the floor, up the steps, and out to the grass. We lifted it again and swung it into the trunk, where it fell with a thud and spilled some of the keys out; but at least we had secured them in the car. We went back for the baby clothes, and we were going to leave our mother's souvenir newspapers behind as we had decided, but in the end Justine convinced me that we should take everything.

We were starting back up the bulkhead stairs for the last time when we heard a man's voice say, "Hands in the air, please," and then Frank Garhart recognized us as we climbed out into the yard. "Oh, sorry," he said.

"It's you," he added, when we were all standing level with one another. His radio crackled at his hip, and he lifted it to speak. I was waiting for some coded lingo out of *Adam-12* , but he only said, "Everything's okay at the Pearl Street address. It's just the Dolan girls." Hearing our name on his lips gave me a stab at my center, regretful and sweet. He looked straight at me.

"Oh," Justine said, realizing suddenly who he was. "You're the one who—oh, yeah." She leaned over and I thought she might vomit, but she took a deep breath and the danger seemed to pass.

Frank looked uncomfortable, as if he were the one who'd been caught at something. "What are you two doing here?"

"Cleaning out the basement," I told him. "We're trying to sell the house."

If it weren't for Justine, I knew he would have asked other things: why I hadn't returned his last phone calls, for instance. We'd talked almost every day after the night we spent together, once I left Ashmont for Delphi. On my first day at my mother's condo, he sent flowers with the message, *Looking forward to next time. Hope you have some peace.* I told my mother and Justine that they were from Ruthie and hid the card in a compartment of my suitcase. I was afraid to see him in person again. Whatever had taken over that night and sent me to bed with him—not only the willingness, but the *need* to be seen as naked as I ever would be—was foreign to me before and since, but I wouldn't have known how to explain this to Frank. He kept offering to drive out to Delphi to see me, and I kept putting him off. Then I just stopped calling him back altogether.

Now it had been a month since we'd seen each other, so it was a shock to have him standing in front of me; in my memory he was shaggy and indistinct, and I had to look away, as if he were a sun or something else it would hurt to look at for very long.

"What are you doing here?" I said.

"Somebody called. I'm not sure who. One of the neighbors; they thought someone was breaking in."

"But couldn't they tell it was us?"

Frank shrugged. "I guess not. Or maybe they didn't really look." He knew we expected him to leave, but he kept his big feet in their black shoes planted on the lawn, where Gwen Schiff or someone in her office had set a sprinkler on a timer to keep the grass healthy in the heat. When his eyes met mine, I jerked slightly, as if he had touched the bare skin of my shoulder. "Do you need anything?" he asked. "A ride somewhere, maybe?"

"I've got my car," I told him, gesturing at the old Horizon sagging under the load of boxes in the backseat. "But thanks."

"Well. Be in touch then," he said, and it wasn't clear whether he was making a promise or a request. He took his time walking back to the cruiser and stretched before he got in, giving me time to summon him back. When I didn't, he started the engine and saluted us, with a solemn smile, on his way out.

Justine knelt and picked up a few stones from the walkway alongside the house. Our father had laid it the summer before he died, and it was from this bed that Justine took the stone to cut herself on the arm, after she'd found him that day.

"Put those down," I told her, the words coming out in a bark.

"I'm just taking a few to remember us by." She curled some pebbles into a soft fist. I tried not to notice the new rolls of fat at her knees, the little dent of flesh in her neck where the nerves were dancing. She gave a nudge of her head in the direction of Frank's retreating car. "You know, he'd have sex with you, if you wanted to."

I started; it was as if she'd looked into my mind and seen the picture on the screen there, me under the covers, clutching Frank into the night. "Why are you saying that?" I demanded.

"Oh, nothing really. I can just tell." She smirked, and I tried not to realize she was mocking my virginity. To the tune of the old jump-rope rhyme she sang, "Frank and Ana, sitting in a tree. F-U-C-K-I-N-G."

"Shut up." I picked up my own stone as a keepsake and put it in my pocket. If I had been anybody else, I realized, Justine would have already figured out what Frank and I had been doing, the night—or morning— he returned me to the motel.

But I knew she never thought of me as a sexual being; she claimed that role, in our sisterhood, for herself. She shrugged. "Fine. Don't listen to me. Even though I know about these things. Better than you do." I

could tell she was only speaking to distract herself, and me, from wanting to look out the car windows as we headed back down the street. The
more provocative her words, the less likely we'd be to notice where we
were and what we were leaving. It worked, too; I barely took note of
turning the corner from Pearl Street to the main road out of Ashmont.

"Who was it?" I asked, our neighborhood safe at a distance in the
rearview mirror. "Was it Skip Junco?"

Justine clucked. "Ha. I'm not telling. Besides, it doesn't matter. I'm
never going to do it again."

"What do you mean?"

"What do you think I mean? Sex. Intercourse. *Screwing.*" She rolled
down her window to let the breeze blow her hair. Looking away from
me carefully, she said, "What do you think I was doing when Meggy got
killed?"

It took me a moment to realize what she was saying. "Really?" I felt
foolish not knowing how to respond.

"Yes, really." She rolled up the window again, her emphatic tone
mimicking mine. "I mean, there's no way of actually knowing, since
they can't tell the exact time of death. But I could have been. I think I
probably *was.*" Her feet brushed against an empty Styrofoam cup on the
floor in front of her, and she flattened it with stabbing kicks.

There were many questions I wanted to ask—*No, really who? Where? Did
he use a rubber?*—but I knew she wouldn't answer. Over the years, when it
came to sex, Justine had always been the one to decide exactly how much
she would tell me, meting out details the way a mother gives children
treats. So I stayed silent after she said she believed she'd been screwing
at the moment Meggy had died. We listened to our father's keys rattling
in their box in the trunk as I took the corners. When we reached the
boundary of Ashmont and approached the exit for the Thruway, I hesitated only a moment and then passed it, continuing on into Albany.

Justine jerked her head up. I hadn't been sure she was paying attention. "What are you doing?" She sounded dismayed.

"You hungry?" I said.

She gave me a quick look of puzzlement before she caught on. Then she smiled slightly, realizing where we were headed, and said, "I could eat," as if it were an old punch line between us.

In the city, I turned onto Madison Avenue. We were about three blocks from Mercer Street, where we'd lived when both Justine and Meggy were born, and we were also near P.S. No. 16, where I had attended kindergarten through the third grade. I found a parking space directly across from the Taft Theater, and Justine and I sat for a moment watching people buy tickets for *Die Hard*.

The Taft was the theater my father went to when he was a boy living in Albany with his mother and his sister Rosemary. Their father, my grandfather, had died when my father was eight and Rosemary was ten. He worked as an electrician, and one morning he fell into a live wire and grabbed it with both hands. My father remembered most vividly his own confusion at being told what had happened. "I couldn't understand how, if he fell into a live wire, he could be *dead*," our father said, on the rare occasions when he talked to us about his childhood.

It was my mother who told me, one day when I was in the eighth grade and pestering her for information so that I could construct a family tree for Social Studies, that there had always been some question about the origin of my grandfather's fall. "I guess some of the men he worked with thought he could have jumped, on purpose," my mother said. "Of course, Daddy doesn't believe that. But I think your Aunt Rosemary might."

My father's mother began working as a legal secretary after her husband died. Her job required overtime, including weekend hours, and my father and Rosemary were pretty much left to bring up themselves. They were good children for a few years until they found no reward in it, and then they began to cut school and Mass at St. Joseph's, and to hang out with other kids who were doing the same thing. West Street was a poor neighborhood, and they got into trouble often, and most of the parents were absent or too tired to do much about any of it. Rosemary began smoking cigarettes when she was eleven, but my father never took it up. Even then—Rosemary told us years later, teasing her little brother when he was a grown man—he was squeamish about the things he would put into his mouth. "Actually, I think you got that from Pop," she told him. It was a source of frustration to my father that Rosemary could remember things about their father, when he could not. All he recalled was a dim shadow passing above his forehead, after leaving a good-night kiss smelling of boiled corn beef and beer. "We never had anything baked or fried or broiled for Sunday dinner. Ma had to boil all the meat and potatoes, and of course the cabbage, before Pop would eat them," Rosemary said.

It was not because of the movies themselves that my father began to spend time at the Taft, to consider it his second home. You hear stories about lost and unhappy children finding solace in the fantasy of film, but my father was not one to escape in this way. He always chose real life over fiction, biographies over invented characters, books about true crime over the tales of Dashiell Hammett or Rex Stout. When we went to the movies, it became a family joke that he usually suggested the latest disaster feature, especially if it was based on a historical event, like *The Hindenburg*.

At first I thought it was just because of the way boys and men were, always wanting to see things blow up or fall apart. But as I grew older, and got to know my father and the world better, I came to believe that he avoided romances, and happy endings, because it was so cruel a shock to come out of the theater and find life as it actually was.

What attracted my father to the Taft was the man who owned and ran it, Mr. Bloom. He was small and bald and gentle, a Jewish widower who had no children of his own and who, when he saw a kid hanging around the ticket booth, alone, assumed that he or she didn't have enough money to come in. In such cases, Mr. Bloom offered free admission. It was not something he advertised, and sometimes kids who actually had money in their pockets tried to take advantage of the old man's benevolence. But he could pretty much tell when someone was trying to put one over on him, and he had been known to take the opportunists aside and ask, with disappointment in his smooth, mild face, if they weren't ashamed.

When Mr. Bloom told my father, one cold November afternoon, that he could come in and see *High Noon* as the Taft's guest, my father grew flushed and said thank you, but what he was really looking for was a job. It was partly true—my grandfather had died without insurance or savings, and since my grandmother had to pay off his debts, in addition to coming up with tuition at St. Joseph's for my father and Rosemary, the family finances were so tight that she would move a bulb from lamp to lamp, depending on what room she needed lighted, instead of replacing the one that had burned out.

But I believe that if my father had been completely honest—and if he had known the truth, himself—he would have told Mr. Bloom that he was looking for a father. And when Mr. Bloom hired him to usher and sell popcorn, on weekends and after school, a father is what my father got. Mr. Bloom helped him with his homework (all except the catechism, of course) and brought in his own supper, whenever he had leftovers from the night before, for my father to eat while the evening movie was playing and concession sales were slack. I think my father liked Mr. Bloom because he was so different from my grandfather, a ruthless Catholic who, by all accounts, could be relied upon only to drink more than his share of Beverwyck Irish Cream Ale. In Mr. Bloom my father found the kind of quiet, steady, paternal love that few of his friends were lucky enough to have in their own fathers. When some of his classmates called my father a Jew-lover, my father had to be told by Rosemary that it was meant as an insult. When my parents got married, Mr. Bloom sat in the pew with my grandmother, and told her privately that it was the only circumstance under which he could imagine ever setting foot in a Catholic church.

Mr. Bloom died just after I was born, so I never knew him except in the stories my father told. The Taft Theater was condemned after his death and scheduled for razing to make way for a Price Chopper. My father didn't have any money to invest himself, but he got a bunch of the St. Joe's graduates working in area businesses to buy it back from the city. The neighborhood around the theater was becoming trendy, he pointed out, popular with young couples and single people who had money to spend. In the right hands, there was a profit to be turned.

Johnny Antonelli, who had been one of the boys who tried to play upon Mr. Bloom's sympathies and get in for free, and who led the calls of "Jew-lover" against my father, knew a good deal when he saw one, and he persuaded his brothers to go in with him on a "Revive the Taft" campaign. They renovated the big theater into four smaller showing rooms and established Antonelli's Pizza in the old card shop next door. Within a year, you couldn't drive by the block on a Friday or Saturday night without seeing a line of customers to the corner.

The Antonellis never forgot that their prosperity was due in large part to my father's perseverance in saving the Taft, and they always tried to wave us in when they saw us standing in the ticket line. But my father refused. The first time he took his billfold out and insisted on paying Johnny, who didn't want to take his money, my father beckoned Johnny closer with a crook of his finger. "God forbid I should be taken for a *Catholic*-lover," my father said. He delivered the last words with an emphasis that sounded threatening, and I felt my stomach clench as I envisioned my father and Johnny Antonelli getting into a fight. But the next moment they were both smiling, then laughing, and Johnny took the bills my father handed him and clapped a thick arm around my father's shoulder. I looked up at my mother, and she was smiling, too. As Johnny Antonelli led us in to seat us for *The Goodbye Girl*, I felt the pride that comes with the discovery that your family is special, and that you are loved in the larger world.

We used to order takeout from Antonelli's at least once a week. It was one of my favorite things then, but I never eat pizza anymore. The smell of the sauce is a physical memory—reminds me always, with a quick nauseous thump, of those nights we spent hunched around the TV, eating slices straight out of the carton while we watched reruns of *Get Smart*, which was our father's favorite. He always used to get red stuff on his chin by laughing at Max when he dialed the phone in his shoe.

Approaching the restaurant, Justine and I moved slowly, savoring the memories in the smells. I didn't particularly feel like eating, myself, but after emptying out our house I craved the comfort I knew I would find at Antonelli's—the warmth from the ovens, the old-fashioned feel of oilcloth on the tables, and most of all a smile from one or more of the Antonelli brothers, who had catered, for no charge, the reception at the Waxmans' house after the funerals. It was still early for dinner, five o'clock, and there were only two other customers eating as we sat down. Justine and I chose our favorite red booth by the window, with a view of the playground at St. Joe's.

We waited for Johnny or another of his family to emerge from the kitchen, but when the waitress came we looked up to see that it was Sibyl McGuin, who had been in Meggy's nursery-school class, and who inherited Meggy's bicycle after she died. For a moment I couldn't figure out what she was doing there at Antonelli's, standing beside Justine and me in a white blouse and black apron, hair pulled back in a ponytail and a pencil poised over a pad. Then I realized that if Meggy had lived, she would probably have started her first real job this year, too.

Sibyl started when she recognized us, letting out an involuntary noise. She tried to smile. "Hi, you guys," she said, as if she were not surprised to see us, as if nothing dramatic had interrupted our casual but continuous acquaintance of the past twelve years. She put down a basket of rolls and packaged bread sticks, and I saw her eyes widen as she took in Justine's newly expanded girth. But my sister was looking down at her menu and by the time she looked up again, Sibyl had recovered. "I didn't get a chance to talk to you at the funeral," she murmured, and then I saw her brow dip as she tried to figure out if this was a stupid thing to have said.

"That's okay," Justine told her. "We know you were there. You signed the book." She flicked a forefinger at the menu. "We'll split a sausage and pepper, okay?" I could tell it was not out of her own discomfort, but a desire to relieve Sibyl's, that she acted as if we were in a hurry. "A Diet Coke, too," Justine added, and I caught Sibyl's raised eyebrows at the word "diet" as she scurried back toward the kitchen.

"We make her nervous," Justine said.

"Gee. I wonder why."

"Like it's contagious or something."

While we waited for the food, I folded the edge of the tablecloth between my fingers and Justine kept taking sips from her water glass, letting ice chink against her teeth.

"They should turn on the air-conditioning," she said, pulling at the collar of her wrinkled shirt. "It's hot in here."

"You think so?"

"Aren't you?"

"Not really." In fact, I felt a chill, though there seemed no real reason for it. We sat without speaking for several minutes and looked out the window at people leaving the five o'clock Mass. A young family emerged—a mother, father, two daughters, and a baby son—and waited to cross the street. The mother was carrying the baby, and both girls reached up to take their father's hand. At the same moment, Justine and I turned away from the window, and our eyes met over the basket of bread. I thought one or both of us would look away, but we didn't, and I felt myself flush.

"Ana," my sister said, seizing what moved in the air between us. "I have to ask you something." Something in her voice made my spine sit up. "Do you think he would have killed me, too, if I had come home earlier from Lake George?" She spoke as if we were merely picking up in a conversation we'd already begun, when in fact neither of us had ever directly addressed, with each other, the details of that day.

A sound stuck in my throat but Justine didn't notice.

"And what about you?" She concentrated on a spot she was rubbing in the tablecloth, so she would not have been able to see that I wanted her to stop. "What if the Melnicks had decided not to go to New York that day, or one of the kids was sick, and they didn't need you to babysit? They said he didn't shoot himself right away, after Meggy. Do you think he was waiting for one of us? Or both?" Just saying it seemed to scare her, and her voice rose on a choked breath.

I had to swallow before I could answer. Although I wanted to tell her the truth, it felt dangerous, somehow, to let her know I had wondered the same thing.

"No," I said, hoping I sounded convinced. "I think Nora Odoni was right when she said he just kind of snapped at the end, and no one could

have guessed what he was thinking." Sibyl McGuin came toward us heft-
ing a round silver tray, and I waited until she set the pizza and drinks
down beside us, then left again, before I continued. "Besides, Meggy was
his favorite."

We'd never said this aloud to each other, but once it was out, I could
see that we both felt relieved. Justine studied me closely, searching for
evidence that I was withholding something, and when she didn't find it,
she sniffled and blew her nose into a napkin. Then she put her fork down
and wiped her mouth hard. I bit the insides of my cheeks and waited.

"Do you think he was always—well, nuts?" she asked, and I saw she
regretted choosing the word. "Maybe we should have seen it coming."

"No," I said, though I couldn't have said where my certainty came
from.

"But the way he was about eggs, and germs, and the stuff in the
pantry—" Her lips trembled and she pursed them around the straw in
her Coke. "Maybe we should have done something."

"Like what?" I lifted a piece of pizza to my mouth, but the smell of
sausage curled my stomach and I put the slice back down. "Like *what*,
Justine?"

She sat back in the booth, not expecting my force. I hadn't expected
it, either. "I don't know."

"If anybody could have done something, it should have been Mom,"
I said.

Justine snatched up a cellophane bread-stick wrapper and pressed it
into a ball. When it began to uncrinkle on the table she jammed it into
the napkin dispenser. "You shouldn't say that," she murmured, so low I
almost couldn't hear.

"There's no way she didn't read that note." I thought of my mother
as she appeared in the photograph on my dresser—surrounded by her
husband and daughters, wanting to say something, but cut off by the
camera's snap. Or maybe I'd been wrong, all these years; maybe, after
the image was captured, she did get to speak her peace. "There's no way
somebody writes you a suicide note and you don't even read it. No goddam way."

Justine said, still muted, "But why would she lie?"

"I have no idea." Rage, acid and aching, rose in my throat, but I pressed it down again. "That's why we have to make her tell us what it said."

"We can't, Ana."

"Why not?"

Justine rubbed a fresh napkin roughly across her lips. "I'm not sure I want to know," she told me. "What was in the note."

"How could you *not?*"

"Do you think," she said, hooding her eyes with her hand, "it's possible, what some people were saying? That Dad was—you know, abusing her? Don't look at me that way, Ana. I'm serious." She drummed her fingers on the table to a nervous beat.

"I mean, do you think it's possible that he lost his mind that way, at the end? If he did, I'm not saying I think he killed her because she said she was going to tell, or anything. First of all, she wouldn't." She raised her eyes to check, in mine, the truth of what she was saying. I nodded; we both knew that Meggy's love for and loyalty to our father would have prevented her from betraying such a secret, if it existed between them.

"I think he could have killed her out of guilt, though," Justine went on. "Himself and her, if he did touch her, even once, in a kind of trance or something."

The image of Meggy hugging a pillow the night before she died, trying to tell me something, darted across my eyes. I shook my head to get rid of it. "No," I said to Justine. "He'd kill himself before—" I stopped short, and to save both of us she interrupted.

"But what else could be in those pages?" She pinched a crust of the pizza between her fingers. "From her diary? I mean, what else could she have written about, that he would have bothered to take out?"

"You said you thought Meggy ripped out those pages," I reminded her.

"But why?"

"I don't know. That's why I'm saying I wish we knew about the note."

Abruptly, she stood up from the table and let her fork clatter on the floor. "Enough," she said. "Let's get out of here."

Sibyl hadn't brought us the check yet, but I took out a twenty and stuck it under my glass. Justine tucked the remaining bread sticks into her purse and we headed toward the door, both of us tasting escape.

But just as we reached it, I recognized one of the two women sitting at the corner table. It was Mrs. Nichols, who worked in the library at the middle school. The kids all called her Hanky Head because she had a scalp disease and wore kerchiefs to cover her perpetually thinning hair. Today it was gingham, the red matching her manicured nails. It was too late to pass her by, because she recognized us, too, and her eyes were briefly startled, then filled with thrill and pity. "Well hello," she said, catching my eye, calling us over to their table with a wave. "How are you, girls? This is my sister-in-law, Phyllis Nichols. Phyllis, meet Anastasia and Justine Dolan." She paused for breath and surveyed us curiously. "How are you, girls?" she repeated.

"Dolan?" The sister-in-law tapped her fingers on her forehead, scrunching up her face. "Why is that name so familiar, Bev?"

"It isn't," Mrs. Nichols told her abruptly. A sudden, spastic move of her body made me believe she had tried to kick the other woman under the table.

"But I could swear," the sister-in-law said, clearly frustrated.

"I'll save you the trouble," Justine said. "Our father killed our little sister last month, and then he killed himself, and it was all over the papers and TV, so that's probably where you know the name from. Yes, that was us," she continued, as the women looked up at Justine with stunned looks on their frozen faces. "By the way, that necklace you're wearing is so adorable I could just puke." It was a thick gold chain supporting a round blue bead, with a bouquet of pink buds painted in the middle. Meggy had barrettes just like it. Justine said all of this very calmly before moving out the door, and I followed her as if this were a normal thing that had just happened, as if she had just told the women she'd made the cheerleading squad and they should try the eggplant parm.

On the sidewalk, Justine told me, "I know that wasn't the right thing to say. In there, to Hanky Head. Do you think I'm nuts, like Dad?" She stood on the corner with her hands thrust deep in her jeans pockets, letting her hair hang into her worried eyes.

"No," I said. I knew she expected me to add something, but I didn't know what it would be. Just: "No."

We were about to cross the street when we saw a line of teenagers on bikes whizzing up the street toward Washington Park, riding no-handed. They shouted to each other over the whirr of many pedals: "Gross—hurry up and pass Spud, he just cut one"; "That's disgusting, Tanner"; "Is Shelly meeting us there, or are we picking her up?"

Justine and I looked down at the sidewalk as they passed. They weren't likely to be friends of Meggy's riding bicycles this far into the city. But just in case, we didn't want to be recognized. "Remember how that used to be the most important thing?" she said, when the kids were out of sight. "Going to the park after dinner in the summer? Remember how Pete at the snack bar used to give us free Nutty Buddies? Oh, God—I actually remember telling Dad I was going to kill myself, if he didn't let me go that one time."

"But he did," I said, finishing the story. I waited a moment, feeling my heart pound, and then asked, "Is that what you were thinking, when you cut yourself that day?"

"Thinking what?"

"About killing yourself." I had never asked her about it before, even after the bandage came off and I could see the sharp, pink line down the inside of her arm. It was fading over time, and she usually tried to hide it under long sleeves, even when it was hot, but sometimes I caught a glimpse of it when she was changing clothes.

"Oh, God. *No.*" She blushed, embarrassed. "I don't even remember doing it," she told me. "I think I was just in shock from—what I saw in there."

I could feel a perverse impulse take hold of me, one I knew, in that moment, I wouldn't be able to keep back. "There's something I've wanted to ask you," I told her, turning the key, and in the seat next to me she went stiff with apprehension. Before she could stop me, I asked,

"What did it look like? When you found Dad?" Justine gave a gasp; the sound made my throat close up, but I couldn't stop. "I mean—just what did it look like?" I put the car in gear and pulled away from the curb without checking to see if anybody was in the lane.

"I can't believe you asked me that, Ana," Justine said, barely able to utter the words. Two months ago she would have told me to fuck off, but now she only swallowed. "Don't ever ask me again, okay?" She reached into her purse and took out the bread sticks she'd hoarded. Then the car was filled with the sounds of my sister's crunching until the sky went dark.

5. Petrified Creatures

Q. How long can a woodpecker peck?
— *D. O'M., Rensselaerville*

A. A woodpecker is an animated chisel. It digs into wood by knocking out small chips with its bill. It grasps the tree with its claws, props itself with its stiff tail, then bends back the upper part of his body to put force behind each swing. It can beat its head against wood 20 times a second, in uninterrupted bursts of almost an hour, and dig holes more than a foot deep into the heartwood of a living tree. In the process, it sets up vibrations in its skull that would probably kill any other bird.

Nine weeks after the deaths, at the beginning of September, we drove Justine off to college in Syracuse. It wasn't that far away, an hour or so, but we all knew it meant the end of something much bigger than the summer. She'd wanted to put off school for a semester, but our mother convinced her it would be better to start on time. Mom seemed in a hurry when it came time to say good-bye. I believed I understood; the last time we had left a daughter of hers, and a sister of mine, it was in that sunny cemetery, the grass so green and vivid that I was aware, even through my numbness, how I hated to flatten it under my feet. I remember pulling away in the backseat of the big funeral car, thinking, *How can we leave her like this?* I found out only later that my mother and Justine felt the same weird consolation I did: at least Dad's with her, he'll keep her company.

In her new dorm room, Justine could see that we were struggling, and she came outside with us to the car. "I'm okay, you guys," she kept saying, though I knew she was scared, about to be on her own in a new place with an alien body and with none of her former glories known. Her assigned roommate had arrived ahead of her and claimed the best spaces. Justine hung the framed photograph of her old cheerleading squad over her bed, and hid Meggy's rubbie in a drawer of the smaller desk.

She lasted two weeks. I was getting ready to move back to Boston, where my friend Ruthie had found us an apartment in the same neighborhood where John F. Kennedy was born. She was particularly excited about this because she hoped someday to marry JFK's son. She'd been sending me the Help Wanted section of the *Globe* every Sunday, with ads she'd circled for jobs I might get with my psychology degree, and I had a few interviews set up.

The day before I was scheduled to leave, I was alone in the condo, packing, when a cab pulled into the parking lot and my sister stepped out. Through the window, I watched her just stand there, looking stunned, while the cab driver removed her suitcases from the trunk. I went outside to help her carry them in, and she mumbled something about how she'd tried but she just couldn't do it, the only things her suitemates ever talked about were sex and money, she wasn't on their planet, she wanted to come home. Her decision gave me an excuse to call Ruthie and say that although I would send a rent check, my actual move back to Boston had been delayed. When our mother arrived home after work that day, she found us both unpacked, settling in again with our books and TV.

We'd put our empty suitcases back in our mother's assigned rectangle of storage space in the condominium basement, next to the box of baby clothes we'd rescued from Pearl Street. (When we'd come home with our load of memorabilia that August day, our mother made us drive her old newspapers, and our father's cache of dead keys, straight to the dump. But the baby clothes she let us keep.) Most of the storage space was occupied by Meggy's things, except what Justine and I had taken as keepsakes, like her rubbie and her collection of seashells from Cape Cod. My mother marked all the boxes *Fragile*, even though most of the things inside them were not.

She pretended it was fine if we wanted to stay with her "a little longer," but we could feel her dread; she'd expected us both to be gone by the end of the summer.

"You know," Justine murmured to me that night in the sofa bed, so our mother couldn't hear, "some people would be glad if their kids wanted to stay home with them, after what happened. They'd like the company."

"I know," I said, and I didn't have to add what we both understood was true in our mother's case: that having us around reminded her of what she was missing. With summer behind us, she couldn't pretend that Meggy was away at camp anymore. But if all three of us were gone, she might be able to concoct a different story for herself.

The day after we came back, she told us that she expected us both to go out and get jobs. Neither Justine nor I had to work, as far as money was concerned—after our father died and his debts were paid, she and I would divide two hundred thousand dollars in insurance. I always thought insurance didn't pay out on suicides, but this isn't necessarily the case. It depends on the policy and when it was bought. In our first phone call I asked Don Whitney, the insurance agent and a member of our grandfather Ott's Kiwanis Club, if our father had asked specifically about suicide when he signed up. Mr. Whitney wouldn't tell me, which I figured was an answer in itself.

So we each had some savings and plenty of cash on the way, but our mother said that if we wanted to keep living with her, we had to pull our own weight. (When she said this I saw Justine—who'd just dropped off a whole bag filled with her old size-eight clothes at Goodwill—give her a dirty look, but it seemed to be an innocent choice of words.) I knew that Justine hated the idea of having to go out every day, giving up the narcotic drone of the TV. But instead of arguing she went down to the Donut Hut and signed up to work behind the counter, because she knew our mother would find it embarrassing.

I began word processing for the lawyer who had handled our parents' separation. I spent a whole lunch hour looking through the file marked *Dolan, T. v. Dolan, M.*, and at first, nothing in it surprised me. *Irreconcilable differences*, it said. The last papers in the file were the unsigned divorce documents. Across my father's name the word DECEASED had been stamped in red.

Then, just before I closed the file, the word "Psychiatric" caught my eye, and I saw that my father had been referred to a specific doctor for evaluation. There were no notes to indicate whether he had followed up on the referral, but several dates—during the month before the deaths— were listed next to the doctor's name. I scribbled the name at the top of the bookmark holding my place in *Revolutionary Road* and, though I wasn't sure what I would do with it, I made sure not to lose the slip.

During other lunch hours I went to the library and read the psychology journals. I thought, again, about graduate school. Slowly, the days regained a shape and texture I remembered from before the deaths: they had a beginning, middle, and end, instead of the amorphous stretch of consciousness during which I yearned only to be asleep. Whole minutes could go by, now, without the electronic marquee in my head flashing the continuous message, *They're dead*. Although I did not admit it to Justine, I was glad our mother had made us leave the house. I was pretty sure my sister felt the same way, even though she always came home smelling like doughnuts and complaining of sore feet.

In the middle of October, our mother suggested taking a trip back to Ashmont to visit the graves over Meggy's birthday at the end of the month. By coincidence, the man at the memorial shop had just called to say that the headstones—he called them monuments—were ready, and would be installed within the week. Although our mother made the trip sound like her own idea, I suspect it actually originated with Paul, the staff photographer at the *Oracle*, whom our mother had started dating around the time of the Toothpaste Burglar pool. He was a short man who always seemed to wear the same hooded navy sweatshirt, brown corduroys, and sneakers, and although he didn't have much hair—he was completely bald on top, but still had tufts at the sides, around the ears— it always managed to look uncombed. Justine and I, to each other, called him Curly, after the Stooge. He was the complete opposite of our father, who kept his body tight and lean by running in the summer and swimming in the winter, and who had a regular appointment at the barber's every three weeks. Paul could make Mom laugh, which was something our father hadn't been able to do for a long time before she left.

At first Justine and I didn't see Paul all that much, because our mother felt awkward having him at the condo while we were still there. But when it became clear to her that we weren't planning to move out anytime soon, she invited him over for dinner. He came a few times in September, and Justine tried to repel him out by eating three or four helpings of everything on the table, but he didn't seem to notice; then one day when he didn't know I was looking I saw him sprinkling parmesan cheese into his throat, followed by a chaser of Reddi-wip squeezed straight from the can, and I understood why Justine's habits didn't bother him. He kept to himself, mostly, and if he had to speak to one of us he did it shyly, mumbling into his plate. We never talked about my father or Meggy, and if the subject ever threatened to come up—like a finger pressing gently, testing an exposed wound—one of us always managed, at the last minute, to snatch the conversation back to the Mets or the merits of Mom's Hungarian goulash.

The reason I believe it was Paul's suggestion that we go to the cemetery on Meggy's birthday is that during one of these dinners, seemingly out of the blue, he made a point of telling us he had to work that whole particular weekend, shooting the Bills in Buffalo and then a freelance job in Niagara Falls. My mother didn't seem to understand why he was bringing up his schedule, but when she got home later that night after they'd gone out to a movie, she sat watching Justine and me without speaking. Sneaking looks back at her, we saw that she was considering something. When a commercial came on she raised a finger to get our attention and said, "Do you think we should go visit Birch Street on the twenty-sixth?" as if she knew it were an absurd proposition but was willing to solicit other opinions. (She always referred to it as "Birch Street" because she seemed unable to bring herself to say the word "cemetery." Our father and Meggy were buried in the graveyard on a corner near the center of Ashmont, where the two main roads, Birch and Euclid, crossed each other at a light. Growing up, we always held our breath when we drove by it, so our bodies wouldn't be invaded by the souls of the dead.)

When Justine and I looked at each other and realized simultaneously what "the twenty-sixth" was, then both answered "Yeah" without qualification, my mother seemed surprised and a little nervous. "Are you sure?" she said.

"I wanted to see the headstones, anyway," I told her, and Justine nodded.

"Well. All right, then." Our mother stood up and put her hands together with the air of one who wants to get busy on a new project. As if to convince herself of her commitment, she went over to the calendar and drew a bold circle around Saturday, October 26.

"I think we should invite Rosemary, too," I said, flipping through my address book to find my aunt's number in New York. My mother hesitated a moment, though she tried not to show it, then handed me the phone.

As the date approached, she kept asking us if we really wanted to make the trip, if we didn't think we might be rushing things, if maybe we shouldn't wait until Christmas or even the spring.

"You don't have to come with us if you don't want to, Mom," Justine told her the last time she brought it up. Our mother replied, *Don't be silly, of course I want to go.*

She didn't get home until late every night of the first three weeks in October. She said she had evening assignments, but we knew she was spending that time with Paul. Justine and I didn't mind, as long as we had each other for company.

The night before the trip, Justine and I stayed up late watching a *Star Trek* movie while we waited for our mother to come home. When we finally turned off the TV and shut the light out, it was three o'clock and she still wasn't there. "Should we call over to Paul's house?" Justine asked. "Just to make sure? I mean, what if she got in an accident?"

"She's not in an accident," I told her. "She's in bed."

"You didn't have to say that." Justine turned over, and I had to keep myself from rolling toward the depression her body had carved into the mattress.

Within minutes I felt my sister's even breath heating the ridge between our pillows. Then, before I even realized I was sleeping, I dropped deep into a dream: Meggy was hiding under her bed in the house on Pearl Street as a rainbow of bullets sang through her room. They were out to get her, but nobody thought to look beneath the bed. The shooting stopped after a while and Meggy began to crawl out. I passed by her room at that moment and saw one gun still aiming, waiting and cocked, to pick off my little sister. I tried to scream her name, but I had forgotten it.

Panicked, I woke to the sound of *The Jetsons* wafting through the living-room wall. Next to me Justine was silent, but the three-year-old girl on the other side of my mother's duplex was watching cartoons. Her name was Deirdre, and my mother baby-sat for her sometimes. She was cute, but—as silly as it might sound—Deirdre's friendship with our mother had felt threatening to Justine and me ever since we found out that our mother gave her one of Meggy's old dolls.

It's not as if it was Meggy's favorite doll; in fact, we didn't even know if it ever had a name. But Justine and I didn't like the idea of letting go of anything that once belonged to Meggy, anything she ever touched. The only other time it had come up was when we considered and then approved giving Meggy's bike to Sibyl McGuin. The bike was a blue three-speed Schwinn with accessories. Our parents had given it to Meggy for her twelfth birthday, and we let it go to Sibyl on the condition that she agree not to roll the odometer back to zero, but save the miles Meggy had left there.

I must have fallen back asleep, listening to *The Jetsons*, because the next thing I was aware of was the sound of my sister taking a shower. My mother entered the house and tried tiptoeing into her bedroom.

"Good morning," I said, and she drew her breath in and dropped her keys.

"Goddammit," she answered. "You scared me." Instead of the work clothes she had left the house in the day before, she was wearing the Mets shirt and sweatpants she generally used as pajamas.

I lifted my head to see what time it was: 7:15. From the other side of the wall I heard Deirdre eating cereal, her spoon banging the bowl. "You scared us, too," I told my mother, even though this was true only of Justine. "We called the hospitals."

"Oh, God. You didn't."

She looked so stricken that I said, "Well, no, we didn't. But we thought about it."

"I just assumed you'd know I was at Paul's."

"Well, that's what we figured. But you could have called."

My mother sank into the loveseat, laughing a little as she shook her head. "Something's backwards here," she said.

"What do you mean?"

"I mean I'm the one who's supposed to worry about you guys staying out too late. You should be the ones having to sneak into the house." She leaned forward, and I could tell she was ready to pick a fight. "Really, Ana. Don't you think it's time you went back to Boston and Justine got a place of her own? We can't put our lives on hold, just sitting around here moping and getting fat."

"We're not moping," I told her. Anger made me sit up. "And I'm not getting fat."

"Well, you know what I mean." She crossed to the windows, stepped over the dog, and opened the blinds before I saw what she was doing. The sun went straight to my eyes.

"Jeez, Mom," I said, making my hand a shade, "do you mind?"

"What?" She looked puzzled.

"It's too *bright*."

"Oh. Sorry." She turned the slats back down, but only halfway. "Don't you want to be getting up soon, anyway?"

"It's not even eight-thirty," I said, reminded that these were the two circumstances—in my mother's presence, and too early in the morning—that caused me to speak in italics.

"Well," my mother murmured, "I know." She added, as if she had not already told us this several times, "Rosemary said she'd be here by eleven," as Justine emerged from the bathroom wrapped in two towels.

"Mommy," Justine said, the word escaping her tongue before she could check it. "I mean, Mom. You're back." I saw in her the same instinct I'd felt, to accuse, but she refrained as I had.

"Yes, I'm back," our mother said lightly. "I didn't know I'd be the subject of an APB."

Justine looked at me, and I shook my head. "Well," our mother said, with a let's-change-the-subject raise of her eyebrows, "I guess I'll make breakfast." She went over to the kitchen and started taking things out of the cupboards. Justine got dressed, and she and I set the table as our mother took down the fancy champagne glasses from the sideboard. She poured orange juice into the glasses and we sat in our usual places. She picked hers up and looked into it, then set it down again without drinking when she realized that Justine and I were trying to forget what it was we had agreed to celebrate.

"It's Meggy's sixteenth birthday," she said, as if we might not know.

When Rosemary arrived, the three of us were in the front yard waiting for her and raking leaves with Deirdre's mother. It was more of an excuse to be outside than it was real work; Deirdre kept jumping in the pile we made, scattering the leaves for us to rake up again. Although it wasn't sunny, the air was warm, and we wore light clothing with our sleeves rolled up. Most of the other people who lived in the complex had also been lured out by the temperature and were sitting in lawn chairs or on their front steps. My mother didn't know any of them officially except Deirdre's family, but she waved or nodded or said, "Beautiful day," and they did the same back, so it felt like a neighborhood even though none of them knew one another's names. Through a screen window, somebody had a radio on, playing baroque music that made it feel as if we were all part of a medieval dream. When we heard a car slowing as it approached the cul-de-sac, Deirdre looked over and then yelled to us, "Is that who you're waiting for? She's wearing big sunglasses and her hair kind of looks like a witch."

"Ssh, Dee Dee," her mother said, though it was an accurate description. When our aunt stepped out of her car, a maroon Mercedes, she appeared mysterious and—especially to a child, I'm sure—scary. Her eyes were hidden and her hair, which was longer now than I'd ever seen it, stuck out in wild strands across her forehead. She took the glasses off as we came toward her, and her eyes looked dazed and puzzled, exposed to sunlight without a shield.

"Oh, Margaret," she said, putting her arms around our mother, who stood closest to the curb. "Ana. Justine." She said each of our names as she kissed our cheeks, as if she were christening us.

"Mommy," Deirdre said, watching from her side of the lawn, "they're all hugging the lady."

"Are you hungry?" my mother asked Rosemary, after we'd stepped back from one another and stood blinking at the day.

"Oh, God, no." Rosemary slid the sunglasses on top of her head and put a hand against the stomach of her sweater, which was made of lace eyelet in a pale green. Whenever I think of Rosemary, I picture her in this color, an American Irishwoman who inherited her father's vivid eyes and bushy hair—which Rosemary kept auburn even after it wanted to go gray—and his appetite for alcohol. "I had a milkshake from Burger King on the way up." She spoke with a thickened tongue, and Justine and my mother and I sent glances at each other, because from the kisses and the way her words came out, we could tell that she poured a little something extra into that milkshake before she drank it down.

Our aunt Rosemary was two years older than our father, which made her nearly fifty, but she looked at least ten years younger. All the time we were growing up, she lived in Woodstock, near the town where the famous concert was held. We used to visit her in the little house-shack where she supported herself by preparing taxes and reading Tarot cards. There was always a man there when we went to visit, but it was hardly ever the same man as the time before. A few years before our father and Meggy died, she moved down to New York City with the one who had accompanied her to the funeral, Harold Webb. A former priest, he now managed the careers of recording artists. Harold Webb had plenty of money (and the Mercedes), and we believed that Rosemary lived with him for this reason, more than for love.

When it was time to start out for Ashmont, we all got into my mother's car, and she started it and shifted into reverse. "Wait," I said, putting my hand out to keep her from moving. She braked. "Where's Deirdre?"

"She went into the house with her mother," Justine said.

"Are you sure?"

"The little girl?" Rosemary says. "I saw her go in, too."

My mother was looking at me with an expression I had seen before only when she sensed that something was starting to take hold of my father. "Honey, she's in the house," she said to me gently.

"Can you wait a second? I just have to see." I opened my door and stepped out and went around to the rear of the car, where I bent down to look under the wheels. Of course, Deirdre wasn't there. I got in the car again, feeling foolish. "I just had a feeling. You know how that happens? I had to check."

"It's okay, honey," my mother murmured. She looked away, but I saw her bite her lip.

We decided to take a secondary road, Route 20, because although it would make the trip slightly longer, it was less boring than our usual route along the Thruway. More scenic, my mother said. It was true: the trees had turned, and when the sun broke over the hills, it lit up the blond fields like every painting of heaven I'd ever seen. Hay bales left over from summer stood in stagnant, luxurious scrolls. The mountains, set back in the sky behind treetops, stretched dark blue and deep. Cows gathered in sluggish bunches; chickens circled themselves at the side of the road. We went by signs that said *Honey & Nite Crawlers, Grampa's Collectables, Firewood 4 Sale.* A long, low-ceilinged house turned out to be the Petrified Creatures Museum of Natural History. "What do *they* have to be petrified about," Rosemary quipped, and the three of us said, *ha, ha.*

It was so beautiful it made our hearts twist. I knew we were all thinking about Meggy; this had been her favorite season of the year. She loved having her birthday so close to Halloween, and until she was twelve, she always had costume parties with her friends. Our father dressed up in the same pirate clothes to host the party every year, until my mother told him that Meggy was embarrassed by it; she was getting too old.

"Of course she isn't," my father said, blowing dust off the eye patch. "She hasn't said a thing."

"She asked me to," my mother told him.

"Oh." The next day he put the pirate suit in a grocery bag and dropped it off at Goodwill.

On our way to Ashmont, my mother noticed a sign for a garage sale in Voorheesville and decided to stop. She bought a set of canisters, two paperbacks, a welcome mat, and a beach chair she said reminded her of the summers her own family used to spend at Lake Independence in Minnesota.

"I'd say that's a pretty good deal," she told us as we pulled back onto the road. "All that stuff for under ten bucks." I was sitting next to her in the front seat; in the back, Justine started reading Presumed Innocent, one of our mother's new books. "Honey, you'll get sick," our mother warned her, speaking to the rearview mirror. In the old days, Justine would have made a face and kept on reading. But now she closed the book with an obedience that made me roll down my window and whisper "Jesus Christ" into the wind.

In the center of Ashmont, the main roads met in a cross at Four Corners. While we waited for the light to change I looked out the window at the Getty station, which stood diagonally across Birch Street from the Reformed Church. Whenever we passed through this intersection, my father used to sing "Getty to the church on time," and Justine and Meggy and I would pretend to shoot ourselves in the head, Archie Bunker–style.

Next to the church stood the flower shop owned by Luanne Oberheim's father. Luanne had been in Justine's class since nursery school; they played clarinet together in the junior-high band, but in high school they split off from each other. Luanne went the way of the Honor Society, while Justine became what the nerds called a Populette. Still, in commemoration of the girls' friendship in their earlier days, Mr. Oberheim had donated all the floral arrangements for the funeral.

"Stop," Justine said, and I thought she wanted to get out and buy flowers, but when my mother braked by the curb my sister didn't move. She caught her breath. "There's Candy," she said, softly, and turning toward the sidewalk I saw a long-haired girl in jeans and an Eagles jacket strolling down the street. Candy Samuelson had been a friend of Justine's all through high school. She was a member of the Cat House gang and the cheerleading squad and the pack of Populettes who, after their senior prom, had to drive the event's King and Queen to Albany Medical Center because of alcohol posioning (the royal couple had been doing shots of schnapps in the janitor's room). Candy and Justine both belonged to the Choraliers. Had it been only four months since I'd watched them stand with the other white-robed graduates, on risers in the gym decorated for commencement, singing "The Lord Bless You and Keep You"? It seemed impossible.

Do you know that hymn? The words move across the music with a sharp, sweet pain, which, once you've felt it, stays as memory in your bones:

> The Lord bless you and keep you,
> The Lord lift his countenance upon you,
> And give you peace
> And give you peace
> The Lord make his face to shine upon you,
> And give you peace.

We watched as Candy stopped, twirling her hair around a finger, to read the sandwich menu posted outside the Leading Roll. Then she pulled money out of her jeans pocket, counted it, and stepped inside.

"She doesn't look very different," Justine said. She sounded surprised. "Don't you think she looks about the same?"

"I guess," our mother answered, though in truth I don't think she had any idea what my sister had asked.

"Well, hell, as long as we're stopped here, let's get some flowers," Rosemary said. She slammed the car door and disappeared inside Oberheim's, then came out with an armful of green tissue paper, which she tucked under her seat.

The cemetery stood on King's Hill, where we used to go sledding before the town built a monument to Ashmont's military men and women who'd died in Korea and Vietnam. Summers, the granite obelisk engraved with soliders' names served as our home-free in freeze tag, until Lois Phelps came through one day, walking her father, and yelled at us for disrespecting the dead.

Even before we parked at the graveyard gate, I realized that we couldn't have timed our visit more poorly. To get to the cemetery we had to drive past the high school, where a football game had just ended. The players were scattered as they walked to the parking lot with their families, but the cheerleaders moved together in loud, giggling packs. The girls had on the same uniform Justine used to wear—black pleated skirt, black knee socks, a white turtleneck under a black sweater with an orange *A* on the chest, saddle shoes tied with orange laces. Some wore ribbons in their ponytails; others had shorter, layered haircuts—they must have all had the same stylist at Shear Amazement—which they flipped back from their faces with slim, confident hands. Their voices started in murmurs, but turned almost triumphant as the words reached the sky. *We are the Eagles, mighty mighty Eagles! Everywhere we go, people want to know. Who we are. So we tell them . . .*

I shifted in my seat so that my sister was in the corner of my eye. Justine stared straight ahead; she'd put on her Walkman earphones, and I saw that she had turned the volume all the way up. Next I looked at my mother. She had the line between her eyes that meant she was concentrating on not feeling anything. As I listened to the cheers, a stray line from Pushkin swam up to me (*Know, at least, the sounds/That once were dear to you*), making my sinuses sting.

It was clear that the football traffic was going to interfere with our visit. People who didn't drive to the school used the cemetery as a shortcut. Sure enough, we saw them coming through the trees as we made our way toward our destination, the northeast corner by the fence.

"Let's wait a minute," our mother said. She paused by a cluster of headstones engraved with the name Parnell. The Parnells were one of the first families in Ashmont; a main street was named for them, and so was the picnic pavilion at the town park. It was an almost cozy feeling, standing among these graves. The older ones—belonging to Thaddeus and his wife Abigail, their children Mary and Forrest and Louise—lay in a half circle under the giant elm tree, where the first plots were struck. You could barely make out their birth and death dates, although you could tell that most of them began with 18, and Thaddeus and Abigail were born in the 1790s.

The subsequent generations of dead Parnells were arranged in a semicircle behind their ancestors. The most recent addition was Stephen, 1937–1984, the father of the most unpopular boy in my class. Doug Parnell had more money than any kid in town, but he always wore the same clothes to school, and rumor had it that he never washed his hair. His father was killed in a boat accident in the Caribbean the year we were in eighth grade. The full story never came out.

The best evidence that the death had happened under questionable circumstances was the slimness of the account that ran in the *Ashmont Star*. The newspaper printed the standard obituary, next to a photograph of a business-suited Mr. Parnell. The obituary said only that he had "died suddenly, out of town." There followed several paragraphs about his life in Ashmont, his survivors, and the civic contributions he and his family had made, along with a bank address for anyone who wanted to send money to a scholarship fund the Rotarians had set up in his memory.

If Doug's father had not been a Parnell, or if he had been a recent transplant to the town, the *Star* would have printed the details everybody knew already by word of mouth—that there was a woman involved who was not Doug's mother; that there were, most probably, also drugs. And that the boat accident was surely not an accident at all, but an explosion planned to coincide with Mr. Parnell's being alone onboard when the bomb went off.

So you could gauge your status in Ashmont, and how much loyalty you were entitled to, by the way the *Star* treated you in its pages. When my father and Meggy died, it was a big story on Albany's TV broadcasts and even in the *Knickerbocker News,* whose publisher called my mother beforehand to say he was goddam sorry, but they were going to lead with it, it was goddam news.

But the *Star* ran only a single-column item at the bottom of page two, saying that Thomas Dolan, 46, and his daughter Margaret, 15, died in an apparent murder-suicide June 29 at the family's Pearl Street home. There was information about the funeral, a line about our father's life ("Mr. Dolan, whose former employers included the Morgan Insurance Co. and Zenith Realty, worked at Wolf Subaru at the time of his death") and one about Meggy's ("Miss Dolan, an honors student at Ashmont High School and a member of the girls' softball league, played the leading role in the Ashmont Repertory production of the musical *Annie* in 1981.").The story ran under a photograph of a mother-daughter fashion show at the Methodist church. Even through my numbness, I remember being grateful that the *Star* had buried the story. In a perverse way, it made me realize that our family must have meant something to this town.

My father hated cemeteries—he would drive miles out of his way to avoid passing one—but I have always, without quite understanding why, felt comfortable around graves. Even before the deaths in my family, I liked to walk through burial grounds and read the inscriptions, like *Gone but not forgotten* and *Called home*. My favorite was on Boston's North Shore, at the edge of Rockport, where my friend Ruthie and I drove to celebrate the day our finals were over in sophomore year. In that graveyard with a view of the ocean, I lingered longest over a stone belonging to a boy who had died in 1789 at the age of two months, twenty-two days. His epitaph read:

> *When the angels shall blow the trumpets*
> *And souls to bodyes join*
> *Millions will wish their lives*
> *Had been as short as mine.*

When I read it out loud to Ruthie, she made a face. "Bummer," she said, and then she laughed, but I could tell she wanted to get out of the cemetery, that she had only agreed to come with me because I promised to drive her down to Hyannis the next time we heard of a sighting of JFK Jr. there. Reading the baby's headstone, I imagined his parents, and how their grief must have been eased by the belief that their baby was better off dead—that they, being alive, were the unlucky ones, still with years of earthly trial ahead before they ascended to Paradise.

So I always felt calm, approaching the gray strength of a stone, and more than that, I believed in the words "at peace," although I had no idea what it might feel like. As my mother and Justine and I made our way past the Parnell family's plot, I knew that whatever Doug Parnell's father had suffered on the way to or during his death, it was over now, as it was for my own father.

The only one I couldn't believe this about was Meggy.

We waited until a parade of bicycles shot past us, then made our way over to the corner where newer graves stood by a row of maples iridescent in the sun. "I'm not sure I can do this," my mother said, sounding as if someone were choking her. The headstones jutted up out of the ground next to each other, my father's closer to the fence. When it came time to choose the burial sites, my mother told the caretaker that she wanted the smaller stone placed where it would never be cast in shadow by the bigger one.

The engraving on Meggy's stone ran the depth of the marble face. *Margaret Olivia Dolan, b. October 26, 1972, d. June 29, 1988.* My mother had gone through my poetry books and selected, as an epitaph, the last stanza of William Blake's "A Cradle Song":

> *Sleep sleep happy child.*
> *All creation slept and smil'd.*
> *Sleep sleep, happy sleep,*
> *While o'er thee thy mother weep.*

At the time, I wondered if she chose that verse because she hadn't, in fact, ever cried over Meggy—at least not that we had seen. Justine said she believed our mother could cry only in private. I thought it was possible she might have forgotten how.

Yet she was affected, clearly, by seeing the words now on the stone. I was afraid she might fall over, and Justine and I both seemed paralyzed at the prospect of catching her. Grabbing air, my mother gripped the top of my father's headstone and leaned against it instead of one of us.

"Jesus," she said when she could get the words out, her throttling complete. "I can't believe that's Meggy."

"It isn't," Justine told her, sounding like someone who had been asleep for a long time.

When our mother stepped away from our father's stone, we read the inscription.

Thomas Edward Dolan
b. February 15, 1942, d. June 29, 1988.
He was loved.

The last line had been added below the name and dates only after Justine and I told our mother that we wanted it there. We would pay for the extra letters, we said. Of course, she didn't take our money. Now it was this phrase that she bent down to trace with a white and feeble finger.

"Oh, God," she groaned, and I knew it wasn't because she hadn't also loved him that she had at first resisted the chiseling of those words. It was because she felt guilty about still loving him, even after what he had done. She fell against Rosemary and let her shoulders go with a shuddering, tearless paroxysm that reminded me of what I learned once about afterbirth, in a film about babies being born. Grief, like the baby, was already out, but there was still something inside that could be dangerous to the system if it weren't also expelled.

Justine and I watched our mother, but we did not look at each other. I think we both knew how much it was possible for us to bear in that moment, and it did not include meeting a sister's eyes.

And yet something about the day—the sharp scent of leaves, maybe, or the echo of cheers in the trees—kept me from being able to summon the measure of sadness I'd felt at the funeral. Glancing at Justine, I could tell she was experiencing a similar surprise. As apprehensive as we had been about coming to the cemetery, now that we were here it was almost a letdown. The surge of grief we anticipated had taken a different route, and we were distracted from death by the insistence of life around us: leaves crunching under our feet, the sound of raised voices in victory, the imagined snap of apples being bitten on porches all over town. Rosemary knelt to place a bunch of baby's breath down tenderly, making a frame around Meggy's name. Instead of the pain I expected, I felt only love, and it would not allow anything else to approach the space it filled in my heart.

My aunt was laying a yellow rose by my father's stone when we heard a woman's voice calling to us from up the hill, near the war memorial. "Margaret?" The voice was familiar, and instinctively I began to smile, though I had not yet caught sight of the person to whom it belonged. "Is that you?" Now we could make out Kay Lonergan in front of the obelisk, shading her eyes as she peered over to where we stood. Her son Matt was still wearing his football uniform, the shoulder pads making him appear monstrous. When he recognized us, he ducked and split off from his parents. The moment before he turned his face away, I saw that he looked scared. Ed Lonergan frowned and then, seeming unsure, lifted his hand in a stationary wave. We saw Kay say something to Ed and he continued on the way Matt had gone, while she began with hesitant steps in our direction.

"Kay," my mother said, as fervent as a prayer.

"Who's that?" Rosemary whispered to me, before Kay was close enough to hear. "She looks familiar."

"Her best friend from when we lived here."

"I think I remember her from the funeral. They're the ones who pulled your mom out of the church when she started throwing things, right?" I nodded.

My mother and Kay hadn't seen each other since that day, though for nearly fifteen years before that they'd been best friends. I expected my mother to exclaim and run to meet Kay, so I was shocked when, instead, she started hurrying off the other way, back toward where we'd parked the car. "Come on," she turned to hiss at us, when we didn't follow. But by then Kay had caught up.

"What's going on, Margaret?" she said, addressing my mother across the expanse of graves between them. "Don't tell me you're running away from me."

My mother took a few steps forward, trying to smile. "Of course not," she told Kay. "How are you? I was just chasing a squirrel." The absurdity of her lie made Justine and me look at each other, though we managed not to laugh.

"Well, talk to me. Come here." Kay reached out and squeezed my mother hard inside a hug, and I saw my mother trying to pull away, though Kay held tight. "Where've you been? Didn't you get any of my letters? And what's with the unlisted phone?"

"We were getting some crazy calls," my mother said. "Didn't I give you the number? I meant to."

Rosemary said to Justine and me, "You guys, let's make ourselves scarce for a minute," and my mother and Kay didn't stop us, so we left the grave site and moved a few rows up the hill, crunching on dropped leaves. We were now standing in front of a family whose stones said merely: "Mother," "Father," and "Baby Daughter." Nearby, at the grave of a child who'd died as an infant in 1949, a jack-o'-lantern that had no doubt been fresh a week ago rotted around a sign that said in elderly cursive, *We miss you*. Behind us, my mother and Kay spoke now in urgent and intimate tones.

"I can't hear them," Justine said.

I reminded her that this was the point, though I had also hoped the sounds of their conversation might carry.

"So what's the scoop?" Rosemary asked. She put her hand out to feel the engraving on a stone decorated with angel wings carrying a skull. "They're best friends, but they stopped talking?"

"I think Mom feels guilty or something," I said, grimacing at the pull in the back of my calves as we sidestepped up the slope.

"Gee," Justine muttered. "I wonder why."

"What?" Rosemary said.

"Nothing."

"Shut up, Justine," I told my sister, feeling suddenly sick. I went over to the edge of the cemetery and fastened my fingers in the fence. It was a dangerous thing to do, because from here I could see the backyard of the Waxmans' house, and this was closer than I wanted to be.

After a few minutes, our mother and Kay came over to where we stood. I could tell from the expressions on both their faces that in that short time, something had already been worked out—erased, explained, reconnected—and that, like a shuttlecock in the air between them, they were eager to keep it in play.

"Kay's invited us over for a little picnic," my mother told us.

"No," Justine said. When our mother raised her eyebrows, she added, "I'm not trying to be rude. But I don't want to go over there." My sister motioned toward our old street, from where we could hear the sounds of children playing.

"Well, I can understand that," Kay said.

"So can I. But I *would* like to go, so we have a problem." My mother folded her arms across her chest. It resembled a gesture of defiance, but then I realized that as the hour grew later, the air was becoming chill. "Ana, how about you?"

I felt completely caught between the two choices. I wanted both and neither; it seemed that our old house was calling me closer, yet at the same time it warned me to stay away.

"I don't know," I said.

"How about this, as a compromise," Rosemary suggested. "Justine and I, and Ana if she wants to, will walk down into town and grab something to eat at that ice-cream restaurant you always liked—what's it called?"

"The Toll Gate," Justine and I answered in unison, and we smiled.

"Right. Margaret, you can go to Kay's, and we'll meet you back here at, let's say, four. Sound good?"

"Oh, Rose, thank you." My mother looked grateful, and I tried to read in her face what she hoped I would do.

"Coming, Ana?" my aunt asked, as she and Justine turned in the direction of Birch Street and the Four Corners. I imagined myself sitting in a booth, folding down the corners of my paper place mat while we waited for burgers, and wondered what it would feel like to go back home.

"I'll go with them," I said, gesturing toward my mother and Kay.

Briefly, my sister looked as if I had betrayed her. But then she smiled again. "Careful," she whispered, as if it were a code.

Justine and Rosemary took off in the direction of town, and I followed my mother and Kay down the path to the edge of the cemetery where the road began. Although it was daylight, only a bit after two o'clock, I felt as if we were moving with stealth through the darkness toward a forbidden place. When we emerged at the mouth of Pearl Street, Kay was already starting down the street, but my mother and I stood still for a moment to take in breath. The house we had lived in was farther down around the bend, and I knew that we were both trying to get ready.

When Kay realized we were hanging back, she waited. "There's a new family in your house," she said. She rubbed a stone back and forth with the toe of her sneakers, and I could tell that she was trying to sound casual, as if none of this were a big deal. "Two boys, two girls. One of those families where all the names start with the same letter—Kevin, Kelly, Kyle, and Kate." She laughed, brushing stray hair from her face. "Or something like that."

Her voice—its familiar kindness, its gentle warmth—invited us onward, and we walked like timid children toward its touch. I kept imagining curtains being pulled aside so that we could be watched and whispered about, and I sensed the same apprehension in my mother as she gave sidelong glances at the houses we knew from carpools and trick-or-treating and open houses on Christmas Eve. She put a hand on my shoulder, and I looked at her with a question in my face until I saw that she only wanted to feel me by her, to make sure I was really there. I could tell that we both felt the same pull coming from our old home— it was like magnetism, or gravity, and we had to fight its force to stay on the other side of the street where the Lonergans lived.

The noises we'd heard from the cemetery, I saw now, came from a game of jump rope in our old driveway. There were five girls playing, two who were clearly sisters—they wore their red hair pulled back by matching headbands and identical sweatshirts from Disney World—and three others, all of whom appeared to be between the ages of six and nine.

"Listen, Ana," my mother said, "that's one of the jump-rope songs you guys used to sing. Isn't it?"

And, indeed, it was—as they turned the rope and alternated jumping into the center, the girls chanted,

> Mother, mother, I feel sick.
> Send for the doctor, quick, quick quick.
> Doctor, doctor, will I die?
> Yes, my dear, and so will I.
> How many days do I have left?
> One, two, three, four . . .

The jumping girl missed on the count of twelve, and one of the other girls squealed and told her, "Don't die before Christmas, retard!" setting off another round of boisterous giggles.

"I never noticed what a sick song that is for kids to be singing," I said, thinking only for the first time about what the lyrics meant.

Russell Stinson was sitting in his wheelchair on his front porch, and when he saw us, he raised his beer can in a salute. "Over and out!" he shouted, across the street. "Rise and shine!"

"Hey, Russell," I managed to call back weakly. The little girls had stopped to listen to our exchange, but I hurried to follow Kay to the back of her house, where her husband was shaking charcoal into the grill.

"Two more for lunch, Ed," she said, and I could tell she was trying to keep her tone light.

"How are you, Margaret?" Then Ed must have realized he was supposed to do something more than just say hello, so he leaned over and kissed her awkwardly at the side of her head. When he let her go, he picked up a can of Budweiser and popped it open. It was the same brand of beer that Russell was drinking, across the street; I wondered if Ed Lonergan kept Russell supplied, and if this is what he meant when, in his campaign brochures for town office, he listed volunteer work with veterans.

"Oh, fine, Ed," my mother answered. "I hope it's not an imposition, our staying—I hope you have enough." She'd spotted the four hamburger patties sitting on the plate by the side of the grill.

"Sure," he said, but the tone of his voice would more closely have matched if his words had been, "Goddammit, Kay. Did you have to? What are we going to do with these people?"

"I'll just run down to Falvo's and get some more meat," he told us, too cheerfully. "Hamburgs okay, Margaret?" He also looked at me when he asked, but I knew he didn't want to venture guessing my name, because he always got my sisters' and mine mixed up.

"Great," my mother said, and I nodded, too. "But don't go to any trouble, Ed, really. I know this is unexpected."

"No sweat. Be back in a minute." He gave the smile again, which chilled me a little in its emptiness, and brushed by us toward his car. My mother and I looked at each other, and I knew we were both thinking the same thing: he had raw hamburger meat still on his hands, and he had only wiped them on a paper towel, no soap and hot water, before he left. As much as I try not to, I always notice these things, now more than I ever did before my father died: how careful (or not) people are to avoid germs, to make themselves clean when they've been exposed to contamination. I knew I would not be able to eat the hamburger Ed served me when he came back and handled the meat with those same hands. My mother would force the bites down, but she would be thinking about my father the whole time. I wished I'd gone with my sister and my aunt, and as soon as I realized this I knew I couldn't sit down on the patio with my mother and Kay and make small talk.

"I'll be back," I said, "okay? I think I'll take a walk."

"Be careful," my mother said, and then she smiled, catching herself in how silly the warning sounded. "It's just reflex," she added.

I went around to the front of the Lonergans' house and paused by the hydrangea bush in the front yard. It was the same one I had hidden behind on the night of Kay's fortieth birthday party, the summer I was nine.

On that night, my parents had left me in charge of my sisters, telling me that if I needed anything, I should just come across the street to the party and get one of them. It was a hot night in August, and I could hear music and laughter through the screens. When Justine and Meggy fell asleep, I went outside in my nightie and flip-flops and walked up the Lonergans' driveway toward the backyard, where I stopped and hid behind the hydrangea bush.

From where I stood, I could see most of the party and hear much of what was being said. The host, Mr. Lonergan, was telling a joke to a group of people in a circle around him at the grill. I didn't hear the joke itself, but it made some of the women blush and put hands over their mouths to cover the smiles. My mother was one of them. So was Mrs. Lonergan. I watched her whisper something to my mother and they both giggled, and then Mrs. Lonergan put her pretty, dark head briefly against my mother's shoulder, and it was then that I saw they shared secrets, and I wanted so badly to be let in on them that I wasn't sure whether the sound I uttered was from this yearning or from the sudden sting of the mosquito on the back of my thigh.

I slapped at the mosquito and was about to turn around for home, when I heard a familiar sound that made my breath grow quick. It was my mother's voice saying, "Stop, Tom. Tom, calm down." She was trying to speak softly, but I realized that if I could hear it from the edge of the yard, then so could anybody at the party. I was afraid to look, but I had to, and what I saw was my father standing by the side of the grill, where raw hamburger patties were stacked high on a platter. He was looking down at the meat as if he were hypnotized. His frozen posture and expression had caught the attention of other guests, and my mother went over to put her hand on his arm, but he shook her touch off gently.

From the plate of hamburger, a fly rose and flittered away into the dark. By looking at my father's face, I could tell that the fly had been sitting on the meat. This kind of thing normally undid my father to such an extent that he avoided anything that had to do with eating outdoors, but because it was Kay Lonergan's birthday and close to home, he'd made an exception. Now, I could see, he regretted it. My mother was telling him, "Steady, Tom. You don't have to eat it. Why don't you get me a beer?" but even her quietest, most comforting tone could not soothe him. So she leaned closer, and I imagined that I knew what she was whispering: "Go on home, then." The party guests who had noticed my father's behavior were raising eyebrows at each other, and a few of them smiled in a way that made me feel angry and, more than that, ashamed.

My father nodded, and he turned toward the hydrangea bush where I was standing. I saw him try to give a little wave to Mrs. Lonergan, but she was already talking to somebody else. My mother watched my father walk away from her to the edge of the patio. I knew I should have run across the street and pretended not to have left the house, but instead of moving I waited for my father to reach me. "Hi, Daddy," I said.

He didn't seem surprised to find me there. "Hi, sweetheart," he answered. His face showed neither disapproval nor pleasure, and the words sounded automatic, like a bad actor saying a line. He put his arm around me and we walked across the street together, and I remember feeling—although he didn't put his weight against me—that I was guiding an invalid home.

Now, across the street, the girls at my old house were intent on their chalk drawings, and the rope lay twisted across itself and forgotten at their feet. I felt myself wanting to hesitate at the foot of the driveway, but I swallowed the instinct and kept going. Russell's mother had wheeled him inside, probably to go to the bathroom. But I knew he'd be back; the cooler filled with cans of Budweiser sat waiting for his return.

Approaching the stone walkway my father had laid the summer before he died, I suddenly remembered a dream I'd been having the past couple of months, since Justine and I came back to the house in August to clean it out. In the dream, I wandered without haste or fear through these rooms. I knew I wasn't supposed to be there, because new people lived in it now, but I was unable to make myself leave. Everything was set up the way I knew it, and as I walked through the house, I marveled at the fact that the new family had furnished its home exactly as we had, even down to the photographs held in place with strawberry magnets on the refrigerator. Even the photos were of our family, not theirs.

But when I reached out to touch the faces, the photographs slipped off the fridge before my fingers made contact, and when I bent to retrieve them from the floor, they slid away as if carried by a breeze. I chased them around the kitchen, but finally they disappeared under the door of the pantry, and I knew I couldn't open that door.

The pantry was where my father collected things—yard-sale flyers, the labels from food cans, old soap slivers, inkless pens, gum wrappers, used-up deodorants. The dead leaves of houseplants. Broken thumbtacks. Pencils worn down to the nubs. I'm sure there was more, but after a while I stopped wanting to know, and I stayed away from the pantry because I could tell that it was a source of tension between my parents. "There's something wrong with this, Tom," I remember my mother saying one Saturday morning when Meggy, trying to hide from Justine and me, opened the pantry door to send a collection of empty vitamin bottles and burned-out lightbulbs rattling onto the floor. "Do you know that? Do you *get* that this isn't normal?" The rest of us kept a wide berth from the pantry from then on. Or, if we had to go in for a can of soup or a new box of cereal, we slitted our eyes and felt our way through.

In my dream, I hurried out of the kitchen and went upstairs to the bedrooms, but when I tried to lie down, I fell right through to the floor; the beds were only illusions. I went back downstairs and tried to sit on the couch, but the same thing happened. When I picked up the phone it evaporated in my hand. Nothing had substance. Outside the front door, a voice instructed me to come out of the house slowly, with my hands in the air. I thought it was a police officer, but when I opened the door expecting to find Frank Garhart, I saw that it was Meggy instead, waiting to accuse me of trespassing. *You don't belong here,* she said.

The girls playing at my old house—*their* house now, I kept telling myself—looked up as I walked toward them. "Hi," I said. I was standing in the exact spot from which my father had launched Meggy's bicycle, the first time she balanced on a two-wheeler. From inside the house I could hear the sound of a bath running, and a television blared news from the family room.

"Hello," the older of the two sisters answered. All five of the girls were writing their names, with elaborate loops and curlicues, on the asphalt. Hers said *Kelly,* and out of the *y* she drew petals and stems.

"Stop it, Kelly," one of the other girls said, looking at me with a suspicion that penetrated my heart. "She's a stranger."

"I used to live here," I said, before I knew I was going to.

Immediately the younger sister jumped up, and she dropped her chalk so violently that it shattered hitting the ground. "Mommy!" she wailed as she started for the house, in a voice that was not as truly frightened as it was self-conscious of its own dramatic effect. The other girls stopped drawing and looked as if they were merely interested in what would happen next. "There's a ghost outside," we all heard the little sister say, and Kelly and her friends smiled at me.

"Courtney's a little rambunctious," Kelly told me. I recognized the calm superiority of an older sister. "She thinks you're the girl who died."

"What's going on out here?" I heard a woman's voice from behind the front door, before it became visible in the form of a mother, holding the younger girl's hand. When she saw me, she held the hand tighter—I saw the short squeeze—and drew the small head in close to her body, her hand covering the girl's ear.

"Oh, hi," I said, feeling ashamed because instantly I did not like her, though I could not at first tell why. Then, in the next moments, I knew: the way she stood on the stones my father had arranged in the walk; the way she reached over, with her sandaled foot, to kick a clump of dirt aside—I hated the way she owned this place, which still felt like my home. "I was just telling your girls, I used to live in this house. I came back for a visit, to see the Lonergans. I just came over to say hello." The more I talked, the more I hated her, because she didn't smile in response to what I was saying; and the other girls must have sensed something in this, because they stood and seemed ready to run.

"When did you live here?" Mrs. Crowell asked. "You mean, right before us?" She paused. "Are you a Dolan?" She made our name sound like a disease.

"Yes." Although I tried desperately to stop it, I felt my face begin to flush.

"Okay, I see." She turned her younger girl's face up toward her, lifted her chin, and said, "Courtney, honey, it's time for your bath. Go on up and get in with Kevin. Kelly, you go in, too. Girls—" she turned to the other three—"it's the baby's nap time, you need to go home." Perfectly mannered suburban children, they all tossed their chalk into a shoe box by the garage and took off across the lawn.

"I didn't mean to intrude," I told Mrs. Crowell, feeling guilty for breaking up the game.

"Then why did you?" she said.

"Excuse me?" I thought I must have heard her wrong, but then from her face I knew that I hadn't misunderstood. "I just wanted to see my old house," I told her, as confusion and anger began to take hold. "There's nothing so wrong with that."

"No, I know." She sighed and pushed her hair back. "It's just that the children—well, other kids tell them things. We thought it was best if they didn't know, when we moved here, but it didn't take long for the whole story to come out." She dropped her eyes and continued talking to the stones on my father's path. "When they heard about it, of course they got scared. They wanted to move out. Not the boys, so much, but the girls. Courtney still has nightmares. She's afraid the girl—your sister?" She looked up, her lips moving nervously, and I nodded. "Died in her room."

"Which room does she sleep in?" I asked, although it was not what I intended or wanted to say.

The woman pulled herself up and took a step backward toward the house. "Look, never mind. I'm sorry to be rude, but I'm going to ask you to leave. I just don't want this whole thing opened up again. The kids were just getting used to it, they were just starting to forget."

If she had invited me inside, I would not have accepted. If she had shown me any kindness, if she had said, "I'm so sorry about what happened to you, if you ever want to come by and visit the house, feel free," I would only have thanked her, put my foot out to touch one of the stones in my father's walkway, and turned around.

But because she was asking me to go—because I was not welcome—I couldn't make myself leave. "Can I come in?" I asked. "Just walk through? It would only take me a minute. I wouldn't say anything to the kids."

"I don't think so," she said. "I wouldn't be comfortable with that."

When I realized she was saying no, I felt a storm in my stomach. "Please?" I said. "Could I just look at the kitchen? Step in the back door?" I began moving toward it as I spoke, certain she would not restrain me physically. But she reached out to touch my elbow, and when I shook her hand off, she did a little dancing end run and blocked the door.

"Don't do this," I said, hearing the plea in my voice and hating myself for it. "Please don't keep me out."

"I'm sorry," she said. "But I think it's better this way." The front door opened and a man called, "Barb?"

"I'm afraid I'll have to call the police," she said, "if you don't leave now." Her voice was shaking, but I could tell she meant it. And I recognized another feeling in myself, along with the desperation: I envied her children for the way she protected them.

"Everything okay?" Mr. Crowell said, coming over to us. He smiled at me, but his expression changed when he saw his wife's face.

"Don't worry, I'm leaving." And I meant it, but as I turned and took a few steps back down the driveway, feeling both sets of eyes on me, I looked over and saw that the husband had left the front door open. Without planning it for even a moment (I was probably more shocked than they were, though their surprise rooted them where they stood, while adrenaline set my legs free), I ran up to the door, slipped around it before they could get to me, and locked it from the inside.

I looked around: all the furniture was arranged differently, but this was still our living room, where we used to eat grilled-cheese sandwiches on Sunday nights, where we pushed aside one end of the sofa to practice cheerleading, where my mother piled her suitcases at the foot of the stairway the morning she moved out.

At the top of the stairs, the girl called Courtney, who was naked, screamed. Then she cocked her red head and asked in a normal voice, "What's your name again?" Behind her a boy came out of the bathroom, wearing fire-truck pajamas, and flicked his wet towel at his sister's backside. *Last one in is a rotten egg.*

"Ana," I called up to her in answer, and the boy, startled, dropped the towel over the banister. I caught it where I was standing, just as the parents came banging through the back door. I felt rather than heard them rushing across the kitchen toward where I stood, and without thinking I threw the towel at them, right in the mother's shrieking face, before I started scrambling up the stairs. At the top, the kids gave out screeches that sounded more like laughter—as if they believed this to be a game—and they darted into the bathroom, slamming the door. Behind me, I felt fingers on my heels and kicked them away, and when I got to the landing I turned down the hall, ran past my old bedroom and my parents', and hurtled into the room where my sister died.

It wasn't a girl's bedroom anymore. The bunk beds against the wall were covered with football bedspreads, and model airplanes hung from hooks on the ceiling, which was painted to look like the sky. Identical posters of the Teenage Mutant Ninja Turtles were thumbtacked over each bed, and the lamp shade, a creepy clown's head, cast the light of a bright orange bulb.

Still—and the shock of it felt electric—I saw traces of Meggy here. In the far corner of the sky-ceiling was the raw patch of plaster where she had once affixed, with glue, a galaxy of stars and planets she'd made out of cardboard and glitter. The window shade held a nick from one of her early experiments with scissors. And in the corner stood the bookshelf my father built into the wall for her eighth birthday. Although the outside frame had been repainted to match the color of the sky, I could see that the shelves themselves remained as my father made them, decorated with *Alice in Wonderland* decals.

All of this I registered in the space of a second or two, the time it took for the Crowells to catch up with me. The door didn't have a lock—none of our bedrooms ever did—so I stood on the other side and pushed back against the two of them. Behind them I heard the children chorusing, "Get her, get her!" Of course, their combined weight was too much for me, and when they forced the door open I was flung backward, off-balance, toward the dresser, where I hit my arm.

Before I could fall all the way to the floor, the father reached out to steady me. His touch was solicitous, intended only to soothe. As soon as I was standing again, he let me go.

"David," his wife said, "hang onto her, for God's sake."

"What?" The look he gave her was annoyed.

"She'll run again."

"No," I said, feeling suddenly airy and without a center, as if I floated above them all. "I'm sorry."

"Aren't you going to call the police?" Courtney asked, sounding disappointed.

"Yes, we are." Her mother backed up toward the door while keeping an eye on me.

"No, we aren't." Mr. Crowell turned to her and shook his head. With both of his hands he took hold of my shoulders, as if meaning to comfort me.

"David—"

"Don't worry, Barbara. I'll take care of it." He nodded toward the door and she led the children down the hall, where I could still feel them hovering somewhere out of sight.

The father was still holding me by the shoulders. "You do have to go," he said, perhaps feeling in my arms the tension between wanting to have him hold me and to push him away. "I'm sorry."

I told him, "I know. Me too."

"Are you all right?" He said it in a low voice so his wife wouldn't hear. I nodded, though we both knew I was lying.

He led me out past his gathered family and down the stairs where Justine once fell and broke her arm on a Cabbage Patch doll I hadn't put away when my mother asked me to. (When we got to the emergency room, the doctor thought I was the patient, because I was crying harder than Justine.) I could hear the kids whispering. One of them said, "Well, she looks regular." From above my head, the mother called down, "Please don't come here again."

"For crying out loud, Barb," her husband said. "I think she gets the message."

"Thank you," I said. Outside, he stood on the stoop and watched, waiting until I reached the end of the driveway before closing the door again. Instinctively, I knew he did this not because he wanted to make sure I was gone. He waited because he knew what I would feel if I had been close enough to hear the door shutting behind me.

I went back across the street to the Lonergans', my legs feeling like waves of water, and told my mother I wanted to leave. Ed hadn't returned yet with the extra ground beef—no doubt his errand would take him to the Shamrock for "a quick one" or two—and my mother and Kay were sitting side by side over a bowl of Doritos and matching glasses of beer. "Well, okay, sweetie," my mother said, and her readiness to agree was what let me know that she was also uncomfortable, because otherwise she would have tried to convince me to stay.

Kay said, "What about lunch?" but I could tell from her voice that she, too, was relieved. This impromptu reunion was something we would all have liked to be able to do, but in the world as we found it now, it wasn't possible. She and my mother hugged and kissed each other, and Kay tried to include me, but I pretended I hadn't noticed. They promised to stay in better touch with each other, and I also pretended not to know, as they made this promise, that they would probably never see or talk to each other again.

"Where did Matt disappear to?" my mother asked, and Kay said vaguely, "Oh, he's around." I remembered that just after the deaths, Kay told our mother that Matt was having a rough time of accepting what had happened, and she asked us to understand if he couldn't make it to the funeral. In the end Matt came, but he left before the service was over. Now, I thought I saw him standing in the shadow behind the curtain of his bedroom, watching us, but Kay said I must be mistaken. She suggested we wait until Ed returned so he could give us a ride back to our car, but my mother and I said, No, it's not that far, and we walked back down the block and through the cemetery, the long way this time, avoiding Meggy and Dad. My mother had a comment about every house we passed, and the family in it—Remember the time they had the fire, did you hear he lost everything in that last crash? Her step quickened; she seemed invigorated by recalling the bad luck of the people we had known. She still didn't ask what had upset me before I returned to the Lonergans', and I wondered if she would.

When we arrived at the Toll Gate, we had to park three side streets away, and coming closer we saw that the restaurant was packed with Pee Wee football players and their families. The line for takeout was long and wide, and when we finally made it inside the door, we saw that Rosemary and Justine were still on the bench where patrons waited before being seated at tables. Justine was in the middle of a sentence, talking to our aunt, but when she saw us she shut up abruptly. "What happened?" she demanded. Then, before we could say anything, she added, "I knew you shouldn't have gone back there."

I told them about the girls in the driveway, the new woman in our house, the way I had sneaked by them, and the way I'd been chased out.

"Oh, Ana," my mother murmured when I'd finished, but I couldn't tell what was in her tone.

Rosemary said, "That bitch." I gave her a grateful smile.

"Look, let's just get out of here," Justine said. She got up, jostling the elbow of the woman standing in line behind her. The woman turned, annoyed and startled, but Justine didn't apologize.

"Sorry," my mother said to the woman.

Justine said, "Mom, don't talk for me." She tried to push her way through the line to the door, but people weren't moving fast enough for her. "Get out, get out!" she yelled at a frightened child who was on the way into the restaurant with her father. The girl's face collapsed and she reached up for her father's hand, which was already on its way down to meet hers.

"Hey," the man said, but Justine had already lumbered by him and through the door.

"I'm sorry," my mother murmured to the man as she went after Justine, and then as Rosemary and I followed we left an echo behind us: *Sorry, sorry.*

Out on the sidewalk, my mother caught up with Justine and grabbed her by the arm. "Hey," Rosemary said, in the same tone the child's father had just used. "Take it easy, Margaret."

But if my mother heard her, she gave no sign. "What were you think-ing?" she said to Justine. With the force of her own anger, she tried to turn Justine to face her, but my sister broke away and kept walking. "That was a little kid."

At this, Justine stopped suddenly. "Jesus, Mom," I heard her mutter. Rosemary and I were behind them both, keeping a distance so they could have the sidewalk to themselves, but close enough to intercede if it were needed. "Since when do you give a shit?" She shouted loudly enough to make us all wince.

"Ssh," our mother said as people turned to look at us.

"Don't shush me!" Justine dug down deep for a breath, and I saw that she was headed beyond control, that she was going to excavate it all; and although I felt scared, the sight also thrilled me. "How can you fuck-ing tell me to shut up? Meggy would still be alive if it weren't for you, and you're telling *me* to shut up?"

My mother shrank where she was standing. Her shoulders deflated, her face drained of color, and the features turned small.

"Justine," my aunt whispered, but there was nothing to add.

We were still standing on the corner. The light had changed twice and we could have crossed by now, but none of us had made a move. Traffic whooshed by and someone beeped, but we didn't look to see if it was for us.

My sister continued screeching, and I imagined her throat rubbing raw against the red words. "I can't believe you just *left* us with him, and look what happened!" She made a broad gesture of display with her chubby hand, as if showing us charred bodies at the side of the road. "Couldn't you tell there was something wrong with him? How could you just leave us there? You're the fucking *mother!*" In her inflection, "mother" was higher than human and closest to God.

At each sentence our mother flinched. She waited when Justine paused for another breath, as if to allow her all the time she might need to finish. Justine wasn't finished, but neither was she about to say any-thing more. She stood with her body shaking. Actually, it looked more like twitching. It was the motion of crying, but no tears came—just a high, dry wail before she pitched over to the trash barrel by the phone booth and vomited into it.

"Jesus Christ," Rosemary said, but it sounded more reverent than profane.

I said, "Can we go home now?" My voice came out high and hysterical, reminding me of anyone but myself.

Justine said, "We don't have a home anymore, Ana. Where have you been?"

"Let's at least go back to the car," Rosemary suggested, turning her face from the window of the Shoe Box, through which people were pretending not to watch our family drama.

"Justine," my mother said. It sounded like a plea. "Justine. Will you look at me?" Justine turned her face a bit more toward our mother, but still not all the way. "I never thought Daddy would hurt any of you. You guys wanted to stay in school here, and it was only for those few months. Remember? I actually thought things might be better—that *he* might be better—when I left. If he didn't have the stress of me bugging him all the time to keep trying therapy, to try medicine, all those things we used to fight about. And *wasn't* it better, for a while?"

The fact that Justine gave no response made me realize the answer was *Yes.* "Well," she said. She seemed to be aware, for the first time, of where we were. "Look, just forget it." It was not a reconciliation, but at least she allowed herself to be led back to the car. We were all silent as my mother made the three-point turn that brought her back to Birch Street. I knew they all felt the way I did—as if we were fleeing, having committed some crime.

"I can't believe either of you went with Kay in the first place," Justine said finally to my mother and me . "I mean, just being back in this town gives me the creeps."

Rosemary said, "You know, I didn't think it would bother me, since I didn't live here." She lit a cigarette and blew the smoke out as fast as she took it in. "But I do have some memories, and they do make it hard. Like I remember being on this street with Tom once, watching you guys in a parade. When you were Brownies. Margaret, you were working that day,

I think. We had Meggy with us, and he put her on his shoulders so she could see. I remember when the band went by, she said her heart had a drum in it." My aunt made a sound like a single sob when she exhaled.

"Stop," my mother said, putting a hand to her own heart. "Rose, I can't."

"Sorry," my aunt murmured.

Then we were quiet again for a stretch, retracing the route we had taken to get there, through Four Corners, past Oberheim's, and out to the Thruway. Next to me I could feel Justine wanting to know what it was like—being in our old house—but I also knew that she wouldn't ask.

In the front seat, Rosemary put her arms up to the car ceiling and let out a stretching noise. "Hmm," she said. "Funny how kids always come back to jump roping. When I was little, we used to jump rope in the middle of West Street, and if a car came while somebody was counting, we made them wait till the person missed."

"Like a cow in the country," I said. "Lying down in the middle of the road."

"Except it'd be easier to move a cow." I couldn't see my aunt's face, but from the sound of her voice I knew she was smiling. "People would get really pissed off, and if they drove in our neighborhood a lot, they learned to avoid going down our street after school or on weekends." She laughed, and we could tell she was recalling an old, favorite scene. "Especially if your father was having a turn."

"Dad?" Justine sat up from the force of her own surprise. "You mean boys played?"

"Well, when they were little. Until they found out it was just for girls." Rosemary lit another cigarette. "Your dad was one of the best— better than most of the girls, even." When my mother said, "Rose, please, the smoke's killing me," she took a long drag and flipped it out the window.

"One day it started raining," our aunt said, sounding as if she were about to recite a fairy tale. "Tommy was jumping, and I was on one of the ends. It started to thunder and lightning, and our mothers called us in. We all made a run for it, except Tommy. He wouldn't stop. He picked up the rope, wrapped the ends around his hands to make it shorter, and kept jumping by himself while the rain poured down.

"Well, of course, Ma was furious. 'Get in here,' she yelled, and you could see people all along West Street at their windows, looking out at him and laughing." Rosemary coughed, but I couldn't tell whether it was because of smoke or the memory. "He wouldn't stop until he'd jumped to a thousand. It had to be a perfect thousand, with no misses, but the rope was heavy because it was wet, and the ground was slippery. You could see his mouth moving while he counted. A few times he got up to five or six hundred, but then he'd get caught in the rope and have to start over again."

"My God," my mother murmured. In the rearview mirror I could see that she looked as if something long unanswered had suddenly been revealed, and I knew what she was thinking: *So he was like that even then.*

"It got dark, of course, and the rain wasn't stopping. Ma went out once to try to force him to come inside, but Tom was already stronger than she was. 'When I get to a thousand, I'll be done,' he told her. When she came back in she said to me, 'That's it. I've had it. He'll be the end of me.'" Rosemary's voice became small, belatedly hurt on behalf of her brother.

"Ma made me go to bed early, but I couldn't sleep. I could hear Tommy's rope hitting the ground outside my window, and I couldn't help counting every time he started up again. I was cheering for him, in a way. Finally, I heard him get to nine hundred. I actually started praying, and believe me, I never prayed. I could feel my heart under my nightie, and I was whispering, 'Please, God, let him make it.' When he got to a thousand, I said 'Thank you.'" Rosemary shook her head, as if to clear it of clutter. "God, I haven't thought about this in a million years, but I remember it like it was yesterday." She turned toward all of us, knowing we'd want to hear more.

"I heard him come in and run a glass of water. I heard him squeeze out the rope in the sink and hang it on the coat hook. He stopped at my door and whispered, 'Rose, you asleep? I did it, Rose.' You know what I said? I have no idea why, because I really was happy for him, but I said, 'Big deal, Tom.' When he got upstairs, Ma whacked him with the hairbrush."

I knew that this story stabbed at Justine's heart as deeply as it did mine, and probably in the driver's seat our mother also felt the cut. But no one said another thing the rest of the way back to Delphi, and after a while the silence took on a weight, like humidity, in the air around us. We were all remembering my father in different ways: as a child, a brother, a husband, and a father.

And when those memories had come and gone in our heads, there was the common image of the stone marking his grave site. *He was loved.* The words became the rhythm of the tires beneath us, growing louder with each mile. By the time my mother pulled into her space and parked, I couldn't wait for the engine to be turned off; I opened the door and stepped out to feel the solid pavement and to take a long breath of the cooling air. My mother asked Rosemary if she wanted to stay over, but our aunt said no, she'd just use the bathroom for a quick pee and then get on the road again. Harold Webb, the ex-priest, was waiting; but besides that (she didn't have to say it), being with us had of course reminded her of our father, and she could only take so much. We all hugged her hard before she left, nobody wanting to let go.

"She looks like Dad, a little," Justine said, as we waved her off. "I never noticed it before."

Although it was not even five o'clock, our mother went straight to bed and turned on the Buffalo game. Justine and I took our usual places in the living room, but I couldn't concentrate on my book and she kept flipping around channels on the remote until finally she switched the set off and announced, "I'm going for a walk."

"A walk?" I looked up from my page as if she had used a word in a foreign language. The Justine I had always known liked my father to drive her to the bus stop, at the end of our block, on his way to work in the morning. For her, exercise was a purely social activity. "You are?"

"There's too much crap in my head," she said, grunting slightly as she bent over to put on her sneakers. "I have to get out of here."

"I'll come with you." I started to close my book, but she put a hand up like a crossing guard.

"Ana, no. Okay? I just want to be alone." She called Bill Buckner over, clipped on his leash, and stepped out into the dusk.

When she didn't come back in forty-five minutes, I went out after her. The air held the nip and shiver of Halloween. I wasn't really afraid that something had happened, but I couldn't feel safe until I knew where she was. I walked around the perimeter of the development, waiting to catch a flash of pale flesh in the twilight or the tune of Bill Buckner's tags. I called Justine's name, but softly, because the residents of Deer Run Gardens could be skittish about noise.

I didn't find her around the condo. Hesitating, I took a few steps into the woods behind the backyard, and heard the sound of ripping paper. Justine knelt at the foot of a tree, biting the head off a Hershey bar. She looked like a communicant, her face turned up to the sky; I thought of the girls in the Salem witch stories who made sacrifices with their teacher Tituba in the middle of the night.

I hid behind a trunk and watched. When Justine finished the piece of chocolate in her mouth, she reached into a clothespin bag tied around a low branch and pulled out a Baby Ruth. As she tore into the candy, she let the wrappers fall around her like abruptly shedded skin. Bill Buckner sniffed at them. "No, boy," Justine told him. "It makes you sick." She snatched up the discarded wrappers and stuffed them back into the bag, which she pulled tight with the drawstring and wound three times around the branch. Then she began to stumble her way toward the path.

I sneaked out of the woods and ran back to the condo. My mother had gotten up and put on her bathrobe and was making tomato soup and tea. "Where were you guys? I was starting to worry," she said, eating a spoonful of soup straight out of the pan. She made a face and I could tell it had burned her tongue. "Goddammit. I have to get that stove guy over here."

"Just out for a walk," I answered, though my mother seemed to have forgotten she'd asked me anything. On impulse I added, "It was Justine's idea."

"Really?" My mother poured soup into an I♥N.Y. mug. "Good for her." She blew vigorously across the red cream surface, swallowed a sip, and said, "You know I don't want to nag her about losing the weight. But she can't go on like this."

"She knows that," I said, though I wasn't sure I was right. I watched my mother crush a fistful of Saltines into her soup. "What about you?" The words came out before I even realized, and she looked up at me surprised. "Can you?"

"What?" Her spoon remained poised over the bowl.

"Go on like this."

"Like how?" But I could tell she didn't really want me to answer.

"Mom." She wouldn't look at me. Intently, she stirred the cracker crumbs around in the soup. "*Mom.*" I reached over to stop her hand from moving, but my own was shaking, and red soup spattered the table between us.

"Ana, what's wrong with you?" Her voice was sharp and she began reaching for napkins, but I caught her wrist so she couldn't move.

"What did Dad's note say?"

"I told you. I never read it." She reached for the sponge and carefully wiped up the spilled soup.

"Bullshit."

"Ana, I don't know what you want from me." My mother lifted the spoon of soup again to her mouth.

"I don't know what you mean."

"You don't know?" Again I reached over to stop her hand, and this time I took hold hard of her wrist. "Mom, what's wrong with you?" Behind me the door opened and I heard Justine come in, but I didn't turn around. "What aren't you telling us?" When she didn't answer, I squeezed harder, and the skin in my fingers turned red. Although my mother winced, I did not release my grip.

"Ana, stop it." Justine dropped Bill's leash and came over to the table, where she pulled at my arm. "Let go of her, goddammit!" My fingers fell away as our mother drew her arm close and began massaging her wrist.

"Look," she told us, pointing down at her skin, but we couldn't see anything. "That's going to leave a mark."

6. Human nature is upon you

Q. What are the doldrums?

 — *C.S., Elsmere*

A. A theoretical line—the heat equator—girdles the globe through its hottest points. On both sides of this shifting line lies the region known since sailing-ship days as the doldrums, but which meteorologists call "the inter-tropical convergence zone." The air over the doldrums has very little horizontal movement; the sun's blazing heat lifts it almost straight up.

The week after our trip back to visit the graves, I went to the Delphi Public Library and took down the Albany-area phone book from the Resources shelf. Under "Physicians" I found the name I'd come across in my parents' divorce file at the lawyer's office: Geoffrey Zeldin, M.D.

I called the number from the pay phone in the library lobby. When I got his machine, I used a fake name, because I was afraid that if I said who I really was, he might not have agreed to see me. I left a message saying that I'd come across his ad in the phone book. I said I was new to the area and was feeling depressed. It was a bit urgent; I hoped he could help. I gave my name as Clarissa Dalloway, knowing it was something of a risk but assuming that even if he did have time to read, it was a pile of psychology journals he kept on his nightstand and not the novels of Virginia Woolf.

He called back the next morning. My mother had left for work and Justine was in the shower, and I stood over the machine, without picking up the phone, while he offered some appointment times. I listened to his message twice for evidence that he recognized my pseudonym, but his tone was annoyingly neutral; it gave nothing away. He said he was returning Ms. Dalloway's call and he had the following hours available in the upcoming week; which, if any, could I make?

I answered by leaving another message, and so the doctor and I had communicated, though not spoken a single direct word to each other, as I sat in the waiting room of his office the next day listening to a white-noise machine simulate air whishing. Or was it sounds of the sea? I held an old *National Geographic* open on my skirt-lap and pretended to leaf

171

through it. I was early by twenty minutes, and there was no one else in the room. I arrived with time to spare because I wanted a chance to calm down, close my eyes, and prepare myself. I realized, sitting in the softest chair with both feet on the carpet, that I was also trying to understand something about my father, who had probably sat in this same chair dozens—perhaps even hundreds—of times. I pictured him counting the tiles in the ceiling, tapping his toes the requisite number of times against the swirl design on the rug to keep the worst from happening. I imagined him hoping that this doctor would have a cure.

At 3:50, the door to the inside office opened and a middle-aged woman emerged, not looking at me as she wiped her eyes with a tissue that wasn't doing the job because it was already soaked. She didn't merely dab; she dug at the sockets as if to stanch bleeding from a wound. The doctor had followed her to the door, and he left it open to watch, surreptitiously, as she fled the outer office. Then he saw me looking at him through the crack in the door. "Do you always have that effect on women?" I said. If you had asked me then, I would have said I was trying to be funny—break the ice—but the truth was that I laughed to chase the fear clotted in my throat.

The doctor seemed taken aback that I had glimpsed him in his sanctuary, let alone dared to address him in this casual, offhanded way. "I'll be right with you," he said, without a trace of a smile, and he closed the door between us, making sure it clicked.

Well, fuck you too, I thought. No wonder my father killed himself. The person who was supposed to help him, to take care of him, was a humorless bastard without compassion or warmth. Who did these therapists think they were? I thought of the last time I had seen Nora Odoni. My mother and Justine had already left therapy (Mom told Nora she didn't see the point, and Justine was afraid not to side with her), but I kept my appointment every week, not so much because it was helping as because I was afraid of what might happen if I didn't. *If I go to her office on Tuesdays at three o'clock, then nothing else bad can happen.*

My last appointment had been on a hot day in August, and the air conditioner in the Delphi Professional Building was on the blink. I sat in the chair opposite Nora and watched my foot in its sandal jiggle above the rug. "I just don't see how he could do it," I said without looking at her and feeling the words surge without my planning them. "I don't understand why."

She looked at me for a moment as if considering whether to let me in on some ancient secret known only to the Greeks. Then she stood and reached to a high shelf above her desk. She brought down a glazed pot, like the one Pooh kept his honey in, which I'd never noticed up there before. It had the word ANSWERS engraved on the front.

"Go ahead, take a look," Nora said. The pot had a lid with a ceramic knob for lifting. I thought that maybe there were little pieces of paper inside, like the fortunes at the end of a Chinese meal; whichever one you picked held a special message intended only for you, a nugget of inspiration or advice. I didn't want to play this game, whatever it was, but I felt that I didn't have any choice. I didn't want to hurt Nora's feelings. Reluctantly, I raised the lid.

But when I stuck my hand inside and reached my fingers around, I felt nothing except the shiny bottom of the pot. I tilted it toward me and saw that it was, indeed, empty. I remember so vividly the shock I felt that even recalling it makes me flush with shame. Nora seemed to be waiting for a reaction as I replaced the lid on the jar.

"Okay, I get it," I said. "There are no answers, right?" She nodded. "I'm completely humiliated," I murmured. I was also angry, but I couldn't say that yet.

"It's not meant to humiliate you." She looked surprised by my response, but it was too late to make any difference. When she took my check that day I don't think she understood how she had failed me, or that I would not be coming back.

Remembering this in the waiting room of Geoffrey Zeldin's office, I put my magazine aside and started to stand, thinking I would just leave and the hell with it, when the doctor's door opened again. This time he stepped outside to speak to me, extending a hand as he said, "Clarissa Dalloway?" He was a big man, built like a barrel with a beard. He did not precede me into his office, but waited for me to enter first. He must have been familiar with this routine—and with the fact that, his stomach protruding as it did, two people could not fit in the doorway at one time; he stepped aside as I passed by him, gesturing forward with a thick-fingered, open hand. He smelled like coffee but also like the peppermint candy he must have been sucking to mask his coffee breath. Because I was looking at the floor when I went by him, I saw that the hem was falling out of one pant leg, and that his shoe heels were worn down at the sole.

But he also wore a vest and a tie, and I appreciated this. It suggested that he took his work seriously, and whatever my father had suffered, it was serious. Dr. Zeldin indicated a chair and I took extra seconds to settle myself in it by arranging and then smoothing my skirt. When I finally looked up and met his eye, imagining that he might have been rummaging for a notepad or writing the date on a fresh page, I saw that instead he had been watching me, waiting. I blushed, and across the space between us I felt that he was trying to place where he'd seen me before.

"So. Ms. Dalloway." He nodded a bit in my direction. His voice startled me; I was accustomed to Nora's habit of silence in opening a session. "Maybe you can start by telling me something about why you're here." His eyes narrowed behind their wire-rimmed glasses and I searched them for scrutiny, but to my confusion I saw invitation instead.

I looked away from him again. His office was neat but dusty; the sun illuminated a fine layer on the surface of the desk. My eyes settled on the nubby fabric of my chair arm, and I began to pick at it. I shrugged, wanting to keep my shoulders raised in protection—though against what, I wasn't sure. "Well," I said. "I'm having some trouble, I guess." Suddenly, I so regretted having used a fictional name that the sensation of shame slithered through me in a nausea I barely contained. Not for my own sake; but it would have embarrassed my father, I knew, to have me mocking the doctor he'd sought out to save his life. I blurted, "My name's not Clarissa Dalloway."

I could see he wasn't surprised. "Ah," he said, giving the nod again. "I thought it was possible your parents had named you after the character in Virginia Woolf's book. Or that you'd taken the name yourself. Then again, it also occurred to me that you might be using a pseudonym, for some reason." He was making a tower with his fingertips, each pressed against its partner on the opposite hand.

"I guess that's how you could say it. A pseudonym." Now I took a closer look around the office. A bookcase lined the far wall, and without being obvious about it, I squinted to make out some of the titles. *The Bonfire of the Vanities* snuggled in next to *Look Homeward, Angel*. So this man also alphabetized his books by author; was that one of the reasons my father had chosen him? Just before I looked away from the Ws, *Mrs. Dalloway* on a slim book-spine caught my eye. "So you *have* read the book?" I asked.

"A long time ago. But yes." He had not followed my gaze toward the shelves, but kept his eyes on me. Then, carefully, as if he weren't quite sure he was doing the right thing but wanted to follow an impulse, he recited, "*She always had the feeling that it was very, very dangerous to live even one day.*"

The words cleaved the air between us. They had struck me hard enough to force me back in my seat. "Where did that come from?" I asked.

"*Mrs. Dalloway.*"

"I know that. But did it just pop into your head?" My voice scaled an octave but I was helpless to call it back.

"Actually, no." Dr. Zeldin shifted slightly in his chair to redistribute his bulk. "I knew someone—a patient of mine, in fact—who liked to quote that line."

I took in too much air on my next breath and had to cough as I exhaled. I knew who the patient was, and now I realized that the doctor knew that I knew. "Tom Dolan is my father," I said.

This time it was Dr. Zeldin who paused before speaking. I wanted to believe that he was overcome by emotion at the sound of my father's name, but a part of me suspected that he was just buying time until he figured out what to say. "I'm sorry," he told me. "Of course he is. I'm sorry." Even in my electrified state, I noticed that he used the present tense, as I had. And instinctively I knew that he was not adjusting his language to mirror mine. My father existed in that room; he was alive between us, and so we referred to him as if he might be outside parking the car or leafing through *Prevention* magazine in the waiting room.

"What are you sorry for?"

Dr. Zeldin looked surprised, as if I shouldn't have had to ask. "I'm sorry for a lot," he told me after a moment, and I sensed that while he struggled to maintain the demeanor of a professional, he was also acknowledging that in this room we were merely two human beings trying to understand the same thing. "What comes to me is 'I'm sorry for your loss,' but that's what people always say when somebody dies. I don't want you to think I'm just mouthing a formality. But I mean it. I know what you lost. *Who* you lost. I mean, in the case of your father. I never met Meggy." At the mention of my sister's name, he paused again, seeming to realize that he and I hadn't yet been officially introduced. "You *are* Anastasia?"

I nodded, wondering how he could be so sure. I imagined my father saying, "Justine is the pretty one," and the vision caused a new clench at the back of my throat.

"And I'm sorry he killed himself," Dr. Zeldin continued. "I'll be honest with you, I didn't see it coming. I'm good at what I do; I'd like you to believe that." He waited until I let out a slight nod, though I resented being asked to give him this affirmation. Whether he was a good psychiatrist was, for me, beside the point by now.

"Why did he come to see you?"

"Well, I can't tell you everything, of course. But I believe he called initially because of your parents' pending divorce. I believed he thought it might make a difference in whether it went through or not."

"And you couldn't tell how much trouble he was in?"

The doctor shifted slightly in his big chair. "I would say that your father presented as fairly stable, if a bit anxious. At least at the beginning."

"Then what happened?"

"Well, I recommended medication, but he didn't want to take any."

"You mean for depression?"

"Some for depression, but mostly—what was a worse problem for him, I'm sure I don't have to tell you—were the obsessions that plagued him, throughout his life."

I nodded again and looked down at the floor as I spoke. "He never talked about it much. We never called it 'obsession.' My mother always said it would embarrass him if we brought it up, so mostly we tried to ignore it."

Now Dr. Zeldin knitted his fingers and made a humming sound. I wondered if this meant he was rendering some kind of judgment about the way our family had treated my father. Did he think we should have done things differently? Did he think it was our fault that our father and Meggy were dead?

But all he said was, "It's very sad. It used to be that people had to suffer. They had no choice—there was no way to alleviate it—but these days there are new treatments for people like your father. Some of them respond beautifully to the new drugs and go on to have normal lives. But your father seemed distrustful of medication. I couldn't convince him even to try."

"What were the obsessions about? I mean, at the end?"

He cleared his throat, shifted again before answering. "I wish I could help you," he said, looking off to the side of me as if reading responses from cue cards. "And I will, as much as I can. But there's confidentiality to consider. I feel comfortable confirming that your father was having obsessive thoughts near the end of his life. But I'm afraid I'm not at liberty to discuss their nature with you."

Was it a smile I saw at his lips as he told me this? In the moment I thought so, I wanted to leap across the space between us and claw the beard off his face. But the moment passed and I convinced myself that the smile had, in fact, been a wince.

"Well, what can you tell me?" I said.

He hesitated. "Maybe it would be best if you asked me specific questions, and I'll determine on a case-by-case basis what I can say."

So it was a game, after all. Of course, he would win if he wanted to, but I wouldn't give up yet. "All I know is that he left a note, which my sister and I never saw. My mother won't tell us what was in it; she says she never read it, but we don't believe her." I was amazed to feel a drop of sweat roll down from my temple, and I slapped it away before I thought he could see. "And there were some pages ripped out of Meggy's diary. Either she ripped them out because she was afraid someone would see them, or—my father did."

Dr. Zeldin remained silent.

"Can you tell me if any of that means anything to you?"

He said, slowly, "I don't know what was in the note."

"But do you have any idea why he did it?"

Again the throat-clearing. "I couldn't be sure." He hesitated. "Have you talked to the boy yet?"

"What boy?"

"The one across the street."

"Matt?"

"That sounds right." He nodded.

"What for?"

The doctor shrugged; that was all he would give me. "He and Meggy were friends, yes? Maybe he can help you."

"I don't know why you'd think that." And yet I realized as I spoke that the picture of Matt Lonergan at the pool, the day my father and Meggy died, had insinuated itself forcefully among my impressions of that day. Although I hated the doctor for having come up with this idea when I hadn't, I tried to keep the feeling out of my voice.

"What do you think he knows?" I asked.

He shrugged again. "I don't even know that he does."

"Goddammit." I didn't mean for this to slip out, but he didn't seem surprised. "What am I even here for? You won't tell me a goddam thing."

"I can tell you," Dr. Zeldin said, choosing his words from the air again, "that if your father could have helped it, he wouldn't have hurt any of you. He loved you all very much."

"Jesus." My leg jerked a couple of inches off the floor. "I know that."

He raised his chin, and I sensed that he was affronted. "Your father suffered from this disorder for a long time," he said. "I gather there was some car-burning incident that goes back quite a number of years?"

"He was that way when he was a kid," I told him, remembering Rosemary's jump-rope story.

"All the more reason, then. Somehow, he was able to control it enough to get married, have children, work at jobs." The doctor leaned forward as if confiding in me. "He must have constructed a very careful grid in his mind that allowed him to do all these things, without letting the obsessions interfere."

"Oh, they interfered," I said.

"Perhaps, but he still managed to hold it together. Somehow he was able to keep them separate, at least most of the time, from his family life. Then something happened to make the grid fall apart. My guess is that it was your mother leaving." The doctor leaned back and sighed. "When obsessions have people in their grip," he said, "it can feel intolerable, and it's not uncommon for patients to consider suicide as a way out."

"But then why kill Meggy too?"

His mouth made a little moue of regret. "That I'm not sure about. I can tell you that he believed she was in some kind of danger. I only realized after the fact that it was from him, but he probably never saw it that way."

Suddenly I remembered that it wasn't Clarissa Dalloway who captured my father's attention in Virginia Woolf's book; it was the character of the war veteran, Septimus, who ended up impaling himself on a fence spike rather than be captured by the doctor who was coming to get him. *Once you stumble,* Septimus wrote, *human nature is upon you.*

But my father wasn't afraid of other people. It was his own nature that tormented him.

Dr. Zeldin said, "What else would you like to ask?" Although I'm sure he didn't intend for me to notice, I saw him sneak a glance at his watch.

"Did you know he had a gun?"

"No."

"Where do you think it came from?"

"I'm afraid I have no idea."

"Why—" I had to stop and swallow before I could get the next words out, "why do you think he shot her in the head?"

"Well." The doctor rubbed his thumb and index finger together, as if trying to start a spark. "My guess would be that he wanted it over quickly. That he didn't want her to suffer." He seemed to hesitate before adding, "And that he wanted to—make sure of the outcome."

"Look." I knew that the urgency of my tone only made me more vulnerable, but I couldn't seem to control it. "Did he ever talk about me?"

He frowned as if he'd expected something far more challenging. "Well, of course."

"What did he say?"

The doctor shifted his eyes. "I know he loved you all, very much. I can't really elaborate for you. Everything your father told me was in confidence, and the fact that he's dead doesn't negate the contract I had with him."

Don't cry, I told myself. *Wait till you get out to the car. Don't let him see it.*

"Fuck your contract." I rose from my chair so quickly that he had to struggle to keep up. "What difference will it make to him? I'm the one who's still alive, I'm the one who needs you." I tried to tell from his face whether I was gaining any ground, but if I was, it didn't show there. I went for broke. "Can't you tell me why he did it? Can't you see that I have to know?"

He reached his hand out and I was afraid he was going to touch me, but he only held it there. My scalp buzzed and the room started shimmering at the corners of my eyes.

"I don't really know the answer," he said. "Please, try to understand this. I want to help you. But—that's all I can say." This time he made an exaggerated point of looking at the clock on the wall behind me. "I'm afraid we have to stop now."

"No shit." I picked up my purse and slung it hard over my shoulder. "I'm not paying you," I told him. "Just so you know. I have the money, but I'm not going to pay."

"That's fine. I wouldn't take it, anyway." He was at the door, waiting to open it for me. "Anastasia—"

"Ana." I would not let him use the name my father had given me.

"Ana, then." He looked down at the floor as I faced him to hear what he had to say. "I just want to make sure of something. This visit wasn't part of a plan to take any legal action, was it?" He let his eyes meet mine, and I saw the fear in them. "Because there really isn't a case. It's a shame, but your father was receiving adequate care. No one could have anticipated what he would do."

I waited until the door was open and I could see his next customer gathering up her things and getting ready to enter the inner sanctum. "Fuck you," I said, loudly, so there could be no mistake about who I was addressing. In the parking lot, I threw a stone at his window. But it must have been made of shatterproof glass because it only made a sharp sound, like a blank or a BB, and bounced right off.

It was five o'clock when I left the doctor's office. I had planned to stay in Ashmont only long enough to keep my appointment, but I knew now, without actually forming the words in my mind, that there were other places I had to go—and other people I needed to talk to—before returning to Delphi. Although it was the end of October, the day was hot, and I rolled down my window to let in air. It smelled of pumpkin and apple and the smoke of somebody burning raked leaves in a backyard.

The first phone booth I saw was the one outside the McDonald's by the middle school, where kids who couldn't yet drive often went on their first dates. I had been taken here myself, in fifth grade, by Gordon Zukowski; he bought me a double cheeseburger and a shake, and spent the whole meal talking about Phil Cunningham, who would, in junior high, be the one to lead the cries of "Fag" and "Buttfucker" against Gordon.

I parked and waited for a teenage girl to get off the phone. She was saying, "I don't give a shit, I'm not walking home. If you don't come and get me, I'll hitch a ride." She hung up with a bang, and when she turned I saw that it was Trish Symmes, who used to play softball back in the minor leagues with Meggy. She ducked whenever the ball came her way and never swung once at a pitch; she always got waved to first base. At Meggy's eleventh birthday party, she'd burst into tears when she couldn't get her teeth around the stem of a bobbing apple, but my father arranged for her to win Pin-the-Fangs-on-the-Vampire (without Trish realizing, of course). Now I could tell that Trish knew me, too, but she was at a loss about how we might connect. She brushed by me, sweeping bangs off her forehead, snapping sweet purple gum.

The phone's receiver smelled of grape breath and Love's Baby Soft. I picked it up and started dialing, but my fingers froze when I saw a line someone had written among all the other old graffiti in the booth: *Justine Dolan is a slut.* Then someone had crossed out *Justine* and substituted *Meg*, and replaced *slut* with *box of bones.* I slammed the receiver into the wall, closed my eyes, took a breath, and turned my back to the message.

Behind me, Trish Symmes was watching. I could feel her eyes on my back. *Careful*, I thought. It was an automatic self-warning, the same one I'd heard in my head when I thought I might break down in front of the psychiatrist. *Don't let anybody see.*

I dialed again. After three rings, Kay Lonergan answered, sounding slightly winded. I imagined she had been outside, putting her favorite Anne Frank white tulip bulbs into the ground.

"It's Ana," I told her, then added, "Dolan."

"Ana. Of course I know it's you." She sounded genuinely glad to hear my voice. "I felt so bad the other day, you two leaving so quickly. I spoke to Barbara afterward—Mrs. Crowell." She paused to let the name sink in. "I'm sorry that happened. I wanted to call you guys, but I wasn't sure—well, you know." She sighed.

"I know." A truck whizzed past, and I waited until it had gone by before I spoke again. Sitting on the bench by the bus stop, Trish Symmes lit a cigarette. "Listen, I'm in town again," I told Kay. "Outside McDonald's. I wondered if I could stop by."

"Right now? Of course, honey." I couldn't tell which was more prominent in her voice—surprise, dread, or curiosity—but I heard them all. "Is anything wrong?"

"Not really. I just kind of wanted to see you. To apologize for how I acted the other day. I didn't mean to be rude." I paused, tried to sound casual. "Also, I wondered if Matt was around."

"You don't have to apologize for anything. But if you want to come over, you're welcome anytime. You know that. And Matt?" I could tell that the question made her nervous. "I'm not sure. Are you coming over now?"

"If that's all right." I pressed my palm against my chest.

"Of course it is. I'd love to see you."

"Okay. Thanks," I said, my heart still beating faster than I knew it should. "Thanks," I said again, and hung up. Immediately I lifted the receiver to call back and say I'd made a mistake, but I didn't have any more change. "Shit," I said, and a man riding by on a bicycle heard me and smiled.

"It can't be that bad!" he called over his shoulder, and I would have liked to smack him right off his seat.

Trish Symmes, exhaling Newport smoke, turned to watch the cheerful cyclist with a contemptuous eye. "Asshole," she said, knowing only I would hear her, and in that way she acknowledged our historical bond.

When I reached my old street and parked at the Lonergans', I saw that Russell Stinson was at his usual station on his family's front porch. Russell had been wounded at the end of action in Vietnam, and he spent most of his days in fall, spring and summer sitting in his wheelchair. As I approached the Lonergans' house, Russell shouted something that sounded like "Speak of the devil!" but I may have heard it wrong. I gave him a wave and then Kay met me at the door, showed me into the kitchen, and went back to chopping carrots. "Can you stay for dinner, honey?"

"No, I have to get back. My mom's expecting me." This was a lie; my mother had no idea where I was.

Kay nodded, and I sensed that she was relieved. "Ana, how is your mom, really? I guess the other day was just too hard for her."

"It was hard for all of us," I said.

"Oh, of course. I know that, sweetie. I didn't mean it wasn't." She blushed over the cutting board. "This whole thing must be a nightmare," she added, tossing the carrots into a pot.

I would have answered her—tried to give her some idea of what it was actually like—but I saw that instead of looking at me she was letting her eyes slide toward the recipe open on the counter. So I just said

"Yeah" and watched as she took more vegetables out of the fridge, then rinsed them. "So is Matt around?" I asked, reaching to pop a strip of green pepper into my mouth.

Kay put the knife down. "Matt," she said. "Of all people. Do you mind if I ask why?"

I shrugged again, trying to appear as if it didn't really matter one way or the other. "It seemed like he and Meggy were spending a lot of time together, right before it happened. I just wanted to ask if he might have noticed anything wrong."

She nodded, studying me thoughtfully. "I see. Well, he never mentioned anything to me. This has all been pretty tough on him, Ana. Are you sure?" I could tell she was trying to change my mind. But when I nodded, she said, "Okay." She went to the back door and called into the yard. "Matt! Ana Dolan's here to see you." She patted me on the arm and said, "At least stop in again before you leave, okay? I want to say good-bye."

I said "Sure," though I had no intention of doing it, and stepped out to the backyard, where Matt was watching me from the top of the tree-house ladder. My father had built the house when Meggy and Matt were in first grade. The house was supposed to be a joint project between my father and Ed Lonergan; they had the best tree for such a structure, and the kids in both our families were supposed to share its use. As it turned out, my father was the one who put the whole thing together because Ed Lonergan never seemed to be around when they'd made plans to work on it. Or, on a weekend afternoon, he'd be so drunk when he came outside and picked up the power saw in the hand not holding a Genesee Cream Ale that my father would have to find some way to get rid of him, or some excuse to suspend work for the day.

I remember one Saturday in particular, when two of the house's four walls were up and my father was getting ready to install the third. Matt had just carried a tray of lunch out to my father, whom he adored—even though I was only ten or eleven, I could see that he admired my father, while his own made him nervous. Watching Matt hand nails up to my father, or hold out a glass of lemonade to him, I wondered, for the first time, whether my father had ever wanted a son; and, beyond that, whether he was disappointed to have only daughters. The idea made me feel tender toward my father, and for about a week I vowed to be a tomboy. I asked him to take me to the Hall of Fame in Cooperstown; I asked him to teach me about woodworking. But I didn't like the fact that you had to measure, so I gave back the role of helper to Matt Lonergan.

On that Saturday, when the tree house was halfway built, Ed came out to the yard with his bottle of Genny and, from the patio, tilted his head one way and then the other to scrutinize what my father was doing. I had been roped into baby-sitting for Meggy and Justine while our mother played tennis, and I was watching them run through the sprinkler my father had set up for them in a corner of the yard. Mr. Lonergan finished his beer and tossed the bottle into the trash can my father was using to collect leftover pieces of wood. "Looks a little cockeyed, Tom," he called to my father, losing the "Tom" in an unsuccessfully muffled belch. "This end over here looks higher than that one." He waved vaguely in the direction of the tree, where my father had paused to hear what Ed Lonergan had to say.

My father rubbed a hand through his hair and then wiped it on the towel he kept hanging from his back pocket. "I think it's okay, Ed," he answered. "I measured it all, and anyway, it's a tree house. Better if it's a little rough around the edges. Gives it some character." He saw that Matt, who was six then, had been looking up at him with an anxious face in the wake of his own father's criticism. He reached over to fake-punch Matt on the shoulder. "Right, partner?"

"Right," Matt said, his glance darting over at his father to see if his defection had been noted. Ed Lonergan stood still for a moment, then nodded as if in defeat. "What the hell," he said. "What do I know about manual labor. I'm just an engineer." Even at that age, I understood that he was taking a dig at my father's job record and the type of work he did. I looked at my father to see if he was going to say anything back, but he had started hammering again, and Matt was proffering nails in a glass jar like an acolyte holding the grail. Mr. Lonergan came over and yelled at

Justine and Meggy for wearing his grass down as they ran through the sprinkler. He yelled at me for wasting the water it took to cool them off.

Hearing this, my father put down his tools and told Mr. Lonergan he was taking us all to a movie. Mr. Lonergan said he was coming, too. My father said he didn't think it was a good idea, and Mr. Lonergan said that was pretty funny coming from a man who thought it was a good idea to tap the bedpost three times before—here, he glanced at us kids and gave my father a sly smile—having carnal relations. (I remember the exact words he used because at the time I thought he said "carnival," and I thought he meant that somebody in our family belonged to a circus.) My father's back stiffened and he took in air with a sound, but he didn't say another word to Ed Lonergan. Instead he just walked out of the yard and we kids all followed him, and after I'd changed the girls into dry clothes he took us to see *Rocky*.

That night my parents had a fight. He was mad at her for telling Kay things that should have been kept in the family. My mother said she was sorry, she really was, but he couldn't know what it was like to have to keep so many secrets.

"Of course I do," he answered, sounding as if he couldn't believe what she'd just said. "Are you kidding?" They were lying in bed—I was listening from down the hall—and after the fight they started to rustle the covers. I heard them kissing and moving around, and my mother began to make little noises in her throat. After a few minutes, my father said, "Goddammit," and my mother told him, "It's okay."

"I'm sorry," he said. I thought I could hear him slapping his own skin. I put my head under my covers then and stopped listening, because I was too close to understanding what they were talking about.

Now Matt Lonergan sat on the tree-house ladder, his big frame dwarfing the topmost step. "I saw you over there the other day," he told me while nodding at my old house. "I saw you go in. What happened? They throw you out?"

"Of course not," I said, too embarrassed to tell him the truth. I wondered exactly how much he'd been able to see from up there, and whether he'd heard some of what went on, too. "It just felt too weird."

"They're kind of jerks," he said. "Except the father. He seems okay." Then he appeared to consider coming down to meet me at ground level, but thought better of it and remained where he was. I didn't blame him; he must have realized he would need some kind of defense—height, momentum—against whatever I might have come to see him for.

"Matt—" I said, putting my hand out to touch the ladder. His leg jerked as if I had made contact with his flesh instead of mere wood. "Sorry," I said, withdrawing my hand. "I don't mean to bug you, Matt. I just never had the chance to talk to you about what happened."

"Talk about what?" He was looking down at his knees.

"Remember that day at the pool, before we knew, and you were looking for Meggy?"

He nodded, flicking his fingers against his shins.

"Why were you looking for her?" I asked.

"I told you. We were thinking about catching a movie."

"Come on. It was more than that—I could tell." I leaned into the ladder's steps, and I knew that at the other end of the wood, he felt the pressure of my plea.

"It's really not a big deal," he muttered, more to himself than to me.

"Matt." He tried to make himself look up, but couldn't. I knew he wanted to help me. "There were pages ripped out of her diary. Do you know what that was about?"

He shook his head. "How would I know what she wrote?" But he was struggling, biting his bottom lip.

"I saw Meggy the night before, late," I went on, pressing my advantage. "After our father went to bed. It seemed like she wanted me to know something, but she didn't know how to say it." I paused. "But I think you know what it was. Please—just tell me, Matt. I promise I won't ever bother you again."

I held my breath as he stood up, towering over me from the height of branches. If he'd wanted to, he could have swung out and flattened me beneath him with a jump.

But instead he plunked down the ladder steps so that we were on even ground. "Okay," he said, and I flinched at the anger in his voice, even though I knew it was directed at something other than me. "I saw her that night, too. Earlier, like around ten. We snuck out here." He raised a finger to point at the tree house.

"What for?"

"Well—" I could see him flushing under the collar of his shirt. "Look, I may as well just tell you. My mother doesn't want me to say anything, but it's really no big deal. We were kind of—going out."

"You and Meggy?" I almost laughed—it sounded so unlikely, and cute—but I caught myself. "Really?"

"Yeah." Matt punched at one of the wooden steps where the footing was coming undone. "It hadn't been going on very long. I mean it was, like, a week. I don't know; we went to the Toll Gate one night with some other kids, and then they dropped us off and we were talking, and we ended up making out." He looked away from me at the last words, as if he felt ashamed.

I tried to imagine Meggy and Matt kissing, but all that came to me was an image from the time when they were five or six and both had the chicken pox. Our mother gave them oatmeal baths together, and they spelled out all the words they knew—cat, dog, mommy—in the glop on each other's backs.

"You did?" I said, realizing too late that I was repeating myself.

"Well, it wasn't for very long. Like I said, maybe a week. We'd come and hang out up here at night. Meggy was pretty bummed out about your mom leaving and everything." He paused and made himself look at me. "But listen, Ana. We never went all the way, I swear to God. You have to believe me."

"I do believe you." And this was true; I was sure there was no way Meggy could have kept it from me if she were having sex, although it was surprising enough to find out what Matt was telling me. "So you were up here that night?" I tried not to be impatient to hear the rest.

"Yeah. Just fooling around, you know, but I guess—I guess she did have her bra off." He coughed on the word "bra." Now the words came spilling, as if he couldn't wait to get them out and done with. "We were just kissing, and fooling around, and a couple of times she stopped because she thought she heard something, but I said it was just the wind.

"But then there was another noise, like someone coming up the ladder. It stopped, and we listened for a while, and she was going to get up to check but I wouldn't let her. I started kissing her again, but she wasn't into it. I could tell something was wrong." He faltered and found his voice again. "At first she wouldn't tell me, but then she got up and put her shirt on and said she thought she'd seen your father's eyes in the doorway, looking in."

"What do you mean?" I frowned, unable to absorb the last part of what he'd said.

"From the ladder. She thought he'd sneaked up to look at us. I said she was crazy, she was seeing things, and she said, *Yeah, maybe. You're right.* But I could tell it still bothered her. She said she had to go home." Matt was staring straight ahead, as if seeing the Meggy of that night in front of him. "That was around 10:30. I told her to call me later, but she never did."

"Jesus." The yard was tilting. I couldn't think of what else to say.

"Matt?" Behind us the door opened, and Kay stuck out her head. "Everything all right? It's time for dinner, hon."

"Yeah, Mom. Be right there." Matt moved so that his back was to his mother, so that nothing and no one would come between us. "The last thing," he said, then choked a little and gathered up a breath. "The last thing she said was, 'If that was him, he'll kill me.'" On *kill* his voice gave out again, but I could still hear it. "I didn't think she meant anything, Ana—I swear to God. First of all, I was sure he didn't come up here. But even if he did—I just thought she meant he might be mad."

"I think that's what she did mean," I told him, though I wasn't so sure of this. But he needed to hear me say it. "I don't think she had any idea."

"Matt?" Kay's voice was more insistent now, sounding scared. He turned away from me.

"Matt, wait—" I didn't really want to hear any more, but neither was I ready to let him go.

"That's all," he mumbled, and he walked across the yard to where his mother held the door open, waiting to close him safely inside.

Between the Lonergans' house and the police station, the digital numbers on my car's clock changed seven times. It was 6:49 when I parked and 6:51 by the time I'd grown calm enough to get out, climb the steps to the front door, pass through it, and approach the reception desk. *Did Tom Dolan really do his daughter?* I held my breath, afraid I would see the same officer that had been on duty that day, but this time it was a woman who looked up to greet me though I still stood a few steps away.

The badge over her breast said Mahalia Vines. "Help yourself," she told me, and I raised my head, startled, thinking she'd issued a command. But then I saw that she was gesturing at a plate of brownies next to the Far Side calendar propped up on the counter between us. "Supposedly they're low-fat," she added. Her lips blew a skeptical sound. "Yeah, right."

"No, thanks," I said. I was hungry, tempted, but I didn't want to ask for a favor with food caught between my teeth. "I wondered if Frank was working today?"

"You mean Officer Garhart?" She squinted and I blushed.

"Yes."

"Well, I believe so. Let me just check." She picked up the phone and dialed an extension. "Young lady to see you, Frank," she said to the receiver. "What was your name again?"

I told her, and she had barely repeated it and hung up before I heard his footsteps coming down the old fifth-grade corridor. "He doesn't respond that fast to 911," Mahalia said, giving me a sororal wink.

"Ana." Frank didn't go so far as to use a formal name to try to fool Mahalia, but neither did he greet me in any physical way, though I had to fight the impulse to raise my face and kiss him. "Good to see you. Come on down to my office so we can talk." He didn't touch me until we had rounded the corner and entered his office, when he put a hand to my face. I closed my eyes for a moment, then opened them when he spoke. "I was just about to go out and grab some dinner. You hungry?"

"No." I shook my head. "I won't keep you."

"Oh, I didn't mean that. I just meant I'm glad I didn't miss you."

"Well. I would have waited." Hearing the seriousness in my voice, he got up to close the door behind me.

"I've been thinking about you," he said. "I've been wondering."

"About what?" For a moment, I forgot that I was the one who'd come with a purpose in mind.

"What do you think? We sleep together and then you disappear, and I'm not supposed to notice?" Then he laughed. "Hey, don't we have it backwards here? I thought the guy's the one who's supposed to not give a damn."

"I give a damn," I told him, though I realized there was no proof of this anywhere for him.

"I didn't mean it that way. But why'd you stop answering my calls? When I saw you at your house that day, over the summer, I thought maybe I could get you alone to talk for a minute. But your sister was hanging around."

"She had every right to be there," I said. I thought of Justine in the yard on Pearl Street, squatting on her freshly plump knees as she picked out souvenir pieces of stone.

"Oh, I know. Of course she did. Ana, I'm not—don't get mad, okay? I mean, no hard feelings, right?" Then he laughed at himself for the triteness of the line and tapped his desk blotter with the sharp end of his pencil, leaving gray dots on the green. "All I mean is, you're not sorry we spent that night together, are you? When you didn't call back, I figured it was no big deal, just something that happened." He leaned forward across the desk. "But you're not going to tell anyone, in an official capacity?" He waited for me to understand what he was saying, and when I didn't, he added, "Because I could get in a lot of trouble."

"Why?" I said. "I'm of age. Besides, we didn't really—you know."

"Well. But you were a principal in a crime we were investigating. It would be seen as inappropriate. Taking advantage of someone at a bad time, you know what I mean?" He looked away, his glance hooded by guilt.

In my best imitation of Mae West I reminded him, "I took advantage of you."

He smiled. "That's not how they would see it, though."

"Look, that's not why I'm here," I said. "Why is everybody so afraid they're going to be sued?"

"Who said anything about suing?" Now he shifted in his chair and pulled back from me. He got up and opened the door. "What can I do for you?" His tone turned official.

"I want to see my family's file."

"I can tell you anything you need to know."

"Why can't I just see it?"

"You can. But I'm suggesting for your own sake that you just ask me whatever it is you want to know." He went over to a filing cabinet and opened the drawer labeled *A–G,* from which he pulled two bulging manila folders and carried them back to his desk. "There are photos of the crime scene in here, for instance," he told me, clutching the folders close to keep stray papers from dropping out, "which I don't think you'd want to look at by accident."

"Oh." My throat constricted, and I coughed to shake it loose. "No, you're right."

"But any specific piece of information—"

"I want to know," I interrupted, "if there's anything in there from my father's shrink. Did you interview him? He won't tell me anything, but I thought maybe you guys would have more." I hadn't felt the tears coming, so they fell before I could catch them. "*Please* tell me. Please, Frank." I sat down hard in the chair. Frank went out of the room and brought me a paper cup of water, which he held to my lips but which I spilled, anyway, on my shirt.

"I don't understand," he said after a minute. "Doesn't the note say it all?"

My stomach went cold, and for a moment I couldn't see his face. "What note," I said.

"The one your father left."

"But my mother burned it. At least, she said she did."

"Wait a minute." He took his arm away, and I heard papers rustling.

"Oh, my God." I stood up so suddenly that I almost lost my balance again, but when he reached out I shrugged away from his touch. "Oh, Jesus. I can't believe I never thought of this." I leaned over the way people are directed to when they are about to faint. "Of course. You guys have a copy. Right?"

"You mean you've never read it?"

"No."

"Oh. Jeez." He lifted two fingers to knead the skin above his eyes. Then he sighed. "Actually," he said slowly, "what we give the family is a copy. We keep the original. But not up here. It's downstairs, in the evidence room."

"Take me."

"Ana, that might not be such a good idea."

"I know. But I have to." I swallowed hard. "Please."

Before he opened the door of his office, he drew me close again and said, "Okay," the word muffled into my hair. He led me into the hall and back to the reception desk, where Mahalia Vines, who was chuckling into the phone, motioned to the plate of brownies and pantomimed eating. I waved to decline, but Frank picked one up and bit in as we continued down the corridor to the staircase, where—when we went to school in this building—members of the Safety Patrol used to be stationed when we filed by our homerooms to the playground or cafeteria.

"God," I said, slowing down as my hand hit the cold rail slanting toward the basement. "I just remembered the time this kid fell and hit her head on the steps. There was blood all over the place." A second later I had the girl's name: Janet Peyser. We were in the middle of multiplication when we heard her screams, and the teachers tried to prevent us from running out of our classrooms to see what was happening. Phil Cunningham was on the Safety Patrol that year—everyone was surprised when he was picked because he was such a troublemaker, but somebody overheard his teacher saying that if they showed some faith in him, he might live up to it. Phil was the one monitoring traffic in the hall that day. Janet, who was in the third grade, lay on the landing with her eyes open, blood seeping out from under her hair. It didn't take long for the teachers to come to their senses and rush us back to our rooms, but when the ambulance came they didn't stop us from watching out the windows.

None of us had known Janet Peyser very well. It was early in the school year, she'd just transferred from somewhere in Canada, and she never came back after the accident. But I had forgotten all this until now.

"I remember that, too," Frank said, pausing beside me on the stairs. He licked brownie crumbs from his fingers. "The one everybody thought the Cunningham kid pushed, right? But there was never any proof."

"He was so screwed up." Whenever I pictured Phil Cunningham's face, it always had the same smooth expression—no frown or smile, no hint in the eyes of affection for anything. "Do you really think he did it?"

Frank shrugged. "Who knows? Probably."

"But why?"

He shrugged again. We were at the bottom of the stairs, and he turned a light on. "I suppose he just felt like it. There are people like that. You know?"

I didn't, but suddenly it wasn't a subject I wanted to pursue. I bit the insides of my cheeks and continued to follow him.

The evidence was not kept in the cafeteria, as I had expected. Our old eating room had been converted to a maze of cork-walled cubicles. Frank led me beyond the kitchen to an even bigger room, without windows, which hadn't existed when the building was a school. There was a desk in the corner, next to a Xerox machine; otherwise, the room contained only shelves, filled with boxes stacked so high that there were stepladders to reach the ones closest to the ceiling.

Without hesitating, Frank went over to one of the ladders and climbed up to remove a box, which I saw was labeled *Dolan, Thomas E. / Margaret O., 6/29/88* . When he put the box on the desk and took the lid off, I backed up a step, as if something might jump out and grab me by the neck.

I kept my eyes averted so I wouldn't catch sight of anything in the box as Frank rummaged through it. He pulled out an envelope. "Let me just make you a copy," he said, moving to switch on the Xerox machine.

"What do you mean?"

"Well, I can't give you the original. It's evidence." He waited as the yellow lights fluttered and whirred.

"That's what I want."

"Ana, you can't have it. It's procedure. Look, this machine works fine. There won't be anything you won't be able to make out." He lifted the copier lid and from the envelope gingerly removed the sheet of paper it contained. Even from a distance I recognized my father's hand-writing, the tiny letters upright and fine.

"No." I went over to stop Frank's hand before he could give me the copy. "I want that." I gestured toward the original. How could he not understand that I needed the actual page my father had touched, the lines of ink he had put there with a pen pressed between his own fin-gers? I reached for the note, but Frank drew it out of my reach.

"What do you expect me to do? Break the rules?"

"Yeah, if you have to."

"I can't do that."

"Well, you'd better. Because if I have to tell them about us, I will." I'd had no idea I was going to say this, and Frank looked as shocked as I felt. But I made no move to retract it.

"What do you mean?"

"Us sleeping together. You said it could get you in trouble."

He let his breath out through lips that almost formed a smile, as if he thought I was joking. "You wouldn't," he said.

"Yes, I would." For a moment I thought I might laugh, because it was like hearing someone else speak, and it felt so scary; but instead I kept it in.

"My God." He stared at me without blinking. "I guess I was wrong about you."

"No, you weren't. This isn't me, I promise. But I'm not taking a copy." I nodded at the reproduced page sitting in its tray.

Frank looked at me for another long moment. Then he shrugged as if he knew he'd been defeated and said, "Okay." He folded the copied sheet in thirds and tucked it into the envelope, then held out the original between us. "I guess it goes without saying that I could get in trouble for this, too."

"I know." I took the paper as carefully as if it had thorns. "But you won't. There's no reason for anybody to ever look in here again, right? The case is closed."

Frank replaced the box with my family's name on it and turned off the copier, and we went back upstairs. This time, he stayed a step or two in front of me. I could tell he was trying not to let his agitation get the better of him. "You going to be okay?" he said, gesturing at the envelope I held in my hand. He had led me to the waiting area. "You can sit in here, if you want to. Take as long as you need."

I had imagined him staying with me when I read the letter, but now I saw that he didn't intend to. I chose to believe, then—and I still do— that it was deference to my privacy that kept him from offering, rather than anger at my blackmailing him. In any case, I knew I didn't want to stay in the police station. The hallway felt suffocating, the ceiling too low. "I think I'll just get on the road," I said, and Frank nodded. He held out his hand. Confused, I pulled the letter behind me, thinking he meant for me to give it back. But he reached down and took my other hand and squeezed it gently.

"Take care of yourself," he said.

"You too." For a moment, I wished he would grab the letter away from me and pull me close to his chest, a heroic movie gesture, the strong leading man saving the deluded ingenue from herself. But, of course, nothing like that would happen. I felt him watch me go down the steps and out to the parking lot, and by the time I reached my car and looked back, he was gone.

The temperature had dropped a good ten degrees since the afternoon. I shivered behind the steering wheel, where I sat without turning the engine on, trying to work up the nerve to open the envelope. Holding it, I felt a freeze as sharp and thorough as if ice had been touched to my spine.

I took the page out. It was a piece of lined paper that had been torn, no doubt, from one of Meggy's spiral-edged school notebooks. My father had trimmed the left margin of his letter with scissors; not even in a suicidal haze would he have been able to tolerate a ragged edge. The page had been folded neatly, and above the top crease was written

Margaret

Anastasia

Justine

The sight of our names struck me hard enough that I had to look away for a few minutes—at the American flag flapping in the breeze above the police building, the phone booth on the corner—while my stomach rolled.

There was no other salutation. But at the top of the first page my father had noted, in his precise fashion, the date and time: *June 28, 1988, 9:42 P.M.* Which meant that he'd started writing it the night before the deaths; and now I remembered that he had shut the door to his bedroom after saying good night to Meggy and me. Had he begun the note then? Had he written it in bed? If I'd waited a moment longer the next morning before going to my baby-sitting job, would he have broken down, shown me what he was writing, and begged me for help?

But wondering these things made me feel sick again, so I focused hard on the page.

> *The time has come the walrus said to talk of many things*
> *of why the sea is boiling hot and whether pigs have wings*
> *Remember? That's not how I meant to start this, but when I put down 'The time has come,' the rest of it just sort of fell out of my head.*
> *It got to be too much. You always said I was all talk no action, Margaret. Well I guess you won't be saying that anymore.*
> *The gun is Russell Stinson's in case you wondered. He has a collection, he showed me one day. I took it when nobody was home. Their fault—they should have left the door locked.*

Here the ink of the letter changed, from blue felt-tip to a black ballpoint. The next section of text had been reheaded *6:07 A.M.*—meaning that he must have picked it up again right after I left to go baby-sitting at the Melnicks'—and the words looked as if they'd come more quickly, with more chaos and urgency than before.

I went out there with Cokes for them. The loving dad. Like milk and cook-ies. What did I think they'd be doing, playing Candyland? He was on top of her, she was pulling his mouth down to her oh God her chest. Right there in the tree house, hadn't been swept since the summer. How dare he? He liked me better than his own father. He told me that once. I had to save her, can't you people understand that?

Seeing Matt's face flash in front of me, I reached up to press at a sudden pain digging into my forehead.

Thank god we have her on video. My Annie. You better make copies, Mar-garet, in case the tape should break someday.

She wrote it down. Not only how he touched her, but how she saw me, look-ing in. I knew she did—it was only for a second but somehow she knew. I caught them.

What happened was an accident. My seeing her. Not then, in the tree house, but a few nights before, outside the Toll Gate. She was getting ice cream with Matt and some other kids. I was taking a guy for a test drive, in a Cutlass, and we went that way. Here he is telling me about his relatives in New Jersey, and I'm looking out the window, not listening but pretending like I am. I see this woman from the back, she's wearing one of those belly shirts, I think you call them—maroon—and she has these perfect shoulder blades. Her head's tilting as she bends to lick her cone. I keep my eyes on her, she looks so good; and then even before she turns so I can see her face, I realize who she is.

There's no way I can tell you what it felt like, seeing Meggy that way. My own baby girl. I wanted to drive straight into the restaurant, a wall, anything hard, to stop what I was feeling. No word big enough for it. Guilt? Too puny. I must have made a noise, because the test-drive guy asked if I was okay, and then he saw what I was watching. "Hey, nice," he says, nodding at Meggy, and my foot falls off the clutch. I made him get out of the car right there. I knew the sale would fall through but I didn't care.

Again I had to stop reading, remind myself to breathe. A uniformed officer led in a business-suited drunk who was shouting to the police station at large that he was being railroaded. I watched until they took him into a room. Then there was nothing else to look at, except my father's words.

I couldn't stop thinking about it. Then last night when she came home and I heard her go outside, I got the Cokes and climbed up the ladder. Why couldn't they just have been talking, like the old days? They used to do their school projects out there. When they were little, play Go Fish. But no. He ruined her. I should have realized, I should have had the gun before it happened, but I was too late. I'll never forgive myself for that.

It was when she came in, after him, that she called you, Margaret. I heard her on the phone. She didn't exactly say what the matter was, but you should have been able to tell. I heard her ask you to come and get her. If you were still here it would have been different, she wouldn't be wearing things like that, belly shirts and things you can see through. A woman's things.

Or touching him in the tree house. Where were you?

Remember the trip to Boston that time, the boat we went on, Old Ironsides? Meggy was five. It was the same day we went to that witch house in Salem, Ana pretending to be a witch, and we saw that retarded boy. Remember?

On the harbor boat that day I was holding Meggy, she asked me to pick her up to see the water. The three of you were standing by the railing, looking down, and I realized I could throw her in. I could do it so fast she wouldn't have any idea until she was over the edge, on her way down to the water.

Think of what it would do to her.

Not dying. That's not what it was about. But her body down there in the water, and I would have done it just because I could. What it would look like, her face turned up to me. That kind of power, nobody should ever have. It scared me so much I had to put her down on the deck and go over to the other side of the boat. I sat on my hands so I couldn't touch her. Remember? You all thought I was sick.

But I was just exhausted from thinking. Trying to get rid of the picture in my brain. Sooner or later, the only way to get rid of it is to make it happen.

There's nothing left for me. I love you but I'm done

The letter ended abruptly, with no punctuation, no signature at the bottom of the final page. I folded it back into the envelope, stuck it in my purse, and pulled out into the road, where traffic had grown heavy with commuters on their way back to Ashmont. Cars passed and beeped at me and flashed their high beams, but it wasn't until I reached the toll booth at the Thruway, many miles later, that I realized I'd been driving without any lights.

7. Asunder

Q. How come my white shirt has inexplicably developed yellow spots?

— S.H., Watervliet

A. According to the International Fabricare Institute in Silver Spring, Md., the cause is likely to be optical brighteners used by some clothing manufacturers. Such brighteners make white garments appear even whiter. But exposure to light can chemically break down those brighteners, causing exposed areas to turn yellow and unexposed areas to remain white.

Unfortunately, once this happens, the effect is irreversible.

B y the time I got back to Delphi it was after nine. The first jack-o'-lantern of the season glowed a grin on the porch of the duplex, in front of three-year-old Deirdre's door. All the parking spaces were taken, so I let my motor die in the Tow Zone and sat watching my mother's condo for a few minutes. Two lights were on—in the living room and kitchen—and white rays from the TV cast themselves through the shuttered blinds. I kept telling myself to get out of the car and go inside. But it wasn't until I started to shudder that I forced myself to move.

At the sound of the door opening, my mother and Justine looked up. The sofa bed hadn't been pulled out yet, and they sat on either end of the couch, their feet on the coffee table, heads sunk back in the cushions. Over both sets of legs lay the afghan Grandma Ott had knitted and given my parents for a wedding gift. A commercial was on, and I knew that if I hadn't interrupted, they'd be watching the ad with as much concentration as they had given the program itself.

"Where were you?" my mother said, and I sensed it was not so much because she wondered about the answer as that she knew I might have expected to be asked. She turned her attention back to the TV, but when I didn't respond, she looked up as if I had done something to irritate her. "What?" she said, and Justine looked at me, too.

"Just a minute," I told them. Ordinarily I would have left my purse on the kitchen counter, but remembering what was in it, I carried it with me into the bathroom. I thought I only had to pee, after the car trip, but instead I realized I was going to throw up. Just in time I turned on the sink faucets to cover the sound. When I came out, my mother turned the volume on the TV down and Justine clucked in protest.

"What's going on?" My mother was sitting up straight in her seat now, and she brushed her share of the afghan aside. "Ana, what's the matter? You're acting strange."

"What else is new," Justine said, but it was only a halfhearted jab because she'd gone back to watching the soundless screen.

Still not answering—I didn't know what the words would be—I poured myself a glass of ginger ale before joining my mother and sister in the chair opposite where they sat. When I lifted the drink to my mouth, I saw that my hand trembled and I spilled ginger ale down my chin.

"Ana." Now my mother clicked the set off altogether, and even Justine seemed to sense something serious. My mother got up and came over to take the glass out of my hand. She got a coaster from the coffee table and set the drink on it, then reached up to take hold of my chin with her cold fingers. "Ana," she repeated, like someone trying to get a groggy patient to stay awake. "What is the matter with you?"

With the same shaking fingers I unzipped my purse and took out the folded letter. Watching myself from the outside, I kept thinking, It's still not too late to say, "Nothing," flush the letter, go to bed. But I knew I wouldn't do any of those things. I saw my mother take the piece of paper out of my hands and unfold it. I watched Justine instinctively gather the afghan closer to her chest.

"What is it?" she demanded. "What the hell is that?"

As if it had scorched her fingers, my mother dropped the paper on the couch between them. Justine snatched it up and started reading. "Oh, shit," she said, when she saw the handwriting and the first words. She closed her eyes, took a breath, and then focused again. Next to her, my mother clutched herself around the middle.

"Where did you get it?" she whispered. She was not looking at me.

"The police had it." They were the first words I'd spoken since entering the house. "I went there. One of them gave it to me." I felt like a foreigner speaking a new language. A simple sentence was all I could form.

Neither of us said anything else until Justine had finished reading. As her eyes moved down the page, she made little noises that sounded—I realized with embarrassment, wondering if my mother thought the same thing—like the noises of making love, tiny grunts as she exhaled, moans she could not have held back if she tried. When she came to the end, she looked up with an expression as thoroughly blank as I had ever seen on a human being.

"What does this mean?" she said, almost smiling in awareness of her own stupidity.

My mother shook her head. I couldn't tell whether she was deferring to me or asking me not to answer. But it didn't matter, because for the moment—thank God—I was beyond being able to care. "It means," I said to Justine, "that Mom lied to us."

"Don't be ridiculous." My mother pointed at me with a long finger. "That makes no sense, Ana, what you just said."

"Of course it does!" I punched at the paper. "First of all, you told us you never read the letter. Well, we knew that was bullshit."

In spite of herself, Justine giggled when I swore. I ignored her.

"All this time, you knew what was in that note. How could you *do* that? How could you *not* tell us?"

My mother began picking strands from the afghan, pulling at the design. "Okay, I did read the note," she mumbled, jutting out her chin.

"Then why didn't you just tell us what it said?"

"Because it's so—crazy. I thought it was better for you not to know." She coughed, then rubbed her fingers against her throat. "I guess I was protecting Daddy, in a way." She reached over and picked up the letter. "Look—'*There's nothing left for me.*' I didn't want the two of you to read that and be hurt."

"Goddammit," Justine said. Her fingers twitched above the remote and she looked at the blank screen of the TV. "It was a perfectly good night until Ana came home."

Abruptly my mother got up and went to her bedroom, emerging a few moments later with a pack of Salems. She'd smoked all of our childhood lives, but quit when Meggy turned twelve and threatened to take up the habit if my mother didn't stop. Seeing the cigarettes, Justine and I looked at each other.

"I didn't know you started again," she said, and my mother said, "I didn't," as she lit one up. "I just need something, sometimes, for the stress." When we didn't say anything, she asked us, "Would you rather I drank myself into oblivion, like Ed Lonergan?" When neither of us answered, she made a *pph* noise and dragged deeply.

"Listen." She let the smoke out in a final-sounding sigh. "I heard the same threat from your father for twenty-five years. It was always *I'm going to kill myself* or *I just want to die*. At first it scared me, I can't tell you how much. I watched him the way I watched you guys when you were little. When he wasn't at work, I hardly let him out of my sight. I was always asking, *You okay, hon?* I had to be the strong one, he got to fall apart." She paused again for another tobacco hit. Her eyes glazed over in the same senseless pleasure you always see in movies about drug addicts getting their fix.

"I talked to him that morning. He called me at the office and said he felt out of control. But you've got to understand, both of you. He'd said that before."

My mother lifted her body from our small circle of seats and went over to the island separating the living room from the kitchen. On the other side of it, she let herself down slowly on a stool, then set her head inside the arch made by her hands. She turned her body slightly so that while Justine and I could still hear her, she was no longer facing us.

"He was seeing a new psychiatrist," she murmured, almost as if we weren't even there; as if she were reciting her reasons to herself. We could hardly hear her. "That guy whose name started with a Z. Your father thought he was good. That morning, I told Tom he should call him—the shrink. He said he would."

"Well, he didn't." My mother and Justine looked at me in surprise. "I talked to him, too," I told them. "Today. I went to see him."

"Hm." My mother had many sounds to convey doubt, and she made one of them now. "That's what he *says*."

"I believed him." I reached over to pick up one of my mother's cigarettes. It was just something for my hand to do; I didn't light it. "He's a jerk, but I believe what he said."

"Liars," my mother said, but it wasn't clear whether she was referring to the psychiatrist or other, anonymous people she suspected of God knew what.

"What I don't get," Justine said, looking at the floor, "and Mom, don't be mad, okay?" I could tell she was nervous. "But is it true that Meggy called you that night?"

After a long moment, our mother whispered, "Yes." She held smoke in her lungs until we could see that it burned, and exhaling she added, "I told her to go to bed, things would look different in the morning." She spoke quietly and reached for a tissue, both hands pressed against her mouth.

"But how could you take that chance?" Justine's skin had begun to mottle around her throat. "If she called and said she was scared of him, why didn't you do something? Come and get her? Or at least call Ana and me?" She could not look at my mother as she asked the questions. Each of the three of us faced a different wall.

Our mother was silent for a moment. Then she whispered, "I didn't think he would have the guts."

"Guts!" My voice rang shrill through the room around us. "Guts!" We heard movement on the other side of the duplex, and a moment later Deirdre's mother appeared at our door, clutching a robe around her middle, stepping a slipper inside.

"Please," she said. Her voice was apologetic but forceful. "The baby's trying to sleep."

The next day, as soon as my mother had left for work, I moved out. I reserved a room at the Fountain Motel, in the next town over, and packed my suitcase while Justine begged me not to leave.

"Come with me, then," I said.

"I can't."

"Well, I can't stay here with her."

The night before, my mother had tried to hug Justine and me before we went to bed. Justine let her, but I moved away. "Don't do this to me, Ana," my mother said. "Honey, please."

"Don't do this to *you*?"

She had refused to carry our discussion any further after Deirdre's mother interrupted to ask us to stop the noise. "There's really no point," my mother said to us, "in talking it to death." Her own word choice seemed to startle her, but she didn't miss a beat. "It's over. They're gone. There isn't a thing we can do."

"Mom," I said, "we're talking about Meggy. And Daddy." I hadn't used the word *Daddy* since I was nine or ten, but now it filled my mouth and heart with an old, deep comfort that had been waiting to be called.

"I *know* that," my mother said. For a moment her face flickered, and I thought with relief that she was going to break down. But then she pressed her lips together and told us she was going to bed.

"Don't worry." Justine murmured so our mother wouldn't hear. "She's just upset."

"Fuck her," I said, loudly, and Justine turned up the volume with the remote.

I stayed at the motel for a week, going out only to my job at the law office. When I went back to my mother's house to tell her I was moving to Boston and to say good-bye, she asked if I would consider putting it off until after Thanksgiving.

"There's something I have to tell you both," she said. Beside me I felt my sister's shoulders rise. "Paul and I are getting married," our mother went on, not looking at either of us.

"*Married!*" Justine blasted out a laugh. She had just finished eating three miniature Mounds bars, and chocolate sprayed from her teeth. "What the hell are you *saying*?"

"You can't get married, Mom," I told her, feeling my chest grow cold. "For Christ's sake. It hasn't even been six months."

"I know how long it's been, Ana." She shook out a cigarette. "Don't you think I know?"

"Then what are you saying?" Justine asked again.

Our mother closed her eyes before she answered. She seemed to be searching for something to say. "The two of you have each other," she told us. "I need him."

She asked our grandparents if she and Paul could have the wedding at their house. My grandmother was ready to say yes, but my grandfather hesitated, and when it came right down to it, he said he'd feel more comfortable helping to host it at the Hyperion Club. Why, my mother asked. My grandfather answered, How long have you known this man? It doesn't look very good, coming so soon after it all.

My mother said, I feel like it's been forever.

Well, my grandfather told her, I guess it's also because of—Tom. I feel a certain loyalty.

You never had that when he was alive.

I know. And I regret that now.

But Dad, my mother said, he killed Meggy.

I know, my grandfather answered. Believe me, I know. I'm not saying it's what I should feel. But I can't help it. I do.

So they reserved one of the smaller rooms at the Hyperion Club and sent out invitations—handwritten by my mother on floral stationery cards—for the Saturday after Thanksgiving. Our grandfather enlisted the Reverend William Corson, from Albany Presbyterian, to officiate. He was the same minister who performed my parents' marriage; who baptized both of my sisters and me; and who conducted the joint funeral service. He was nearing eighty by the time of the deaths, and he wore hearing aids behind both ears. Occasionally, if he spoke before a microphone, the aids started whining with electricity. I had seen Mr. Corson actually cry from the pain.

Of course, I don't remember my own baptism, or Justine's either. But Meggy's is still clear to me, both in image and resonance. Mr. Corson called our whole family forward in front of the congregation and took the baby in his arms. It was the first Sunday in December, and a single Advent candle flickered behind us at the altar. High in the ceiling, above the pulpit, was the round stained-glass window that always mesmerized me whenever I walked into the church. From the time I was old enough to discern it from the pew, I had fantasies of being married in this church someday, walking down the aisle toward its starburst of color and light.

I never imagined a funeral.

For her baptism, Meggy wore the antique christening robe that went back to Great-Grandmother Ott. Justine and I had on matching dresses, which our grandmother made for us: I remember that they were red and green, in the spirit of Christmas, and we wore red velvet ribbons in our hair. Justine's ribbon looked properly beautiful in her long curls, but my hair wasn't long enough for the ribbon to stay in place, and it kept sliding around on my head until my mother finally reached over and pulled it down so I could wear it like a necklace.

My parents linked arms next to each other, with my mother's parents behind them, and Justine and I stood in front as Meggy squirmed in her lace blanket against the minister's black robe. Mr. Corson asked us, "Do you, in receiving this child, promise with God's help to be her sponsor, to the end that she may confess Christ as her Lord and Savior, and come at last to His eternal Kingdom?" Behind me I heard my parents murmur, "We do," and I added, with extra fervor to make up for my tardiness— "we do," so that my six-year-old voice rang through the sanctuary and made everybody laugh. (It seems to me that I remember this moment— the big room, my family in front of an audience—but of course it's possible that the details have just been filled in so many times, through the family telling of it, that I only think I remember.)

With the hand not holding my baby sister, Mr. Corson patted the top of my head, smiled out at the congregation, and said, "Now that's the kind of faith God's looking for." A little confused, I reached up to rub Meggy's bootied foot with my fingers, and when I heard sniffled tears I was astonished to see that they came from my father. It was the first time I had ever seen him cry. My mother handed him a tissue from her dress pocket and said, "Ssh, ssh," the way she often did to the baby.

Mr. Corson raised Meggy above his head and asked members of the congregation if they would also receive this child. "We will" came the murmur back, echoing against the shiny glass, and—this I know I remember—I felt the power and strength embracing my family as we faced our friends and other people who wished us well. Even as I watched my father flinch to see his baby being sprinkled with water from a communal font, I believed I understood what God was, and it was a moment of perfect peace.

I remember when I learned the phrase "perfect peace," and who it came from. One day when I was in the ninth grade, we had a substitute for English. Everybody was relieved because we were supposed to have started *Great Expectations,* and nobody had done the homework except me and Delia Leonard. I'd read the first two chapters, as Mrs. Berg had assigned us, but I didn't have the sense or patience to care for Dickens yet and if Mrs. Berg had been there, Delia and I would have had to do most of the talking; that was the punishment for being prepared.

So we were all intrigued and shy and on the cusp of obnoxious when we came to the classroom that day and found a new substitute waiting for us behind Mrs. Berg's desk. Usually, we got Mrs. Crummey, whose name and high hair cracked everybody up. But this was somebody new, a man who'd written his name in big capital letters on the blackboard: Mr. Martino. He was dark and thin, with a bald head and mustache. He wore a pale pink oxford shirt, which had sweat stains under the armpits, and a red tie. I heard John Shea whisper "Fag-a-lina," as we sat down, and a couple of kids snickered.

Mr. Martino let us settle in before he said anything. Then he told us to take out a pen and a piece of paper. His voice made him sound even more effeminate than he looked, and behind me the same people did not even try to contain how funny they found him. Mr. Martino ignored the laughter; he seemed to have expected it. "I want you to write an in-class essay," he said, "on the following." He picked up a piece of chalk and blew across the top of it.

"Blow me," John Shea whispered, and this reached everybody, including Mr. Martino; I could tell by the way his ears wriggled as if they were wincing and turned red at the tips. But again he ignored what he'd heard, and as he turned to the blackboard, we could see sweat wrinkled in the back of his shirt. *The best thing that ever happened to me,* he wrote, and he looked at it for a few moments before turning around to face us again.

"Twenty minutes," he said. "I suggest you write like hell, and in the last half hour of class, you'll read them aloud."

Around me, I could feel everyone else freezing in their seats, the same way I was. We had all been impressed by the fact that he had said *hell*. Then, across the aisle, Ginger Cox scribbled something, put her pen down, took out a bottle of nail polish, and began touching up her manicure. I lifted myself from my seat far enough to make out what she'd written for her essay: "I was born." Mr. Martino came down the row and read over Ginger's shoulder. "Let me clarify," he said. "What I'm looking for is a memory, something you were a part of that makes you happy to look back on, that made you glad to be alive." This time only John Shea made a snickering sound; the rest of us were trying to figure out what to think.

"I'll give you an example." Mr. Martino pushed aside Mrs. Berg's stack of folders and sat on the teacher's desk, facing us. "I'll tell you what mine would be. When I was twelve, my family took a trip to the Grand Canyon. We camped out one night because everybody said it was so beautiful. But the whole time we were there it rained. The tent leaked, and my parents were fighting, and my little brother got sick and started coughing and couldn't stop." He had all out attention now, even John Shea's. A grown-up who would talk about his own parents fighting had something to say to us.

"It was late, after midnight, maybe two in the morning. I couldn't stand it anymore." Mr. Martino's tasseled fag-a-lina loafers swung against the desk as he spoke. "The noise was driving me crazy—my brother coughing, my parents sniping at each other." (In the margin of my notebook, I wrote down *snipe*, to look up later.) "So I went outside, and they didn't even notice. It was pouring, I mean like buckets of water on your head, but it drowned out all the sounds from the tent. I couldn't hear any of them anymore. I found a rock not very far away from where we had camped, and I sat on it and let the rain come down on me. I pretended I was a frog, or something in nature that *liked* to be wet. It was a hot night, and even though I was soaking, I didn't feel any chill. I turned my face up to the rain, and after a while I started laughing. The weird thing was, though, that I couldn't *hear* myself laughing—I could only feel it. I don't know whether it was because of the rain, or the wind, or what. It was the oddest thing." Mr. Martino paused, and looked as if he were seeing that night again, right there in front of him, instead of all of us in Mrs. Berg's ninth-grade classroom in Ashmont, New York.

"*You're* the oddest thing," John Shea muttered, but by now the class had been converted to Mr. Martino's side because we sensed that he was describing something important, inviting us into a private room to which other adults never opened the door.

"At that moment, I was completely happy," Mr. Martino told us, and we could tell by his face it was true: remembering the moment was almost as good as having it happen the first time. "It was like nothing could touch me, or make me unhappy, or—this was probably the biggest part—make me afraid. I think human beings spend their lives being afraid, most of the time." Nobody in the classroom was moving. We were all looking straight ahead at him, waiting to understand, but also understanding at the same time.

"Then it was over," Mr. Martino went on, "and I was just sitting there on a rock in the rain, shivering. I wanted to get that feeling of perfect peace back again, but it was gone. It started going as soon as I realized how good it was." He turned again to the blackboard and picked up the chalk. I think he wanted to be alone with that part of the memory. "T.S. Eliot wrote about those moments—that kind of fleeting illumination— in a poem called 'Burnt Norton,'" he said. "I mean, I don't know if that's what he meant to be writing about, but that's what it always means to me, every time I read it." His voice cracked on the word *poem*, and a couple of kids laughed, because the air had gotten too heavy. Mr. Martino wrote:

> Dry the pool, dry concrete, brown edged,
> And the pool was filled with water out of sunlight,
> And the lotos rose, quietly, quietly,
> The surface glittered out of heart of light,
> And they were behind us, reflected in the pool.
> Then a cloud passed, and the pool was empty.

He put the chalk down and turned to us. "Write about that moment," he said. "You've all had them. Try to get it back again and put it
on the page." Then he pulled the chair out behind Mrs. Berg's desk and
rearranged the papers he had messed up by sitting on top of it.

I heard John Shea say, "Yeah, right," but when I turned my head to
look from the side of my eye, he was staring at the piece of paper in
front of him. He took a quick glance around to see if anyone was watching, and then he began to scribble. The fact that John Shea seemed to be
doing the assignment made everybody sit up a little straighter and bend
forward over their desks. John Shea doing the assignment meant something serious was going on. I began to panic, because although I recognized the sensation Mr. Martino had just described to us, I couldn't attach
it to any specific experience of my own. I closed my eyes, and tried to
squeeze a memory into my head. I opened them and read, "the pool was
filled with water out of sunlight, / and the lotos rose, quietly, quietly, /
The surface glittered out of heart of light." Then I had it.

Christmas Day, the year I turned ten. We always celebrated at my
grandparents' house, and it started to snow in the morning. By the
middle of the afternoon, after dinner, enough fresh powder had fallen
on the field behind the house for my grandfather to pull the old toboggan out of the shed and announce that it was time to christen winter
with the season's first ride down Hangman's Hill.

"Too dangerous," our father said. He was already nervous because
the radio was warning people to stay off the roads, and he believed we
needed to start for home. When he felt my grandfather giving him a
look, he added, "I mean, people have accidents on those things. Look at
Ethan Frome and his girlfriend, whatever-her-name-was." He was trying to make a joke, but I didn't get it until eight years later, when I read
Edith Wharton's novel in Freshman Lit.

"There won't be any accidents," Grandma Ott said. "The point is to
have fun. Are you going to keep them away from everything that might
ever hurt them, Tom? You may as well build a bomb shelter in your
backyard."

"Well, I'll go with them, then." My father picked his gloves up from the radiator, where he had set them to dry.

"I'll go, too," my grandfather said. Justine and I looked at each other. We sensed in the men's tones something more than the mere desire to have a good time, and we weren't sure we wanted to go out and play anymore.

"Let's all go," our grandmother said, suddenly seeming to have a fresh burst of energy. She was already untying her apron and reaching to turn off the stove. "Come on, Margaret. The fresh air will do us good."

"What are you talking about?" My father was holding Meggy on his lap. "What about the baby?"

"Bundle her up," our grandfather said. "Besides, she's not a baby anymore, Tom. You'd better wise up to that."

"Margaret," my father said, pleading with that one word for my mother to do something. But my mother went over to take Meggy from him and started packing her into her snowsuit.

"Look how much padding there is," she told my father. "She'll be fine."

"You people are all crazy." But my father seemed to realize it wouldn't do any good for him to object. We all put on boots and jackets, mittens and hats, laughing at how we looked—Grandma wore a stocking cap she'd knitted herself, in the Mets' colors, and she wrapped the tail around her neck—and trooped outside to the toboggan, where my mother sat on it holding Meggy while we all took up the rope and pulled her across the ground.

It was one of those crystal winter days, the air cold but sunny so that you squinted up at the light even as the frozen hairs crackled inside your nose. Outside, our grandparents looked like whole different people. You wouldn't have guessed they were old from the way they looked—all bundled up and laughing, leading the way across Wildwood Lane.

The adults had come on the sledding trip to protect us children, as much from one another's influences as from the momentum down the hill. My grandfather worried that my father would make us afraid of too many things, so he came along to remind us we were having a good time. Our father came to make sure Meggy wouldn't die from exposure or a crash. Grandma probably wanted to save us from any argument the two men might have, and our mother, besides not wanting to be left in the house alone, no doubt felt like the fulcrum at the center of this family; without her, somebody might fall off.

But within a few yards of leaving the house behind, all these invisible reasons disappeared, and we were seven people on our way to the top of a hill on a December day and anticipating the rush of flying, for a few moments, faster than the things we were afraid of. There were three other people at Hangman's Hill when we arrived, a father and his two boys. But all they had were saucers and those plastic mats that kept turning sideways a few feet into their run. They hadn't even been able to pack a very good path down the hill, so my grandfather pulled the toboggan over to a fresh patch of snow and said to us, loud enough that the father and the boys might have heard him, "Let's show 'em how it's done."

Or maybe it was just the look of our toboggan—its obvious experience and history, the sleek and powerful design—that made them stop to watch us as we prepared for our descent. "Meggy stays with her mother," our grandfather said, motioning for our mother to stay where she was, in the center of the seat. "Grace, you get behind Margaret, and the girls get in front of her. That's it. Now, Tom, you get on behind Grace."

"Carl," my grandmother said, even as she was obeying his instructions, "you can't possibly be thinking of us all going down at once?"

"Why the hell not? Just because we believe in God doesn't mean we can't have a good time!" My grandfather never swore, and his suddenly raucous mood made Justine and me, and even our mother, laugh. "Hold on, everybody!" he shouted, and the next thing we knew, he had given the toboggan a push before jumping into the last space on the cushion, sending us on our way. I heard my father say, "Oh, my God," and I knew he would be clutching my mother and Meggy, holding them as close as he could as we hurtled down. I felt myself laughing and gasping as we closed our eyes and let the wind carry us toward the bottom. I felt lighter than I ever had, and it was okay to scream because the grown-ups were doing it, but screaming in a good way as we pressed into one another and the toboggan slithered and leaned.

When we finally stopped because the ground leveled out, I felt the toboggan tip over at a slow speed, trapping us all underneath. I expected Meggy to cry, but instead I saw that she was staring straight ahead, sideways, still tight in my mother's arms. I saw her smile. The wood made a cover over our heads, blocking the sun, but around us we saw the bright snow, and we were warm lying on it, heated by nestled bodies and the exhilaration of the trip down.

Everything was completely still, the only sounds our hard breathing and, in the distance, the call of a single bird. I sensed all seven of our hearts beating in the same row. I closed my eyes thinking that this would make the sensation stronger, but instead it made me feel alone. I opened my eyes and saw my grandfather's hand flung over my father's shoulder, his other arm under my mother's back. On the other side of me, strands of Justine's brown hair and my grandmother's gray were packed with each other into the snow.

But after a few seconds we all began shifting, untangling our limbs and pulling away into separate spaces, claiming again what was ours. My father took Meggy from my mother to convince himself that the baby was all right. My grandfather righted the toboggan and began pulling it up the hill, but we all knew we wouldn't be going down again. Grandma touched my father's shoulder, and I saw him look up at the tender pressure, but then she changed it into a gesture of brushing snow from his sleeve.

At Meggy's baptism, Mr. Corson's voice had been strong and sure as he declared, "Whoso receiveth one such little child in my name, receiveth me." But nearly sixteen years later, conducting the funeral, he faltered over the words from Ecclesiastes, and by accident he repeated the line, "Better is the end of a thing than its beginning." This time it was me who tried to bite back tears with the tissue my mother offered.

On the day of my mother and Paul's wedding, Mr. Corson looked nothing like the vigorous man of faith who had lifted the infant Meggy above his head to present her for a blessing. He had grown hunched with age, and I couldn't tell whether he recognized Justine and me, even after our mother reminded him who we were. The guests gathered among the chairs set up in modest rows at the front of the reception room, where the ceremony would take place. Altogether there were about twenty-five people, including my grandparents, who sat in the front row; most of the others were coworkers of my mother's and Paul's from the newspaper. Deirdre, the child from next door, was carried in by her mother at the last minute, and they took seats in the rear. No one from Ashmont had been invited. When the guests filed in they were handed computer-generated programs, on the cover of which was a rose.

The Hyperion Club provided an organ, and shortly before two o'clock a woman with crooked hair and a corsage pinned to her chest sat at the bench and began playing Bach. When it was time for my mother to walk down the "aisle," Justine and I preceded her, clutching bouquets of lilies and baby's breath. Paul had combed his hair into two wet sheets at the side of his head. His brown suit didn't fit right, but at least he looked like himself. Our mother moved toward her new husband by herself—no one would give her away—and joined him at the makeshift altar, where Paul reached to take her hand. I had to look down and take a breath to compose myself as Mr. Corson stepped forward and the ceremony began.

"We are gathered here today to join in the celebration of matrimony between Margaret Ott and Paul Richter," the minister said, referring to notes he had scribbled on an index card. Justine and I looked at each other. We had not been told that our mother would use her maiden name, rather than the one we shared with her, in these vows. "Let us pray."

I stole a look around the room and was surprised to see so many heads bowed. "Heavenly Father, we ask that you look down on us today in a spirit of welcome and thanksgiving," Mr. Corson said, and I felt reassured to hear in his voice some of the reverent authority I remembered. "Be with us as we ask for Your guidance in sanctifying the marriage of Margaret and Paul, keeping in mind Your teachings of infinite love and the almighty power of forgiveness." When he said "forgiveness," my mother looked up in surprise, but the minister didn't seem to notice. "What God has joined, let no one put asunder." Through his prayer, we heard the noise of dishes clattering in the kitchen next door as the chefs prepared the buffet. Something heavy fell to the floor, and a few of the waitresses standing by the door covered laughter with their hands.

The ceremony was short and my knees shook all the way through it. At one point, I felt Justine reach out to steady me. My mother and Paul pledged their promises to each other, leaving out until death do us part. Next came the benediction. "The peace that passes all understanding," Mr. Corson pronounced. I waited for him to explain what this meant, until I realized he couldn't, and, further, that this was the point. Then my mother and Paul kissed each other to the sound of uncertain applause.

8. All our best love

Q. Why can't you tickle yourself?
— B.R., Esperance

A. No one knows the answer for sure, but neuro-anatomist Richard N. Grote speculates that your brain sends out inhibitory messages when you tickle yourself, and that these supersede the messages sent from the nerve endings in—for example—your belly or the soles of your feet. Grote says that the sensations of itch, tickle, and pain are probably linked. The brain can send messages to the spinal cord to modulate pain transmissions, which can inhibit how painful you perceive a given stimulus to be. (This is the way narcotics work.) The same may be true of a tickle.

If you move your hand in space, many receptors in your skin are activated, but you don't feel much sensation unless the hand touches something. Similarly, Dr. Grote says, if your brain knows you're trying to tickle yourself, it can send an inhibitory signal to the spinal cord that will block neurons in the tickled area from responding.

"Basically," Dr. Grote concludes, "whether or not you feel the tickle may depend on whether or not you see it coming."

After five months of not bleeding, I got my period back during my mother's wedding reception (I had to leave the Hyperion Club to find a drugstore) and Justine's returned shortly after New Year's. My mother and Paul spent their honeymoon in Florida and ended up buying a house in Madeira Beach, where they've lived ever since. Paul opened a little shop in a strip mall, where he takes passport photos and develops one-hour film. My mother got her real estate license and has done very well. She wanted everything to change when she moved south, she told us, including her career. She had her pick of agencies, based on tryouts, and she chose Century 21. Every time somebody buys a house from her, she brings them a Tiffany key ring as a housewarming gift.

For months after the wedding, Justine remained in the condo in Delphi, until it was clear that our mother wasn't going to come back. Our mother sold her unit to Deirdre's parents, who moved Deirdre's grandmother into my mother's side. Justine came to live in Boston with me and Ruthie for a while, but the way she ate made Ruthie nervous— little Clark bars, Mallomars hidden all over the house—and Justine realized this and left before I had to say anything. She drove around the country for a while, sending me postcards and leaving phone messages on my machine (she seemed to call when she knew she wouldn't get me in person). She settled in Tucson, where she did the opposite of what, in all the jokes, a woman is expected to do: she got married and then lost the weight. Not all of it, but she'd been too thin to begin with, so she ended up just about right.

To keep herself in shape she runs every day, no matter what the weather or how she feels. In this way she reminds me of our father. His compulsion—the thing that ultimately killed Meggy and him—shows up in both my sister and me from time to time, but it doesn't scare me the way it did at first, as on the day we set out to visit the graves, when I couldn't let the car move without checking to make sure Deirdre wasn't underneath. Although it may sound strange, when I sense my father in one of my own behaviors (for example, *if I skip every other step on the stairway, it will be a good day*), I find it an odd comfort, like an unexpected but familiar hand on my shoulder, an old friend waving from the bus. It's as if he's still around somehow, as if we didn't lose all of him when he died.

The last time I visited Justine in Arizona and she went out for her regular six-point-two-mile run during a thunderstorm, I asked her if she remembered the day they called us from the YMCA because our father wouldn't get out of the pool at closing time. He told them he'd only swum fifty-four laps and couldn't stop until he reached one hundred. My mother went down to try to talk him out, but even when the lifeguard tried to drag him physically from the water, my father pulled away, and with his legs pushed himself mightily off the wall. Later, he told us that if he hadn't swum exactly one hundred laps, something bad would have happened. We didn't ask him what. The lifeguard let him finish, but they revoked his membership after that.

Justine said she didn't remember this story. Only half-teasing, she accused me of making it up.

Her husband is a psychiatrist, and because of my old resentments toward his profession, I had a chip on my shoulder the first time I met him. But it fell off as soon as I saw the way he kept looking at my sister: with gratitude, as if she were a gift he never dared ask for and couldn't believe he'd received. They have two sons, Jake and Robbie, and are expecting a daughter (Justine will finally get to use all the baby clothes we rescued, including the christening dress). I see them about three times a year.

Now that there are new children in the family, we all come together occasionally. When it was just grown-ups, it didn't work. Justine and I could talk to each other, and she and my mother were in touch.

But I didn't see my mother and Paul for two years after the first time we tried to have a family Christmas in Florida, which was a disaster. Nobody had anything to say to one another; or there was too much to say, but nobody dared. After that, we just sent cards (always the so-called humorous kind) and talked on the phone some Sundays. There was a tacit acknowledgment that this was the easiest way.

But Jake and Robbie changed things. They give us something to focus on, beyond what we have suffered together in the past. Instead of screaming at one another, we change diapers. Instead of asking questions nobody can answer, we read aloud from *Green Eggs and Ham*.

Distractions, yes. But that's what life comes down to, I'm beginning to understand.

The boys know one grandfather and aren't old enough to ask about the other one yet, and Justine says she's not sure what she will tell them when they do. In the meantime, we take pictures and put them in albums dating back only as far as the day of Jake's birth. My nephews call me Ana Banana. I send them each a new book every month, and I look forward to their being old enough to read *Alice*.

For a while after we moved from Ashmont, I kept a subscription to the *Star* because I liked following the news of people I knew. Two years after my father and Meggy died, an item under Unions announced the marriage of Heather Shufelt—whom I had once smacked in the ear with an errant cross-fire ball—to Officer Frank Garhart of the Ashmont Police Department. I stared at the announcement for a long time. For a moment I considered cutting it out, but instead I picked up the phone to call the *Star* and cancel my subscription.

My grandfather died a few years ago, of a heart attack, and my grandmother moved into a place that advertised "assisted living." When I helped her move in, I smiled at the sign and said I wouldn't mind some assistance with living, but she was beyond getting the joke.

If anyone had told me in high school that I would end up becoming a scientist, I would have said they'd been reading the wrong report card, not to mention the wrong heart. I had never paid much attention, or energy, to science and math. It was literature I loved—from the first book I ever memorized and feigned reading aloud to my kindergarten class, a long verse about manners called *The Goops* ("The Goops they lick their fingers, the Goops they lick their knives; they spill their broth on the tablecloth—oh, they lead disgusting lives!"), and later, *Jane Eyre* and *Tess of the D'Urbervilles* (which was my favorite because it was so delicious to know Tess's secret, and wait for it finally to come out), I would have said I preferred spending my time with made-up people in pages than with just about any live human being I knew.

When I started college, I planned a double major in literature and psychology. It almost seemed wrong to me that they were separate disciplines, because there was so much of each in the other. That was before I learned more about the distinction between the mind as the seat of the soul, and the brain as an organ. In my second year I decided to focus only on psychology, because—oddly enough—of the professor who hadn't let me use my anecdotal research, on people's earliest memories, for a term paper. Although I thought she was being unfair at the time, I began to understand that she was trying to make me understand the beauty of psychology as a science. And she did. In my junior year, I worked as a lab aide for an assistant professor who was convinced that memory could be transferred from one animal to another. He was trying to reproduce experiments from the 1970s in which researchers trained one set of rats to avoid dark spaces, then injected a peptide (scotophobin, from the Greek for "fear of the dark") from those rats into an untrained set of rats. Supposedly, the untrained set would become afraid of the dark strictly by virtue of the injection, thereby proving that memory had been transferred between brains.

It turned out that this particular professor was a cokehead—he ended up having to abandon the experiments, and losing his job, when they found him stealing cocaine from another researcher, who was testing its effects on monkeys. And the scotophobin theory had pretty much been debunked twenty years earlier, so nobody picked up where my boss left off.

But I was hooked. If it was possible to see the process of memory taking place in a sea snail's nervous system preserved in a petri dish, didn't this suggest that there might be more secrets of the human mind to be uncovered, if we studied long enough and hard?

My first exposure to the vagaries of memory came from the story of the Russian Anastasia, and the idea that a person could forget, entirely, the foundations of her life. I remember watching the old Ingrid Bergman movie, *Anastasia*, with my father on a Saturday afternoon, the winter I was twelve. I was supposed to have a piano lesson, but my father convinced my mother to cancel it so that I could watch the movie with him. We sat on the couch together and ate graham crackers as we watched Yul Brynner trying to persuade Helen Hayes, as the Empress, that Ingrid Bergman was really a member of the imperial family. My favorite part was when the Empress finally believed that the woman presented to her was her long-lost granddaughter—she flung her arms around Ingrid Bergman and welcomed her back to the family. At the end of their emotional embrace, the Empress whispered, "And if it should not be you, don't ever tell me."

"God," my father said, suspending a quarter of graham cracker in front of his mouth. He ate them that way, split along the cracker-folds, to avoid spilling crumbs.

"What does she mean?" I said. "'Don't ever tell me'?"

"She means, if Ingrid Bergman is lying to her, she doesn't want to know." My father put his cracker down instead of eating it, and this seemed to me a gesture of deference to what had just happened on the screen.

I put my cracker down, too. "You mean, she doesn't want to find out the truth?"

"Not if the truth is what she doesn't want to believe." My father put his hand on the back of my neck and squeezed. It was a touch he saved only for me. "Not if it's too painful."

Aristotle believed that memory was located in the heart. He said the brain was too cold, too bloodless, to nurture emotion and thought.

But in the past ten years I've taken tremendous solace from studying the brain's functions connected to memory. Sometimes, when it seems that my feelings might overwhelm me, I close my eyes and picture what an emotion actually looks like: an intricate confluence of cells and chemicals, proteins dancing in a round. In the year after my father and Meggy died, I found a peculiar comfort in the embrace of science and its hardedged, solid-sounding words—*hippocampus, anterograde, fugue.*

In January, six months after the deaths, I took the entrance exams and applied to graduate-school programs in experimental psychology. I always stress "experimental"—the scientific branch—because if I just say psychology, people assume I'm a therapist. At parties they start asking me questions about their own therapies—how the shrink won't say whether he's married or not, or if he has any kids, and do I think it's fair of him to withhold such basic information, when he expects the client to spill her guts?

Or, if it isn't therapy they want to talk about, it's dreams. *What do you think it means,* my landlady asked me, when she saw "psychologist" under Occupation on my rental agreement form, *that I keep having dreams about cows with no faces? Over and over, the same dream every night. Well, one time one of them had a face, it was my ex-husband. But usually there's nothing—just this big, blank white space where the eyes are supposed to be.* It was after this encounter that I began saying I studied the way the brain works, whenever somebody asked.

Although I knew I had scored well, I believed when the acceptances came that I had been let in because the admissions people felt sorry for me. I felt guilty about having used Meggy—my loss of her, and our father's obsessions—in the essay I submitted with my applications. What else could I write about?—they asked, *What made you interested in the study of the mind?*—but I was aware, as I wrote it, that mine was a story that would get noticed.

So I pictured the review process for graduate school this way: the committee members sat around a table and examined files, and when mine came up they murmured, "Oh, yes, the murder-suicide," and out of pity and benevolence, they let me in.

In my essay, I wrote that along with the feelings you are forced to endure when something changes forever the good world you have known, there is a little bonus thrown into the bargain by God. It's not worth a fraction of how much it all hurts, but at least it's something—the expression you see in somebody's eyes when you tell them your whole story or a piece of it, and what is reflected back to you is the small comfort of the truth they understand then, that you are set apart by your suffering. That feeling is something you come to expect and depend upon. And, yes, to *use*, when you need it, when the words—*my sister's dead, our father killed her*—are not enough to hold onto, they are a fact floating through the gray water of your day, sinking like soap to the one place you will never reach.

Ruthie and I were roommates for three years, until to her surprise she fell in love not with John F. Kennedy Jr. but with the woman in the next cubicle at work, and they moved to San Francisco. Since then I've lived alone, except for Bill Buckner, who is nearly thirteen years old. He and I stayed on another year in the place Ruthie and I had shared, and then, when the rent got too high, I found an apartment in a house outside the city, near the Cambridge town line.

I earned my doctorate at the university five years ago, and now I have a junior appointment here. I teach a seminar on the science of memory, and spend a lot of time on research. Usually my partner, or *co-investigator* as it says on the grants, is my colleague Ben Sokol, who went through the graduate program a year ahead of me.

Although he's never told me directly, I know Ben hopes one day to discover evil. A compartment in the brain like the ones for art or calculations; he believes it can be located and identified, crouched behind sympathy or lust. His grandmother was at Auschwitz, one of the dozens of child twins allowed by Josef Mengele to survive so that Mengele could try out different things on duplicate gene sets, surgeries and injections and other experiments as they suited his Nazi whims. Ben's grandmother came out from the liberation with a tendency to faint, from the transfusions. Her twin sister grew a beard for the rest of her life.

Although he tries to hide it, I can tell that Ben is nervous about himself, how the effects of those dark tests near the chambers might have seeped into his blood. It's why he eats so carefully; why he avoids the rat labs and wears earmuffs into spring. He carries a pocket mirror in his backpack, along with his books, and a couple of times I've caught him peering close at some new blemish when he thought nobody could see. He reminds me of my father in his cautious, thoughtful ways. When I met Ben, I thought there might be something more between him and me than friendship, but then he started dating a postdoc in the biology department, a woman named Helen who doesn't look anything like what you'd expect of an expert in the sex life ("reproductive behavior," on the grant applications) of tobacco horn worms. They got married within a year, and this made sense to me. I didn't really expect Ben, or anyone else for that matter, to love me the way people believe they can be loved. I don't know whether this comes from my father's suicide and his murder of Meggy—from the conviction that if he had really loved us, he couldn't have done what he did—or from finding out that you can't, after all, trust what you thought you could.

I go on dates sometimes, and I sleep with some of the men to make myself feel normal. But after the third or fourth time with the same person, I find some reason not to see him again. It's too frightening, that feeling of losing control. I'd rather be lonely than scared. I guess I believe that someday the balance will tip in the other direction, and I'll try therapy again.

Or I won't; maybe I'll just keep busy until everything's too late. It's odd how our brains are constructed—isn't it?—giving us flashes of truth and then, thank God, allowing us to forget what we've seen in that split second the window was open. All I know is that right now, even after so much time has passed, there are days when it's all I can do to look at the photographs on my dresser without falling back into bed.

And yet there are moments—hearing one of my nephew's voices on the phone, for instance, or feeling sun on my face through the trees— when I know it is possible not just to survive, but to live. I don't remember this all the time, but I remember it often enough, and if it isn't precisely hope I feel, it's a close enough cousin.

Ben and Helen are my best friends in Boston, and their daughter Catherine is my godchild. She's five now, and I spend a lot of time— weekends, holidays—with their family. Catherine has fine black hair that has never been cut, and she likes me to braid it. When I do, I close my eyes and think about Meggy. I imagine myself brushing long, soft hand-fuls away from my sister's forehead, gathering it into bunches, and weaving it into braids. There is an over-and-under rhythm to braiding which the fingers, once fluent in it, never forget.

Sometimes when I open my eyes it gives me a start to see my hands twining through Catherine's hair, because I could have sworn it was Meggy's. I love my little sister as much as I ever did when she was alive, but her presence is fainter to me now; it makes me sick to admit it, but she's grown more distant, she floats farther from my shore. I have not seen her or hugged her or touched her in more than twelve years. She would be twenty-seven now; when she was little she used to say she wanted to be a nurse or a cowboy when she grew up, but I can't imagine her as an adult. Of course, I remember what she looked like—I almost slipped, just then, and said what she *looks* like—but those visions go in and out of focus, over time.

Ben and I have made a name for ourselves, at least as young re-searchers go, in the memory-disorder field. A year or so ago, we pub-lished a paper about a forty-seven-year-old man whose wife had come home from grocery shopping one Saturday to find him twitching and unconscious on the kitchen floor. In our study we call him Pete, though that isn't his real name. When Pete woke up in the hospital, he thought he was twenty-three, and he didn't remember a thing about the intervening years; he thought he had a baby, when his son was ac-tually twenty-five, and of his sixteen-year-old daughter he knew noth-ing at all.

The doctors couldn't find any neurological damage or injury to the brain. In the course of our research, we conducted interviews with just about everyone in Pete's life, and found out that just before the onset of his amnesia, he'd learned that people at work were beginning to be sus-picious about the qualifications he'd listed on his resume—which he had, in fact, been fabricating since he graduated from college and began his career. Based on the interviews, and the tests we did on Pete, we made a pretty good case for the hypothesis that his amnesia was due at least in part to his unconscious having taken over and—by erasing his memory for the years he had been, essentially, a fraud—saving him from having to face this discovery.

Pete's case has been a godsend for Ben and me, the perfect experimental subject just when we needed one. It would have been impossible to write our paper based on theory alone. A lot of people in our field reject psychogenic theories about amnesia out-of-hand; they insist on physical sources, even of psychic pain.

It always amazes me when I hear this, because it makes perfect sense to me that there could be something so intolerable that the mind, in its infinite complexity and with every beneficent impulse toward its host, would take care of the problem by simply eliminating what refuses to be borne. It can't be chosen, but (Ben and I believe) some of us have the capacity to lose track of the thoughts and memories that make life—as we would experience it, otherwise—impossible. My father didn't have this gift, but I think my mother does. Of course, there's a trade-off, which wouldn't be worth it to most of us; in Pete's case, if he's telling us the truth, he's had to give up most of his conscious history as an adult. We still haven't determined why, but we're working on it.

And, of course, we have our doubts. As much as we believe our own theory, it just doesn't make gut sense that a person could lose, or put away somewhere inaccessible, the majority of his life. We're like kids in nursery school who have been informed of the death of a classmate's mother. We know it must be true because adults are crying, but our hearts aren't stretched enough, yet, to allow a loss so large. We look at our friend and know it is some trick we will understand later; that it didn't really happen, because no one could still be breathing whose mother wasn't, too.

Then we learn about survival, how breath and life go on. We learn how people manage, even if it means giving up what they have come to count on, like sanity and love.

I'm not sure how much my mother sacrificed for her peace of mind, if she has any. All I know is that what she surrendered did not belong only to her.

We test Pete at three-month intervals; our grant pays for him and his family to come to Boston from Cleveland for a week at a time, so we can update his progress. So far, he's only been able to acquire new information since the amnesia. He's never remembered anything from what he calls *the gap*.

But one rainy afternoon in November, as I'm sitting in the cafeteria grabbing a sandwich while Pete takes a nap, Ben comes in and sits down at my table with a grin so outsized that I see people at the next table noticing it, too.

"What?" I say, dropping egg salad on my napkin. "You look like a retard."

"Enough with the political correctness," he tells me, pulling my square of carrot cake toward himself.

"What are you so happy about?"

"You will be, too. I was just upstairs with the daughter—"

"Whose, Pete's?"

"Yeah. I always forget her name—Kali? Some goddess name. The one with the nose ring."

"You think those hurt when you blow your nose?"

"I asked her. She says no."

"You *would.*"

"Well, it was just idle chatter. At least, I thought it was, until she started telling me this. I didn't have time to call you, it would have interrupted the flow—" He pauses to take a bite of my cake. "Hm," he says. "Needs carrots."

"Would you tell me what she said, already?" I slap the sleeve of his lab jacket and he holds his hands up, feigning fear of further attack.

"Okay. So listen to this. She was the only one in the room; they took Pete out for some blood work, and his wife was down here getting coffee or something."

"Yeah. I saw her."

"So Kali's standing by the window, just looking out at the rain, and I ask her if she's okay. I figure she's going to say fine, right? but instead she says *No, not really,* and she has to tell me something." He makes a little drumroll with his fingers on the tabletop. "You know how we were looking for something besides the fake resume that Pete might have wanted to forget?"

"Yeah?" I let the word rise on a question mark, feeling chills dimple my arms.

"Well, Kali was snooping around in her father's desk, and she found a letter from some girl—some woman, I guess—claiming that he was her father. She's the same age as Pete's son, twenty-five, and from what she wrote, Kali figured out that Pete must have had an affair right after he got married." Ben pauses to take another forkful of frosting.

"You're kidding," I say, because this—if it turns out to be true—could be further evidence of why Pete's memory went back to the age it did. Our theory is that in certain types of amnesia, the patient's mind returns to a time *before* the stress, or stresses, that might have caused the amnesia in the first place. We think the person goes back to a safer, happier time of life.

And the letter from his illegitimate daughter could give us a clue about what precipitated Pete's condition. "When was the letter dated?" I ask Ben.

"This is the best part." He leans in closer to deliver the *pièce de résistance.* "Three years ago, June seventeenth."

My brain darts back to the date of Pete's first hospitalization: June nineteenth. "So he would have gotten the letter that *day?*"

"Bingo." Now Ben points as if aiming a pistol at me, and pretends to shoot. I duck my eyes without thinking and he says, "Oh, shit, Ana. I'm an idiot."

"It's okay," I say, though any mention of guns still gives me a quick jab in the heart. I try to concentrate on what Ben's just told me. "Jesus. We couldn't have invented a better script." The deadline is approaching for submissions to a big psychology conference next spring, and we'll be able to whip up an abstract based on this new information.

"I know." We sit there without speaking further while Ben finishes my cake. He takes his time licking the last of it from the fork tines. "Do you think," he says, after a few moments, "that if you had the choice, you'd ever want to be like him?"

"You mean Pete?" Once again I marvel at the way Ben has intuited my most secret of thoughts. I've never mentioned to him the perverse jealousy I sometimes feel when I think about the possibility of painful memories being completely banished from the mind.

"If you could. Forget everything." Then he puts a hand out and covers mine with his own. It's a very un-Ben-like gesture, and the feel of his touch brings me tears. "Would you?"

I think of my nephew's first day of nursery school. Jake was silent on the whole car ride over, Justine told me; when she kissed him good-bye, he wouldn't look at her. On the ride home, she asked him how it had gone. "Well," Jake said from his car seat, meeting her eyes in the rear-view mirror, "when you left I was annoyed, and in the middle I was nervous, but then we had Circle and I was happy."

The memory of Justine telling me this makes me smile. "No," I tell Ben, and he nods, as if I've given the response he expected. It would surprise him to learn I've surprised myself with my answer. But it's the truth. And knowing this causes a cave to widen inside my heart, as if making room for something to move in.

Driving to campus every day, I always take the same route along the river. There's a certain office I always look for, on the third floor of a ten-story building behind a nursery-school playground. The office belongs to a woman who appears to be a little older than me, but not by much, and if she's sitting at her desk I can watch her, especially if traffic is stalled to a crawl. To myself, I've named the woman Charlie, because she reminds me of the glamorous lady executive in those old Charlie perfume ads.

Most of the time she is sitting at her desk, with her back to the window, when I drive by. I watch her hunching over her papers with a pen twiddling between her fingers, and I wonder what she is reading—are there words on those pages, or figures? Projections for the future, or appraisals of the past? A couple of times I have seen her get up from her desk to stretch or walk out of the office, and other times I've watched as she talked on the telephone while walking back and forth in a path on the carpet, the cord twisted around her hand. She wears a navy blue suit more often than anything else, and she rotates the color of scarves around her neck. In winter she leaves her hair long, but in warm weather she fastens it back with barrettes or a band.

Once, last summer, she was leaning her forehead into the window and looking out at the river with her fingertips pressed tight against the glass. Her posture was one of despair, and I waited to see if she would wipe away tears. But she didn't move until someone else, another woman, came into the office, stood on the other side of the desk, and seemed to say something. Charlie took her fingers down from the window and turned, and then I lost her because traffic forced me to move forward. Her office was dark for three weeks after that day, but of course I never knew whether her absence had anything to do with the moment I'd witnessed. She might have had a vacation already planned for that time. I preferred, though, to believe that something had shaken her soul—something it would take her a long time to get over, or to get through. It's not that I wished anything bad on her. But other people's distress tends to comfort me. I used to feel guilty about this, until I realized that such comfort is a form of sympathy—"the one poor word," George Eliot wrote, "which includes all our best insight and our best love."

Today, Charlie seems to be in a good mood. She hangs up the phone laughing and shoots a rubber band at the wall. It's a Friday in November, it feels like snow, and maybe she is thinking of leaving work early, before the roads get jammed. I watch her neaten the stacks of paper on her desk, sharpen a pencil, jot a few things onto a pad. She shrugs into her coat and hesitates with her hand on the light switch to look out the window, as if she knows someone is watching. And then the room goes dark.

On Saturday night the snow is still falling, but the newscasters have stopped warning people to stay off the roads. I am twelve, no one has died yet, everything is still possible in the world. We drive into Albany to see *Jaws II* at the Taft Theater, then buy a pizza from Antonelli's to take home. It turned dark while we were inside, and we ride back to Ashmont in high spirits as the windshield wipers whine across the glass.

Justine hums the shark theme music as she tiptoes her fingers across my lap to tickle Meggy, who shrieks even though she has seen it coming. In the front seat, my parents smile at each other and touch hands in the space between them.

At home, my mother runs a bath while my father puts out the pizza. *Last one in is a rotten egg.* The three of us get wet quickly, briefly, then step into our towels. We put on our pajamas and pitch like madmen downstairs to the family room, where he's set up the TV tables for dinner. My father catches my mother around the waist and draws her close in a kiss. Justine goes "Ooh, ooh" and Meggy says "Yuck" and makes a face. My mother moves to pull away, but my father tightens his grip and whispers a line from that old movie, the one I've heard them quote from so often over the years.

"'Life's a funny thing,'" my father says, and my mother, wriggling, picks up her cue: "'Compared to what?'" Then they laugh and my mother tries to escape him. But he holds on; he will not let her go.

Acknowledgments

For their sustaining support and encouragement during the writing of this book, I am indebted to, among others, the following: my family (especially my sister, Molly Treadway Johnson), Kathleen Wolf and Michael Glenn, the Elizabeths Berg and Searle, Debra Spark, Joan Wickersham, Charlotte Troyanowski, Kay Sweeney, Dawn Skorczewski, Jean and Jim Lucey, Donna and Larry Stein, the third-floor group, the Sunday-night group, and my own dear Anastasia; Richard Parks, the kindest, most patient agent and buoy; and, finally, Fiona McCrae, editor and friend nonpareil.

My gratitude, as well, to the Bunting Institute of Radcliffe College, the Massachusetts Cultural Council, and the National Endowment for the Arts.

JESSICA TREADWAY's first book, *Absent Without Leave and Other Stories*, received the John C. Zacharis First Book Award in 1993. A native of upstate New York and formerly a reporter for United Press International, she teaches creative writing and literature at Emerson College in Boston. She was a Fellow at the Mary Ingraham Bunting Institute of Radcliffe College and is the recipient of awards from the Massachusetts Cultural Council and the National Endowment for the Arts.

The text of *And Give You Peace* has been set in 11/15 Joanna,
a typeface designed by English artist Eric Gill (1882–1940)
and cut by the Caslon Foundry, London, in 1930.

This book was designed by Wendy Holdman, typeset by Stanton
Publication Services, Inc., and manufactured by Bang Printing
on acid-free paper.

Graywolf Press is a not-for-profit, independent press. The books we publish include poetry, literary fiction, essays, and cultural criticism. We are less interested in best-sellers than in talented writers who display a freshness of voice coupled with a distinct vision. We believe these are the very qualities essential to shape a vital and diverse culture.

Thankfully, many of our readers feel the same way. They have shown this through their desire to buy books by Graywolf writers; they have told us this themselves through their e-mail notes and at author events; and they have reinforced their commitment by contributing financial support, in small amounts and in large amounts, and joining the "Friends of Graywolf."

If you enjoyed this book and wish to learn more about Graywolf Press, we invite you to ask your bookseller or librarian about further Graywolf titles; or to contact us for a free catalog; or to visit our award-winning web site that features information about our forthcoming books.

We would also like to invite you to consider joining the hundreds of individuals who are already "Friends of Graywolf" by contributing to our membership program. Individual donations of any size are significant to us: they tell us that you believe that the kind of publishing we do *matters*. Our web site gives you many more details about the benefits you will enjoy as a "Friend of Graywolf"; but if you do not have online access, we urge you to contact us for a copy of our membership brochure.

www.graywolfpress.org

Graywolf Press
2402 University Avenue, Suite 203
Saint Paul, MN 55114
Phone: (651) 641-0077
Fax: (651) 641-0036
E-mail: wolves@graywolfpress.org

Other Graywolf titles you might enjoy are:

Rainy Lake by Mary François Rockcastle
A Four-Sided Bed by Elizabeth Searle
Ana Imagined by Perrin Ireland
How the Dead Live by Alvin Greenberg
Central Square by George Packer